ROADS AND BRIDGES

GLYNNIS HAYWARD

CONSTANTIA PRESS
Los Gatos, California

For further information, write Constantia Press
constantiapress@gmail.com

Library of Congress Control Number: 2021953059

This book is dedicated to the memory of
Elizabeth Moley (1939-2021).

All the characters in **Roads And Bridges** are fictional, except for Mrs. Liz. There wasn't a person that Liz couldn't help. Her generosity assisted countless institutions and people world-wide; refugees, the oppressed and underprivileged, received her special care and attention. Funding from her provided for the building of an orphanage outside Durban, South Africa, and helped many Zulu children receive an education, even at a tertiary level.

She tried to make the world a more just and better place. Thank you, Liz.

My thanks to Mr. McCall Smith

for his permission to be quoted,

as well as his encouragement to write

ROADS AND BRIDGES.

Thank you also to my editor, Jessica Powers,

for her commitment to the book.

ROADS
AND
BRIDGES

GLYNNIS HAYWARD

PART 1

Journeys are not only about places,
they are also about people—
and it may be the people,
rather than the places,
that we remember.

Alexander McCall Smith: *Trains and Lovers*

CHAPTER 1

Mandy Walker sat on a rock with her back turned to her companion, too hot to move. Neither of them spoke as they waited alongside a dirt road for a taxi to arrive. Eventually, Ryan Thompson broke the silence.

"Sorry about last night," he began. "I had too much to drink. But it wasn't just the alcohol talking; I really meant what I said..."

"Please stop," she said, her hands flying up to block her ears. Covered in dust, her face was flushed as she spun around to face him. He was unshaven and hungover—and looking at his bleary eyes made her stomach turn. As she pushed her fair hair aside, she replied, "I accept your apology, but don't say anything more. I also meant what I said; I'm glad we're traveling together, but we're just friends. Let's keep it that way. Otherwise, when we get to Durban, we'll have to split and go our separate ways."

He opened his mouth to speak but she cut him off sharply. "Friends, Ryan; that's all. Without privileges."

Despite the heat, she felt herself shiver as she recalled the previous night, fending him off in his drunken state. His advances weren't welcome, even if he were sober. When they'd just been phone buddies working in the Peace Corps, she'd looked forward to their calls—but since they'd started traveling together in South Africa, things had changed. "Perhaps it was loneliness that colored my thinking," she thought. "I was deluding myself, wanting it to be something special with him. But it isn't. It just isn't."

He looked so crestfallen that she took pity on him and tried to explain her feelings. "We had such fun when we met in training. And when you think that we could've been sent to work anywhere in the world, it was lucky we were both sent to Namibia—even though we were far apart. It was tough, working for two years in remote villages. I felt isolated—I don't know about you. It got to me at times. And although we didn't get to see one another much, phone contact with you was a life-line. It was a connection to home. Your friendship meant a lot, Ryan; it still does."

"Right. You've made your point. Just friends; I get it."

"What I'm trying to say is that relationships grow—they don't just explode. We hardly know one another really."

His eyebrows shot up. "Are you kidding me? Two years—you don't think a relationship has grown in two years?"

"Yes, but not the way you were thinking. You misinterpreted things. Two years speaking on the phone isn't the same as being together. We've spent very little time face to face. I...I'm sorry."

She didn't think she needed to apologize, but she didn't like hurting his feelings. It was an awkward situation, so she forced a smile and changed the subject. "Maybe we should've rented a car instead of trying to get a taxi. We could be stuck here forever."

He shrugged, resigned. "I'm not sure where we'd get

one in the middle of nowhere, but a guy at the campsite took care of it for us. I heard him on the phone speaking Zulu. He assured me a taxi will get here in due course. It's going to take a while, though. We're miles from the main road."

"I guess," she replied, saying nothing further—until it looked like he was about to start in on the subject of relationships again. Steering the conversation away, she added, "You know, I'm glad we've still got a bit longer in South Africa; I'm not ready to head home just yet. Grad school's waiting for me next year, but it only starts in the fall."

He couldn't resist saying, "That's promising. There's still time to change your..."

"Haven't you been listening? It's got nothing to do with you. It's everything to do with Africa."

"OK, OK, I was kidding," he said. "You've got a short fuse, Mandy. Don't take everything so seriously."

She gritted her teeth. If anyone had a short fuse, it was Ryan. She ignored the jab however and tried to keep the conversation civil. "I miss California, but Africa has a special place in my heart. I mean if you think about it—it's Thanksgiving back home and I can just imagine everyone stuffing themselves, saying what they're thankful for. Then they'll spend the rest of the weekend at the gym, working off excess calories. Yet look around us here; people are starving."

He couldn't hide his irritation. "So, do you want to stop everyone from eating turkey and pumpkin pie because people are hungry in Africa? How will that help?"

She frowned. "Doesn't it make you feel even a little bit

guilty? It's not fair."

Taking a deep breath, he groaned. "Life isn't fair, but you can't blame America. We give millions in foreign aid each year, and people like you and me volunteer our services. We're trying to help. Can't we enjoy Thanksgiving without feeling bad about it! Lighten up."

It was too hot to argue. Her blue eyes were steely as she turned her back on him again and silence enveloped them once more. For a long time, the only sound Mandy was aware of was her heart pounding—until eventually she heard a grating, mechanical noise that was quite jarring to her ears. Straining to see what it was, she discerned a cloud of dust approaching in the distance and, without bothering to disguise her feelings, she muttered, "Oh God, please let that be a taxi."

CHAPTER 2

A yellow Kombi came to a stop alongside them and a young man jumped out of the driver's seat. With a broad smile, he said, "Are you the Americans needing a ride to Durban?"

Mandy and Ryan nodded as the man informed them, "I'm Joseph Hlangani. Sorry to keep you waiting. This is my taxi. I kept two spaces for you on the back seat; other people took the ones in front. Sorry."

Her heart sank as Mandy looked at the dilapidated vehicle that had *Speedy Passenger Service* written across its side. However, the driver was courteous so she steeled herself; the ride would only be a couple of hours and anything was better than baking in the sun, bickering with Ryan.

Noticing the look of astonishment on Joseph's face when she paid him, she smiled and said, "Keep the change." He deserved the generous tip. She knew it was customary for passengers to either signal at the side of the road, or meet at a taxi rank, but he'd come out of his way to fetch them—by special arrangement. Her heart sank again, however, once she looked inside the vehicle. There was really only room for one person in the far corner, because two people were already on the back seat with a basket of chickens taking up another place.

She groaned softly, "Ah man, we should've rented a car."

"Too late for that," Ryan muttered. "You might be small, but you'll have to sit on my lap. We'll never fit in otherwise." She wrinkled her nose, looking hesitant—which prompted him to say, "Would you prefer it if I sit on your lap? I'm probably only about 60 lbs. heavier than you."

It was the last thing she wanted to do, but it was the only option. She rolled her eyes and let him climb in first, following him reluctantly. The man in the back nearest the door had the best seat in the taxi; he could stretch out. As she climbed over this man's legs to reach Ryan's lap, the woman next to him smiled and said, "Sorry about my chickens; I hope they won't worry you." Mandy shrugged and half-smiled in response. When she turned away, however, she was frowning.

Suddenly, before Mandy was even properly settled, the taxi took off at speed along the corrugated road. She almost suffered whiplash injury as Joseph put his foot down flat on the accelerator in an attempt to skim over the potholes. The noise was deafening. Furthermore, with no air-conditioning—and all the windows closed to keep out dust—the heat soon became suffocating. The taxi lurched and swerved like a dodgem car and Mandy gripped the seat in front of her, trying to steady herself.

As she bounced around, she attempted to observe the other passengers. They were all Zulus. A wizened old man with white hair sat next to a window behind the driver, muttering to himself. Next to him was a young man, attempting to steady his phone as it jumped around in his hands. Behind them sat a priest with a small boy. The child's eyes just reached window level and his head bobbed around as he looked out. Lastly, there was a woman next to the driver; she was wearing a bright scarf on her head to match her dress. Nobody spoke however, because nothing could be heard as the vehicle shook and rattled over the dirt road.

Soon Mandy began to feel queasy. She tried to concentrate on looking out the window, hoping it would make her feel better. It didn't. She was carsick. Terrified of throwing up, she looked around frantically for a receptacle—just in case. There was nothing available, except perhaps the basket with chickens in it.

She was desperate to get out of the taxi until suddenly the speed seemed to be diminishing. As it did so, the ride became smoother, bringing her relief from the nausea—but making her anxious about something else. What was happening? The driver also appeared anxious. He was frantically changing gears, though nothing he did seemed to alter the fact that the taxi was slowing down. After a while, the vehicle was just rolling along, carried simply by its own momentum, until finally it came to a complete stop.

There was an outburst of consternation as Joseph scratched his head and turned to his passengers. "Don't worry, please. I'll see what's happening." He was smiling as he spoke, but Mandy could tell that he wasn't smiling on the inside.

"God," she muttered to Ryan. "Let's just get out and walk. I can't stand this any longer."

"Hell, you think you're uncomfortable...I can hardly breathe under here. Yeah. Let's get out."

But nobody moved. Mandy and Ryan were stuck.

She watched in horror as Joseph first checked the gauges, then climbed out to inspect the engine. When he unlocked the cap on the petrol tank and gave it a nudge, she groaned. His progress was slow as he climbed back inside and his voice was grave when he announced, "My friends, I am very sorry, the petrol—it is finished."

"Oh geez, I knew it," she muttered. "Just when I thought things were bad, they go and get worse."

She stared numbly as everyone, except the priest and the child, began to shout at the driver. Joseph attempted to smile and speak above the clamor. "Please, don't worry. This is not a big problem. I can get more petrol in Ixopo," he shouted. Pointing to the bicycle tied to the front of the taxi, she heard him call above the din, "If I use that bike, I'll be there and back quickly. Then I'll go very fast. We'll be in Durban on time, you'll see."

The shouting died down as everyone turned to look at the young man with the best seat, the owner of the bicycle. He looked reluctant until Lindiwe, the woman with the chickens, smiled at him. It was then that Mandy noticed how beautiful the woman was; her long hair was braided in corn rows and she had high cheekbones underneath big, dark eyes. Her smile was warm—and the young man immediately relented. "OK, you can use it," he said to the driver, "but be careful."

"I will, my friend," Joseph reassured him. "Here, I've got some tea and biscuits for all of you. Why don't you go and sit under that tree? Before you've finished drinking, I'll be back; then we can carry on to Durban." He pulled out his emergency supplies from under the driver's seat, proffering them a small camp stove, some water, tea, sugar, and biscuits. Noticing the priest, he added, "And because it's Sunday, maybe the umfundisi can say some prayers."

Mandy's heart sank further at the thought of that. She watched as Joseph jumped on the bicycle and rode off in haste.

Resigning themselves to their fate, the other passengers slowly began to disembark. Mandy wanted to yell at them to hurry up, but she restrained herself as she waited her turn. The moment she was outside, free from the confines of the taxi and thankful for fresh air, she inhaled deeply and looked around. Everyone remained standing, looking at their phones, except for Ryan; he was obviously avoiding her, stretched out on the ground with his eyes closed and headphones over his ears. Well, she didn't want to be with him either. She wanted to be alone, away from all these people.

Whenever she was stressed, she usually found relief by doing yoga—so she found a spot hidden by bushes, pulled a towel from her backpack, and laid it on the ground. Closing her eyes, she lowered herself onto her stomach, arched her back and raised her head, proceeding to do a complicated "salute to the sun." It wasn't long before she heard loud comments in Zulu and realized that she wasn't concealed by the bushes after all; she was being watched. A little embarrassed, she stopped her routine.

It was fortunate she didn't understand what was being said. Mpilo, a young man with lots of opinions, was offering a suggestion. "Maybe it's a mating ritual, like some birds do. Maybe she's sending signals to that guy over there," he said, pointing to Ryan.

Whatever had been said caused laughter, which stopped when Mandy heard a deep voice speaking sternly. It sounded like someone preaching, so probably the priest, she thought. "That's unkind. She's doing yoga. People do it in the Church Hall every week," he said in Zulu.

"So, why's she doing it here?" the same young man muttered. "This isn't the church hall!"

Mandy heard more laughter and blushed. She didn't understand their language and didn't care that much; she'd probably never see them again, anyway. Embarrassed nonetheless, she lay stretched out on the towel, thankful for the solitude as she reflected on her time in Africa. Teaching in Namibia had been worthwhile, although not as fulfilling as she'd hoped it would be; she'd felt a bit of an outsider, never totally part of the community. But she was happy to be in South Africa now—it had a different vibe and she wouldn't let it be spoiled by Ryan. She did feel a bit aimless without a job though; six months seemed a long time to do nothing but explore.

Her thoughts were suddenly interrupted by a loud boom—a crash of thunder, sounding like a massive explosion, reverberated through the valley. The ground under her seemed to vibrate. Mandy shot up and looked around, her heart pounding. Although the flash of lightning that followed was far away, she felt a need to draw closer to the group; the weather could change quickly. As she approached, she heard the woman with the headscarf say, "If a storm's coming, we should go back to the taxi."

Mandy agreed. The rubber tires would keep them safe. Sitting under a tree was a dangerous place to be. But a young guy looked up from his phone and shook his head. His voice sounded like the one who'd made comments when she was doing yoga. "No, it's far away. That storm won't come here. See how dark it is near the hills over there, but the sky here is blue. Don't worry."

"He's right," replied the priest, settling himself on the ground under the tree. "We'll be fine here."

Mandy watched him remove his spectacles and wipe them with a white handkerchief, squinting as his eyesight adjusted. A name tag on his pocket stated that he was Reverend E. Dlamini from Saint Augustine's Church. Replacing the glasses, he beckoned the young boy, who obeyed and quickly settled on his haunches nearby, staring at the ground in silence.

She stood watching the boy; it was the first time she had got a good look at him. He was barefoot, wearing khaki shorts and a tee shirt that were both too big for him. When Reverend Dlamini patted him gently, the kid glanced up, looking bewildered, but she saw that he relaxed when the priest smiled reassuringly at him. As she moved closer, she continued watching the child; he reminded her of one of the lost boys in *Peter Pan*, nervous and unsure of himself.

Reverend Dlamini began to talk. "Thunder can't hurt you, you know. The lightning...now that's very dangerous."

She was not particularly interested in a conversation about a storm that wasn't going to materialize, but listened politely.

The guy who'd previously commented got drawn into the conversation and said, "You're right, Mfundisi.

Last year a terrible thing happened at the place where I was working. Here, near Ixopo, everything is green, but there, near Josini, it's dry bushveld. I was working on a game farm for a man called Joubert. He had a very bad temper and we workers were afraid of him. One day, he parked his truck outside the kitchen door and went inside to eat lunch. When he saw how dark it was getting, he decided to put his truck in the shed and he shouted at me to move the tractor. I was scared of the storm that was approaching fast, but I was even more scared of him. I jumped to it and we sprinted to get the vehicles under cover. Just as we got there, the rain started. You could hear it hit the iron roof like someone was dumping rocks. Hey, I was afraid. I stayed in the shed, but Joubert wanted to finish his lunch. I warned him it was too dangerous but he ran back laughing at me. I stood there watching him; he was halfway to the house when lightning flashed across the sky. He was like a magnet. It went straight for him."

Mandy gave an involuntary gasp and murmured, "Oh my God." Glancing at the distant clouds to make sure they really were far away, she decided it was safe to sit down and hear the rest of the story. From where she sat, she was able to watch the little boy without it being too obvious. She didn't want to embarrass him.

The storyteller swallowed hard before continuing. "The lightning lifted him just like that." He snapped his fingers to show the speed with which it had happened. "That man went up in the air and landed flat on the ground; you could smell his flesh burning. He was cooking." Mandy shuddered and those in the group who'd

12

remained standing began to sit down as he continued. "Joubert was wearing boots with thick rubber soles; that was lucky for him. Those rubber soles saved him; he didn't die. But he was sick for a long time."

As everyone stared at the storyteller, he murmured in a voice that was almost inaudible to Mandy, "Some people said it was my fault. They called me umthakati, because they said I made lightning strike the farmer."

His words produced shock waves. She saw those near to him pull away and the child looked frightened when he registered that one Zulu word. She didn't know what it was and wanted to ask, but people were obviously afraid—so she chose not to interrupt the storyteller.

He looked up and said in a desperate tone, "It wasn't true. There were lots of people who didn't like Joubert; he had a bad temper. It could have been anyone who went to the sangoma for a curse—but it wasn't me."

Immediately forgetting about her irritation with Ryan and the taxi running out of petrol, Mandy held her breath—fascinated to hear the priest's reaction. He frowned and said nothing at first, but after a while he replied in measured tones. "I don't believe you can harm other people with witchcraft. That's just superstition. The danger is that you harm yourself by wishing evil things to happen. It makes you sick inside."

"But I didn't do it," the man protested. "Please believe me, baba."

She felt sorry for him; he was so earnest. The priest was obviously sympathetic as well. In a kind voice, he said, "My friend, what is your name?"

"Mpilo."

"Well, I can see you are honest, Mpilo. I believe you."

The young guy looked relieved, but he frowned when Reverend Dlamini spoke again. "If you think about it, it's strange how sometimes a small thing makes a big difference. If that farmer had taken off his boots when he stopped for lunch, it would've been a different story. It's a miracle he didn't die. Those rubber soles saved him, for sure. Some people might say it was chance, but I think it was God. God didn't want him to die that day."

Mandy tried to hide her smile when she heard Mpilo mutter, "God made a big mistake. I didn't like that man."

CHAPTER 3

Reverend Dlamini cleared his throat, preparing to continue speaking, and Mandy sighed. She was sure a sermon was forthcoming and was relieved when the old man, Bongani, interrupted. "I'm tired of waiting for this stupid taxi driver. I'm never going to ride in his *Speedy Passenger Service* again. There's nothing speedy about it. Mfundisi, you are quite right. A small thing can make a big difference. It's because Joseph didn't fill up with petrol that we're sitting here under a tree."

To her surprise, Mpilo responded gruffly, speaking in Zulu as he inclined his head towards her and Ryan. "And if he hadn't turned onto this dirt road to fetch those two, we wouldn't be sitting here either. They've got legs; why can't they use them like the rest of us? Why didn't they walk to the main road?"

Mandy grew alarmed. Although she didn't understand what had been said, it was obvious he was speaking about them. Despite their earlier altercation, she leaned closer to Ryan, who put an arm around her and glared at Mpilo. "If you've got something to say about us, dude, can you say it so that we understand?"

There was an awkward silence while everyone looked first at Ryan, then at Mpilo. Mandy bit her lip, waiting for a further outburst. She hoped they weren't on a collision course and frowned at Ryan, willing him to keep quiet. They were visitors in this country and it wouldn't do to get into an argument. To her relief, he nodded and said nothing more.

She was thankful that attention turned away from them when the old man, Bongani, turned to the priest. "So, tell me. Are you going to pray for us, Mfundisi?" he asked, nursing a flask in his hands. "Can you ask Nkulunkulu to bring us some petrol? I would like to see if your God listens to you."

Mandy groaned inwardly. The last thing she wanted was a prayer meeting. Her eyes narrowed when the old man coughed loudly and spat out some phlegm; she promptly turned away to look at Reverend Dlamini. He seemed to be carefully considering his words.

"I have already asked God to help us but I cannot tell him what to do. That would be wrong. Nkulunkulu is in charge; not us," he said, finally.

The old man spat once more and Mandy was thankful to be sitting far away from him. She was interested when he challenged the priest again and said, "Why can't you tell him what you need?"

"God doesn't fix people's mistakes. They must do that for themselves. Our driver forgot to fill up with petrol; it wasn't God who did that," the priest said.

"Well, we didn't make the mistake. Why won't God help us?"

Despite his foul habits, Mandy admired the old man's bluntness.

"I'm sure he will, but it might not be the way we expect. We must let God show us the way—not the other way around." She watched Reverend Dlamini turn to the young boy and put an arm over the child's shoulder once again. "For example, I have asked God to help Jabulani here. His parents died of the terrible sickness that is everywhere in our land. His father died first, and now we have just buried his mother. Nkulunkulu has given me the job of looking after this orphan. I don't know how, but God will show me the way."

Mandy was watching the child. He didn't understand what was being said in English and continued to stare at his feet, embarrassed by the attention. She swallowed hard. Not yet comfortable to address the rest of the group, she turned to Ryan and whispered, "Look at that little boy. So much grief in his life and he's still so young. That's what I mean about life being unfair."

There was nothing Ryan could say, but he seemed glad they were back on speaking terms.

She said nothing more either, as the priest continued talking. "I'm taking him to a house near Durban now, where he'll live with me and six other boys. I'm their guardian." He shook his head and added, "We've got too many orphans in our country; it's very sad, very sad. This thing, AIDS, it's killed too many mothers and fathers. But the people with the disease aren't the only victims. Their children also suffer. Some of them live with grandparents—if they have any; but lots become street children with nobody to take care of them." She saw the priest gaze at the boy with compassion, before he added, "My friends, I was also an orphan so I know what it's like. My parents were killed in an accident when I was young. We were in a bus. There were only a few people who survived; all my family died that day." There were murmurs of sympathy and he paused before adding, "Even though my body wasn't injured badly, it was bad inside me. I was only eight years old. The same age Jabulani is now."

Mandy paled and clenched her fists. She opened her mouth to speak, but no words came out as she listened to the priest.

"I was lucky because the priests at Marianhill Monastery looked after me. That's why I started this orphanage; I must help these boys, otherwise they'll end up on the street."

Finally, Mandy found the words she was looking for and murmured, "How can you say you were lucky when you lost all your family?"

It was the first time she'd spoken to any of them and the priest smiled at her. He liked her soft voice and kind eyes. "I *was* lucky. Those priests gave me a good education; they loved me and gave me a purpose in life. Now I'm returning the favor. The first thing I have to do is find a school for Jabulani. His name means happiness in English, you know," he explained. "I'm going to make sure he'll be happy again. He hasn't had any schooling and he can't speak English, but we'll fix that. We must be patient."

Mandy swallowed hard. "You're a good man," she said. Suddenly she didn't care about the priest's sermons; she cared about that little boy. Her eyes rested again on the child, taking in his brown eyes and small body. He seemed so sad. Would the priest ever be able to replace what the boy had lost?

She became aware that Lindiwe was staring at her. When she glanced the woman's way, a look passed between them that made Mandy feel connected to her for just a moment. They smiled—and the Zulu woman nodded at her before turning to ask the priest, "How do you pay for all these things?"

The owner of the bicycle added his thoughts. "Yes, school fees, uniforms, books; they're expensive—and then there's transport too. Where does the money come from? I've got Grade 11 and I want to finish school. Someday I'll finish Grade 12, I hope."

Mandy swallowed hard. It hadn't crossed her mind that the priest would have to find money from somewhere to carry out his work; she presumed it came from the church. Education wasn't free for these people and none of their lives were easy. She was still watching him when the young man muttered, "The trouble is, I'm getting married and the lobola is too much money—eleven cows."

Out the corner of her eyes, Mandy saw Lindiwe recoil. She'd noticed the two of them, this man and Lindiwe, looking at one another in the taxi. She'd presumed they were a couple, but it appeared that wasn't so. Her thoughts were interrupted when Bongani, the old man, exclaimed, "You're lucky, my friend! Grade 11 or 12, what does it matter? But a wife is important."

"Grade 12 means a lot when I apply for a job. And I don't even want to marry this girl; it's my parents who need her to help them. They're the ones who want her, but now I must pay the bride price to her family." He looked somber. "Her family wants twelve cows. They're crazy. My father and uncle told them I'll only pay for eleven—that's still a lot of money."

Mpilo laughed and said, "You know, there's an app for you to calculate how much lobola you should pay. Why don't you download it? Maybe you can knock off some cows."

Mandy had heard about lobola, but was it possible Apple would have an app for such a thing—or was Mpilo joking? "Are you serious?" she asked him. He just carried on laughing and didn't answer her question.

Everyone else laughed too, but she saw that the prospective bridegroom wasn't amused. He turned to the priest and said, "It's very hard for us to get money; we're poor people. Where do you get money to pay for so many boys to go to school, Mfundisi?"

"And why do you only look after boys? There are orphan girls too," added Lindiwe. Mandy had thought exactly the same thing; it didn't seem fair.

The priest nodded. "Yes, it is expensive. And you are right, girls are also orphans. I hope one day to have a different house for girls—because, you know, it wouldn't be right to have teenage boys and girls living in the same house. But we get donations. For example, an American lady, Mrs. Liz, heard about us. She gave us money to build a house. She also pays for two students to attend school each year. She's very good to us."

Mandy listened with even more interest now as the priest continued. "Every day hundreds of people die from this disease, but everyone is afraid to admit what's happening. They won't talk about it. Ignorance will kill our people as much as AIDS. We have too many children without parents. I look after a few orphans, but there are thousands more. We're lucky to have Mrs. Liz. Now we must find someone to help Jabulani. I'm sure God will take care of it. He's watching over the child. His spirit goes out to people and someone will help. It's ubuntu." Pointing to the owner of the bicycle, the priest asked, "What's your name, young man?"

"Philani," he replied.

"Well, you know about ubuntu, Philani. You lent Joseph your bicycle. I could see you didn't want to, but it was good for all of us—so you agreed. Thank you."

Mandy saw Philani's face light up, proud to get praise from the priest. His pleasure grew when Ryan patted him on the back, adding his thanks. He beamed even more when Lindiwe nodded her approval and smiled at him, prompting Mandy to also say, "It was kind of you. Thanks." Then, looking around at the group, she added, "And thank you, everybody, for speaking English so that we can understand. I really appreciate that."

She was gratified to see them all smile at this acknowledgement, but before anything more could be said, the priest spoke again to Philani. "Tell me, my friend, why are you worried about getting married? I can see it makes you unhappy?"

The young man's smile turned to a frown immediately. He shook his head and muttered, "I don't want to talk about it."

This puzzled Mandy; why would he would agree to marry the woman if he didn't want to do so? She opened her mouth to ask him but stopped herself. It would be presumptuous of her. She noticed, however, that Reverend Dlamini paid no attention to Philani's protest. Why would he not respect the young man's privacy? It was rude to pry.

As if he'd read her thoughts, Reverend Dlamini said, "It's always better to talk about something when you're worried about it. Don't be shy, Philani. We're here with time to chat while we wait; maybe we can help you. Problems are always better if you share them. You see, although I'm not a married man myself, I'm sure some of these other people are married." As he looked around the group, looking for confirmation, Mandy began to understand why he was questioning Philani. The priest wasn't being inquisitive, he was trying to help.

Bongani was the only one who didn't shake his head. Instead the old man grinned, sat up straight, and announced, "You can ask me anything about marriage. I have two wives."

Reverend Dlamini's disapproval was apparent as his eyes opened wide behind his spectacles. It seemed as if he was about to say something in response, but Philani muttered again, "I don't want to talk about it."

Mandy thought that would end the conversation but the old man had other ideas. "How can you talk about it when you don't know anything about marriage? Me—I can give you all the advice you need."

CHAPTER 4

Bongani wore a tattered white shirt, khaki shorts, and sandals made from discarded rubber tires. His legs were thin and bony, like the rest of his body. He raised a flask from his lap, took a swig of the liquid it contained, and sighed with satisfaction as he smacked his lips before he began to speak again.

"Now this is an important reason to find a wife." He held up his flask to show everyone, caressing it as if it were a woman, and chuckled as he took another sip. "She can make you utshwala."

Mandy was intrigued; the old man was like a caricature. She could see the priest's disapproval, however. He was frowning, even though others in the group began to smile. Looking at Ryan, Mandy saw that he was clearly amused by it all. Furthermore, he turned to Bongani and inquired, "Sir, what exactly is utshwala?"

The old man looked at him askance. "You don't know what this is?" he gasped, tapping his flask. "That's too bad; you must try it now. And my friend, you are lucky because you'll be tasting the best brew first. You'll never taste utshwala like this again."

"But what is it?" Ryan persisted.

"Utshwala, my friend, is Zulu beer. We always drink it when we want to celebrate, but sometimes we drink it just because we like it. We don't need a reason."

Ryan nodded and smiled. "I get it," he said. "We do a similar thing, but we have to buy it, not make it."

"Here, try some. I've got more in my suitcase," urged Bongani. He took another swig and passed the flask across to Mandy and Ryan, adding, "We've got time to drink together and my number one wife will be happy. She made this. Come, have some."

Everyone watched Ryan as he lifted the flask tentatively to his lips and held it there for a moment. Mandy was willing him to decline the offer—he still looked hungover—but Bongani continued urging him to drink. While everyone waited, Ryan put his head back and took a gulp. Immediately, his eyes opened wide and he gasped for breath. "Man, this is strong!" he exclaimed, wiping his mouth. "Holy shit, what does she put in it?"

Nervous that they would be insulted, Mandy held her breath, relieved when everyone laughed loudly. Bongani clapped his hands. "Ah, that's a secret, my friend; not even I know all the ingredients, except that she uses sorghum and it takes three days. After she makes it, it must ferment before you can drink it. Please, have some more and pass it on."

"It's fermented all right." Ryan laughed and took another gulp before handing the flask to Mandy.

Her hair was falling in her eyes and she brushed it aside, holding the flask in trepidation. Her stomach turned at the thought of drinking out of this thing, but she didn't want to insult anyone. Taking great care, she wiped the opening with her shirt before steeling herself to take a tiny sip; her face registered no reaction as she nodded politely and hurried it on to Lindiwe.

The Zulu woman laughed and gulped some down before giving her verdict. "It's good. Your wife makes a good brew. You're a lucky man. Maybe she'll give me the recipe."

The old man shook his head and said, "If you want the recipe, you'll have to be my third wife. Hey, that's a good idea; a beautiful Zulu woman like you will give me even more children. You've got nice hips for having babies."

Lindiwe spat out her response. "I can get recipes on-line without doing that. You must be mad."

Bongani winked at her and grinned, prompting Lindiwe to shake her head and turn away. She wasn't sure whether he was joking or not, but Mandy could see that the Zulu woman wanted it to be quite clear she wouldn't be the object of his salacious remarks. Nobody else seemed concerned, but a look of understanding passed between the two women before Lindiwe passed the flask to Philani like a bucket of hot coals. From there it did the rounds, with everyone other than Reverend Dlamini and Jabulani partaking. Instead, the priest set about making tea.

Bongani was delighted that his beer had been well-received and was unconcerned by Lindiwe's scorn. He turned and said, "Young man, don't be afraid of marriage. It's a good thing. If I had more money, I would even take another wife—like this beautiful woman here," he said. "A wife will bring you children; she'll look after you when you're an old man and she'll keep you warm in bed." He chuckled and winked at Lindiwe, adding, "And that's the best part. No lobola is too much for that."

Mandy frowned. In the USA, this would be considered sexual harassment, but he seemed to think he was handing out compliments. It was apparent that the priest was also displeased; he frowned and cautioned the old man, gesturing towards the child sitting next to him.

She'd never known such a brazen character. Bongani ignored the priest's warning with a look of disdain. "He doesn't understand English, so he doesn't know what I'm saying. What are you worried about? Is it because you don't want to talk about these things that make a man happy in bed?"

She wondered how the priest would respond, but Reverend Dlamini chose not to engage. Instead, he boiled some water and inquired who wanted tea. Mandy accepted the offer with thanks, noticing that as he drank his tea, periodically dunking a biscuit in it, the priest stared at Bongani with a furrowed brow. Suddenly he stopped chewing, swallowed hard, and cleared his throat. "Tell me, why do you want more than one wife? Don't you know that it's wrong? God tells us that we must only have one wife; he says we must forsake all others."

So, Reverend Dlamini had decided to engage after all, she noted. Curious to know what Bongani would say, she was pleased the priest had challenged him.

She saw the old man shrug and take another swig from his flask. "Mfundisi, it is you who tells me what God says—but did God really say that?" he said, sniffing loudly as he cleared his throat. Turning to everyone else, he asked, "Can any of you see him? Me—I cannot see God. Where is he? I don't see him anywhere. I've never seen him. I have got no time for church or God. And actually, I've got no time for the sea either."

Mandy's curiosity was piqued. She couldn't contain

herself and said, "I can understand your feelings about God and church, but what's your problem with the sea?"

He grunted. "When I was a boy—like Jabulani here— my father was working on the mines in Johannesburg and my mother was working in Durban. I lived on the farm here with my gogo. My mother joined a church and she wanted me to be baptized, so she came to fetch me. I was excited to see the sea for the first time, even though I was a bit afraid. I remember the waves were big and loud. My mother and all her friends were dressed in white robes and they were singing and dancing like it was a party. I didn't know what was happening, but I danced with them. The priest was singing too. Suddenly he stopped and called two helpers. They grabbed me and took me into the sea; I wasn't expecting it and before I knew what was happening, they pushed me under the water and held me down. Hey, I thought I was going to die. Just when I was about to give up struggling because I was running out of breath, they pulled me up. I gasped for air—then they did it again. Three times they did it. They said they were getting the devil out of me. I think the devil was in them."

"Geez, I don't blame you for the way you feel," Mandy said. "That must've been very frightening."

"Yes, it was," he replied. "I came back to the farm here and I've never been to church again. I've never been in the sea again either." But he hadn't finished talking about marriage—and after this digression, he returned to that subject. "Remember that president we had once, the one with five wives? He's a Zulu like all of us, except them," he said, pointing to the Americans. "If I had as much money as him, I'd also have five wives. That's our tradition; we mustn't forget our old ways. He's a lucky man, but I'm poor. I can only afford two wives."

Everyone was watching Reverend Dlamini, eager to hear his response. The priest appeared to choke on his biscuit and take another mouthful of tea to clear his throat. Mandy watched him mop his brow as he began to speak. "It's hard to understand how poor people become rich and then forget about poor people. They get greedy. And some men get greedy for wives."

Bongani responded loudly, "It's our Zulu tradition to have many wives."

She thought she heard an unusual sharpness in his voice when the priest began to speak again. "But remember our great king, Shaka. He had no wives at all and sometimes he forced his impis—his soldiers—to go without women. What about that tradition?"

Mandy was interested when Mpilo added his voice to the discussion; he always seemed to have something to say. "Well, the thing is, we can't afford to have lots of wives and children anymore. The old Zulu ways—they're finished. We live in a different world now."

It was a conflict between old and young, unlike she'd ever heard before. She smiled when Mpilo turned to Philani and said, "Hey, who knows, maybe lobola will disappear." The reluctant bridegroom gave a fist pump and the two men laughed.

Bongani responded immediately. "No, that mustn't change," he shouted. "You don't know what you're talking about. Think about Nelson Mandela. He had three wives."

At the mention of that name, everyone stopped and

listened. Mandy noticed there were some angry glances aimed at Bongani, but the priest caught her attention the most. He looked up at the canopy of leaves above his head and closed his eyes for a moment, before saying quietly, "Yes, he had three wives, but not all at the same time. And it's not for us to judge him about that. He had his reasons for divorcing two of them." Reverend Dlamini then removed his spectacles, surreptitiously wiping his eyes at the same time, before continuing. "You know, I was on Robben Island with him for a while. Nelson Mandela taught me, taught us all, how to forgive. Twenty-seven years in prison didn't make him bitter."

Mandy was spellbound. What an interesting afternoon this was turning into.

Nobody said a word, waiting in awe for the priest to continue. He took some time cleaning his glasses and only when he'd replaced them, did he look around. "When I was a student at Fort Hare University—before I went to seminary—I was jailed on the Island for four years. Nelson Mandela had already been there a long time when I arrived. It was a terrible place; we worked in a limestone quarry every day and then we were locked in cells at night. The jailers treated us like dogs, but Nelson—he never lost his dignity, not for one moment. We all looked up to him.

"I nearly gave up on Christianity then. I was disgusted with people who called themselves Christians. I thought, *How can there be a God who will let these things happen?* But Nelson helped me regain my faith. He made me see that you can't blame God for people's bad ways; it's the people you must blame. It was because of him that I went into the seminary and became a priest. Like I told you, I was first influenced by the monks who raised me at Marianhill, but it was my time with Nelson Mandela that convinced me to follow this path. He changed my life."

Mandy listened in awe. As everyone remained silent, she realized that some of them were from the "born free" generation, born after apartheid ended; they didn't know exactly what those dark times had been like. They learned their history by listening to stories like this.

"We weren't supposed to have time to talk, but we had ways of communicating," he continued. "That's what kept us going. We tapped on walls, we whispered, we sang, we left messages for one another. We shared the little reading matter we were allowed to receive and in that way, we were able to study all sorts of things. It was strange, being so close to Cape Town that we could see it, yet so far away that we were totally isolated. Despite that, we all learned a lot during the time we were there. We called that place our university. We were its graduates." There was not a sound to be heard from anyone else in the group as they listened to the priest tell of his time in the presence of Nelson Mandela. It was as if he had absorbed some of the hero's greatness by osmosis.

"One of our fellow prisoners was very clever. He had the complete works of Shakespeare hidden inside his Koran." The priest shook his head and chuckled. "He told the jailers it was his daily religious reading; fortunately, they didn't look too hard and they believed him. He shared that book with us and we all marked our favorite passages."

Mandy couldn't stop herself from speaking. "You

weren't allowed to read Shakespeare?" she asked, amazed. "Why couldn't you do that?"

The priest shrugged. "The jailers weren't English speakers. I doubt they'd heard of Shakespeare, let alone read any of his work. They probably thought it might be 'subversive literature.' Anything you don't understand can be a threat, you see."

Mandy continued to stare at the priest, but said no more. Despite being disinclined to listen to his "God talk" beforehand, she found herself drawn to hear every word he said now. She noticed that even the child appeared to be listening, although he didn't understand English. The name Nelson Mandela got his attention.

Reverend Dlamini continued, "Nelson marked something from *Julius Caesar* that I remember well. They were words about courage." He stared at the leaves above his head again as he recited in a solemn voice:

"Cowards die many times before their deaths.
The valiant never taste of death but once."

His voice trailed off and he said simply, "There was more...We loved it when he quoted that passage to us."

Looking around at all of them, he continued. "Nelson Mandela was the greatest graduate of us all; he learned something that you can't learn in books—wisdom. You see, he went into prison young and angry, but he came out old and wise. He figured that education is necessary for people to be free; he said our jailers were also prisoners, trapped by ignorance and prejudice. He was right—and that's why I work with these boys at the orphanage.

"I'm not a teacher in their schools; I'm a teacher in their lives. Like a parent, I help them learn how to live together with respect and dignity. That's what matters most. It's the biggest lesson of all. That's what Nelson Mandela taught me and that's why I must do my life's work with them. They are the future."

Mandy felt drawn to the priest; it was as if she was hearing Nelson Mandela himself speaking as he continued.

"That great man maintained that the most important thing in any struggle was stamina. He said, 'Every day you must get up and see the distant horizon, not all the potholes along the way.' Remember that, my friends. Be patient." He gave a wry smile and pointed to the dirt road. "Forget about the potholes. We'll get to Durban eventually."

She wished she had a pen and paper to write down every word this man had said—instead Mandy consigned them all to memory.

CHAPTER 5

As she sat thinking about the priest's words, her eyes never left Jabulani. The child had been listening intently, even though he didn't understand, but every now and again he glanced at Mandy. He had bright eyes and she could tell that he was eager to know what was being said. When Bongani began to snore, he grinned and she smiled at the boy. Their eyes met for a moment before he quickly looked at the ground again.

Bongani had dozed off, but he suddenly snored so loudly that he woke himself up. Mandy was still watching the boy when the old man started to speak. Having missed most of the discussion he'd initiated about Nelson Mandela, Bongani rubbed his eyes and said to nobody in particular, "My son lives in Durban. I'm going to visit him now, but there's another reason I'm going to the city."

Mandy didn't really care and it seemed nobody else did either. Annoyed, the old man shouted, "Are you all asleep? Has the tsetse fly been biting you?"

Heads began to turn. Once he had everyone's attention, Bongani started to regale them with a story—whether they were interested or not. Mandy was definitely not interested, especially when she heard what he said. "You know, it's difficult when you get old. Sometimes your knees get sore, or you can't see and hear well; but the worst thing is when you can't keep your wives happy in bed. That's a terrible thing. And that's really why I'm going to Durban."

The solemn mood began to lift for some, but Mandy grew uncomfortable. He continued, "Sometimes old men are like tractors that've been around a long time—you know how those things don't start every time. They've got work to do, but they can't do it." Her discomfort was unnoticed as Bongani's words were met with loud guffaws. He spoke sternly in response. "It isn't funny, my friends. You'll also get old one day; then you'll understand. And I have two wives to keep happy, don't forget that.

"My wives are beautiful; I'm a lucky man. Number two, she is still young enough to have more children; she says she doesn't want more babies, but that's how a man shows he's a man. My number one wife...well, no more babies for her because she's old like me, but I must still keep her happy. So, I went to see the sangoma—our traditional doctor," he explained to the Americans.

Mandy wished he was telling his story in Zulu so that she wouldn't need to listen, but he obviously wanted the foreigners to hear. She looked away as he continued. "The sangoma wanted to see my wives first. They were in her rondavel for a long time. Then she called me inside and threw the bones for me. Those bones said my wives would soon be happy but first, the sangoma told me, I must go and see a man in Durban to get some western medicine. I've been to see him once already. When I went that first time, he gave me two blue pills—one for each wife. They were expensive, so I only bought two to see if they'd work. I didn't want to waste my money."

His lack of inhibition was surprising to Mandy. She'd

spent two years in Africa and had encountered many situations that she'd found strange—situations where privacy was not given a consideration—but nothing compared to this encounter with Bongani. She squirmed when he looked directly at her saying, "You look like you don't believe me, but I'm telling you, my friend, they worked well. I was like a young man again. My wives, they were very happy. So now I'm going back to buy more."

He continued looking at her, as if wanting her to say something, but she remained silent. What could she say to an old man using pills for erectile dysfunction?

It was a relief when Philani said, "Well, I definitely don't believe you. How can a pill do that?"

Lindiwe spoke up. "Actually, it's true. You can get pills for that problem."

Philani raised his eyebrows. "How do you know that?"

"Because I work in a chemist shop." Her tone was sharp when she added, "I see men buying them all the time with prescriptions."

Noticing Philani's relief at Lindiwe's response, Mandy guessed there was some chemistry between them. She was eager to find out more about Lindiwe, if only this old man would stop talking, but he seemed determined to hold the floor.

Bongani ignored the interruption and continued to speak. "I don't know *how* they work, but I'm telling you they *do* work. And my wives, they wanted me to get more. The doctor told me I must be careful and only take one when I'm in bed, otherwise they're dangerous. I don't know why, but that's what he said. Here, this is the box—

you can see for yourselves." He passed it around for everyone to look at the empty container.

"I don't wish to see it," Reverend Dlamini said when it came towards him, "and please do not give it to Jabulani either. He's just a child."

Mandy agreed with the priest wholeheartedly on this matter. An old man's sexual impotence was not a thing Jabulani should be hearing about. Now she was pleased that Bongani hadn't been speaking in Zulu.

"Mfundisi," the old man responded, waving his hand as if shooing flies. "You—you can't see well, so you wear glasses. Now you can see. Is that wrong? Me, I need help keeping my wives happy."

The priest muttered, "I think you're keeping yourself happy, not your wives."

But before Reverend Dlamini could continue, Lindiwe began to giggle. When Bongani frowned at her, she quickly placated him. "It's nothing, don't worry." Then, turning her back on the old man, she whispered something to Thandi.

Mandy thought she heard the words "sleeping pills." She must have overheard correctly because Thandi gasped and her face broke into a smile. "That sangoma is very clever. The old man takes the little blue pills, then he goes to sleep and dreams about...you know...and he thinks his dreams are real," she whispered.

The two of them started to giggle and Mandy couldn't stop herself laughing out loud when she heard Lindiwe say, "That's why his wives are so happy."

The three women's laughter became almost uncontrollable, much to Bongani's annoyance. Unable to hear what they were saying, he frowned, drank more beer—and glared at them.

As she glanced at his frail shape, a thought struck Mandy. She tried hard to control her laughter but she was still giggling when she said to the two women, "It's fraud though...The old guy is paying a lot of money to buy pills that are just placebos. It's a rip-off."

Lindiwe laughed even more. "No, that sangoma was clever. She found a solution for everyone, him and his wives."

"It *is* dishonest, though, you have to admit. I mean you could call it elder abuse," Mandy replied, attempting to stop laughing.

"Why is it abuse if it makes him happy?"

Mandy opened her mouth to say something further, but stopped herself. Maybe it was karma.

CHAPTER 6

All phones were forgotten and the air suddenly seemed carbonated with laughter—except from Bongani. "I don't see any respect here for an old man," he grunted, looking at the three women. "I share my beer with you, and what do you do? You drink it and then you laugh at me. Young people don't know what respect is anymore."

Lindiwe swallowed hard and tried to look serious. "I'm sorry, baba. I'm happy for you and your wives."

Mandy felt awkward at the rebuke from Bongani, but she was surprised to hear Lindiwe stop laughing and say, "The thing is, baba, I respect your age but I don't respect your ideas."

"Whoa, that's heavy," Ryan murmured to Mandy. "This should be an interesting discussion."

"I like Lindiwe more and more; she's got fighting spirit," Mandy whispered back. "She's my kind of person."

"I don't want my family to choose my husband for me. I'll never let my family do that," Lindiwe continued.

The old man gasped. "But your family must get lobola for you. You cannot change that." As an afterthought, he added, "Even if you choose your own husband, he must still pay lobola."

Mandy held her breath.

"You're wrong," Lindiwe said. "I know that lots of women feel proud about it. They accept it, but I'm not one of them. Nobody's going to think he owns me. And my grandmother agrees. She's not stuck in the past like you. She's the one who gave me these chickens to take to Durban. She says she doesn't want lobola for me. She trusts me. My grandmother knows that I'll look after her now that she's old—just like she looked after me when my parents died. I was also an orphan, you see."

Reverend Dlamini reached out to the Zulu woman saying, "I'm sorry to hear that, sisi. I can understand how important your grandmother is to you." He was a man full of empathy; Mandy could see that.

Lindiwe nodded. "Yes, Mfundisi. My grandmother looked after me; my auntie also helped. I finished twelfth grade because of them. Now I work at a chemist shop during the day and study at Technikon every night. I'm going to be a pharmacist." There was indignation in her voice as she uttered these words. "If I marry one day, I'll marry someone I choose for myself."

Bongani shook his head.

"Have you got a boyfriend in Durban?" Philani inquired.

Mandy smiled. Chemistry was definitely working.

Lindiwe's response was curt. "I've got no time for boyfriends. I work and study. That's all." Her tone suddenly changed as she added, "But now a terrible thing has happened and I have to get money to find my auntie's body."

Everyone stared at her and Mandy wondered if she'd misheard. Eager to understand better, she was pleased when Reverend Dlamini asked, "What's this about your auntie's body?

"Yes, what do you mean?" Mandy added.

"Ah, my friends, it's terrible what some people do. My auntie was sick, so I took her to the hospital in Durban. She was getting better, then suddenly when I went there—the nurses told me she was dead. And they told me her body was gone. The undertaker had taken it away. I asked them, 'Why didn't you call me to say she was dying?' They said it happened too quickly and they needed the bed, so they had to move her straight away. I know there are lots of sick people and not so many beds, so the hospital had to move her fast. But when I went to the mortuary, they said I must pay two hundred rand for them to find the body. Now my gogo wants to bury Auntie here in Umzimkulu with our ancestors. It's already a lot of money to do that, but first we must pay to find her body before we can bring her home."

Frowning, Mandy said to Lindiwe. "How can that happen? Don't you have to identify her body?"

The Zulu woman shrugged. "Those people at the mortuary don't care. They won't listen to me. They said the hospital had already identified her body and I must pay for them to find it."

The priest said, "That's not right. Like I said, it's terrible when people are so greedy that they forget right from wrong, sisi. That's a bad thing they're doing. That makes me angry. If you like, I'll come with you. We'll get your auntie back and we won't pay anything, I promise you. They won't argue with an umfundisi."

As Lindiwe nodded her thanks, Mandy's heart went out to her. It was terrible that such corruption existed, exploiting people who could least afford it. She didn't know how, but she wanted to help as well—but before she could say anything, Philani spoke up. "I'll help you too," he said. "If you give me your phone number, we can arrange to meet in Durban."

Mandy wasn't surprised by Philani's eagerness to help, nor by Lindiwe's acceptance of his offer. She felt a warm glow, loving every minute of the afternoon and thankful they hadn't rented a car. And, the more she watched the little boy sitting quietly next to the priest, the more she wanted to see him smile.

Lindiwe pointed to the basket of chickens and told the priest, "I was going to sell those in Durban to make some money, but now you've saved me two hundred rand. So I want you to take these birds and feed your orphans."

Reverend Dlamini clapped his hands together. "Sisi, you're kind. Young boys are always hungry."

He explained to Jabulani in Zulu that they had been given a gift and soon would be eating chickens. Mandy's heart warmed to see the boy smile—just what she'd wanted to see. When he answered the priest in Zulu, they both laughed and Reverend Dlamini patted him on the back, informing everyone that Jabulani wanted to keep the hens in a chicken run. "That way," he said, "we'll have eggs for many months, not just meat for a few days. He's a clever boy."

Mandy longed to reach out and hug the child, who looked pleased when everyone applauded him. He almost smiled.

Bongani was still frowning, however. "What those people at the mortuary are doing is wrong, I agree. They shame the ancestors. But it's also wrong to ignore our traditions. Aren't you proud to be a Zulu woman?" He glared at Lindiwe. "Your grandmother needs payment when you get married. You've just told us what she did for you; lobola is her right."

Listening with baited breath, Mandy watched the Zulu woman grit her teeth before she replied. "I am very proud. But that doesn't mean I must do everything the way it was done a hundred years ago. Do you still expect women to walk around with bare breasts just because that's what traditional Zulu women used to do?"

Bongani eyes brightened and he nodded. "Yes, I wish they would. Why do you women cover your breasts now? Breasts are beautiful. I'm proud of my wives' breasts. They are too. They don't cover them. Why do you want to hide your beauty? You don't hide your face. Breasts are just as beautiful as faces." After a moment's thought, he chuckled and added, "In fact, they're even better than some faces."

Mandy turned her head to hide her smile. He was so outrageous that he was funny—but he was creepy at the same time. It was unexpected that one so frail would be so fixated on sex. When she glanced at Lindiwe, she could see that the Zulu woman's anger was about to explode; before that could happen, though, Philani spoke up.

"It's different now, baba; breasts are private. One day when I marry, I don't want other men looking at my wife's breasts."

Lindiwe spun around and gave him a high five, before turning back to continue her argument with Bongani. "Zulu men should accept change. You're afraid to do that," she told him.

"Rubbish. Zulu men are never afraid," he retorted.

Her voice was calm, but firm, as she spoke. "Men aren't always in charge anymore. Women are judges and cabinet ministers and…"

Mandy was tempted to back up Lindiwe, adding her thoughts about women's rights, but she kept quiet when Reverend Dlamini coughed and put his hands together as if in prayer. He interceded, saying, "Please, stop arguing. Show respect for one another. People are born and they die and the world seems to change, but still the sun comes up each morning and goes down each night. That doesn't change. The sun cannot escape the sunset. Our time here is short, but people waste it fighting. Let's not do that. It's better to laugh than cry—we all have a lot to cry about already, so why not make each other happy instead?"

CHAPTER 7

As she listened to the priest speaking so profoundly, tears welled in Mandy's eyes. The people she was traveling with were more interesting than she could ever have imagined. She'd spent two years in Namibia, yet in all that time, she'd never felt what she was experiencing this afternoon. Lindiwe was a woman with whom she felt a connection—there was something about her that made Mandy want to know her better. And the priest, whom she thought was going to be a drag, was profound. She looked at him in admiration; he was a peacemaker and a caregiver. But most of all, little Jabulani had captured her heart as he sat in silence, watching and listening. She was thankful to be here with them all.

However, she'd been sitting outside for a long time, first waiting for the taxi, and now waiting for petrol to arrive. She'd also been drinking a lot of tea and water. Feeling uncomfortable, she whispered to Ryan, "I need to pee badly."

He muttered, "Me too. That beer is going straight through me." He looked around and suggested, "What about behind a bush over there in that field?"

Their fellow passengers barely noticed Mandy and Ryan's departure when they slipped away. Once they'd relieved themselves, the Americans kept their distance— close enough to see whether Joseph returned, but far enough to have some space.

"I've been watching you," Ryan said. "You've hardly taken your eyes off that kid. What's the big deal?"

Mandy shrugged. "Nothing. I just like looking at him. He fascinates me. He's such a beautiful child, don't you think? Those big eyes of his..."

"Yeah, he's a cute kid, I suppose, but one kid's much like another to me. I didn't enjoy teaching young ones very much, much preferred the older ones. Little kids are too needy and whiny."

"Well, I wouldn't say Jabulani is whiny. The poor child is almost catatonic, he's had so much to deal with."

"I guess," Ryan replied. "To be honest though, I wouldn't mind a break from all of them. Why don't we wait here for a while? It's nice and peaceful. Let's just stay here and chat."

"OK. What do you want to chat about?" she said with a laugh as they sat down and made themselves comfortable on the ground.

"Anything you like. How about, why did you join the Peace Corps?"

She looked away. "Oh, that's a long story. I'm not sure I want to talk about it."

"I've got time to listen. Come on..."

As he pressed her to speak, Mandy's expression changed. She wasn't smiling any longer. First, she looked past Ryan, staring into the distance, then she rubbed her temples and looked at the ground. Realizing he'd struck a nerve, he said nothing and waited for her to speak.

She sat thinking about the priest, how he'd encouraged Philani to share his troubles, recommending that it would help solve problems to talk about them. Maybe she should take Reverend Dlamini's advice as well. It felt awkward, but perhaps speaking of her pain would ease it.

Eventually she looked up at Ryan and sighed. "When I was seventeen, I took my Mom's car to a party one night while my parents were out. My best friend, Michelle, came with me. I didn't have permission but we were sure we could get away with it. Oh boy, how wrong we were..." She swallowed hard. "There was alcohol at the party; I didn't have much because I was driving. I wasn't drunk or anything, I just had one small drink. Michelle had a few drinks though, and then she vanished. When I found her outside, there were two drunk guys all over her and it looked like she'd passed out." She shook her head, saying, "That's why I really hate it now when people have too much to drink. It reminds me of that night."

Ryan flinched, but he said nothing as Mandy continued with her story.

She looked up and said, "I screamed and pushed them away—I'm sure they'd spiked her drink. I needed to get her home. They didn't want her to leave and tried to stop me pulling her clothes back in place. I was really angry and shouted at them, but they didn't care—and Michelle hardly knew what was happening. She came around enough that I could get her to the car, but they followed us; I was driving fast to shake them off. By then Michelle was wide awake, laughing and telling me to speed up. She was hanging out the window, shouting at them. I tried telling her to put her seat belt back on, but she didn't hear me, and the guys were getting closer. We were almost home, so close—just around the corner." She stopped and swallowed hard again. "I don't know what happened exactly, but I lost control and we slammed into a tree." For a few moments she said nothing, before murmuring, "Michelle was thrown out of the car. She died instantly."

Her face was buried in her hands and her voice was barely audible when she added, "The guys took off immediately; I didn't even know who they were. They never came anywhere near to help. Oh God, I wish I'd been the one who died. I had broken bones, lots of deep cuts, and I lost some teeth, but like the priest on the bus, I survived."

Ryan said nothing. He just listened.

"I was a mess. I wanted to die. It was my fault that it happened...I shouldn't even have had one drink. I shouldn't have taken the car. I was such a fool."

She was silent a long time before able to speak again. "After the accident, I became good friends with Michelle's sister, Cassie. I guess our shared grief brought us closer. We're still in touch. She and my parents encouraged me to see a therapist. I fought against it, but it was the therapist who suggested I join the Peace Corps." Mandy scratched her head. "It's not easy to forgive myself, though. Even after teaching in Namibia for two years, I still feel the scales aren't balanced. I owe more than I can ever give back."

At this point, Ryan couldn't stop himself from speaking. "Mandy, you can't torture yourself. Try to leave the past behind and move forward. Don't bring it with you like heavy baggage."

She shook her head. "It's easy for you to say that, but it didn't happen to you—and I hope it never will. I can't stop feeling this way, though. The past made me who I am. I carry it with me. It haunts me." Starting to shake all over, she hugged her arms across her chest and continued. "I realize that I have to make peace with myself; I'm trying to do that, but it's not easy. I caused someone to die; someone with her whole life ahead of her. Every day I'm alive is another day she didn't have. I have to make my days worthwhile." She squeezed her eyes shut and murmured, "Anyway, to answer your question, that's why I joined the Peace Corps. It was for Michelle."

When she opened her eyes again, she said in a voice little more than a whisper, "I'm ashamed of the person I was before the accident."

Ryan shook his head. "You were young, that's all. There's nothing wrong with being young. If you don't grow up, that's a shameful thing."

They sat for a while in silence until Mandy said, "I'm going for a walk—I need to be on my own for a bit. Don't let them leave without me if our driver comes back." She didn't wait for an answer but stood up and walked away.

"Stay where I can see you," he called after her, reluctant to let her go alone but aware that it was useless to argue.

A few hundred yards away, Mandy slumped to the ground, sobbing. The flood gates opened and years of sorrow came pouring out. The agony of loss and self-recrimination attacked her again with the same force they had seven years ago—and a little voice came back to haunt her. *It was your fault, Mandy Walker.* It was a voice that wouldn't be silenced.

CHAPTER 8

When Ryan and Mandy returned to the shady tree, Lindiwe beckoned them. "Come and sit with us," she said. Noticing the American woman's red eyes, she frowned and patted the ground next to her. "Here's a place next to me. Come."

Mandy was taken aback. She wanted to make this woman's acquaintance, but hadn't expected the Zulu woman to make any overture. She smiled weakly at Lindiwe, who reached out and patted her arm as she sat down. "I wondered where you were. I thought maybe you were walking back to that place where we found you. I'm glad you came back, my friend," she said, smiling.

Warmed by such unexpected kindness, Mandy murmured, "Thanks." Lindiwe's hand was still on her arm as Mandy reached across to grasp it in her own. "Thank you very much," she said again. The two women looked at one another for a few moments, but said nothing more.

It was easier listening to other people's stories than thinking of her own and so Mandy quickly turned her attention to Thandi. She was tightening her head scarf as she approached the priest and asked, "Can I speak to you about something?"

Reverend Dlamini nodded and beckoned her to come closer.

Settling near him and pulling her dress carefully over her knees, she said, "I am forty years now. I'm too old to have more babies. But the thing is, my boyfriend won't marry me unless I give him a child. Samuel says Zulu men want children and I must prove that I can have babies. But I have got two children already; they're grown up, Mfundisi. And not only that, I've got a good job at the post office in Ixopo. I'm on my way to Durban for training so that I can take over my boss's job when he retires next year. I don't want another baby. I like my job too much." She sighed and added, "What can I do?"

"Wow," Mandy murmured to Ryan, "even in this remote place, women want careers." Her sadness was pushed aside as she listened to Thandi.

"I know what advice you'd give her," Ryan replied in an undertone.

Her eyes were still red as she nodded and whispered, "It's a no-brainer." Then she added, "It's turning out to be an afternoon of confessions and confidences, isn't it?"

He nodded and smiled at her. "Thanks for telling me your story, Mandy. Did offloading it make you feel any better?"

She shrugged. "No, not really."

He leaned over and put an arm around her. "Hang in there. You're a strong woman. I reckon you were spared for important things; you just don't know what they are yet. You'll figure it out though. I know you will."

She nodded and looked away, thankful for his kindness and friendship—despite their many disagreements. She was at a loss for words though and was pleased to be spared further discussion when she heard Reverend

Dlamini begin speaking to Thandi.

"Do you want to marry this man, sisi?"

Thandi nodded. "My other children have different fathers. They were no good—they paid nothing for their children. Samuel is different. I like him too much." Her voice wavered as she spoke. "But sometimes he has too much to drink and then I'm scared. He gets angry." Shaking her head, she added, "It makes him mad that I haven't got pregnant."

As the priest put his hand in front of his eyes and rubbed his forehead, Lindiwe turned to Mandy and whispered, "It's hard for us women. We're left with babies while men go and make more of them somewhere else. How does she know Samuel will marry her if she has his baby?"

Mandy nodded in sympathy.

The priest cleared his throat before saying, "How old is Samuel?"

"He's also forty."

"Has he been married before?" he asked.

"He had a wife, but she died. She was having a baby; she and the baby died that same day. It was very sad for him; that's why he wants another child."

"I understand," said the priest, "but he can't bring back that child and his wife." Reverend Dlamini frowned and removed his spectacles to clean them. "And it's better to have a baby after you are married—not before." As Thandi stared at him, he said simply, "I'll pray for you, sisi."

Prayers hardly seemed helpful when Thandi had asked for advice, Mandy thought. She turned to her and said,

"Have you told him that you don't want another baby?"

Thandi shook her head. "How can I do that when he wants one so badly? I feel sorry for him. I suppose it will be OK if I get pregnant again, but I'm too old. I don't think it's going to happen. I like him too much. I really want to marry him, but I don't want to lose my job."

Frowning, Mandy leaned towards Thandi and said, "Wouldn't you be able to get maternity leave?"

Thandi shrugged. "Yes, I could," she replied. "But I'd be away for a long time. They might find somebody else to do my work, like the junior clerk. I know she wants promotion."

It came as no surprise when Bongani gave his opinion. "You're a beautiful woman, sisi. If this man doesn't want to marry you, he must be crazy. I tell you what. If Samuel won't marry you, you can be my third wife."

Mandy was getting used to the old man's ways and came to expect remarks like this from him. He meant no harm and she smiled at his joke.

"You must be clever about this," he continued. "Listen to me, sisi. You know a man always wants what he can't have—and Samuel, he'll be the same. You must tell him that if he only wants you so that he can have a baby, then you will find someone else. Tell him that you already have two children and you don't mind if you have more or not."

It was obvious to Mandy that the old man was no longer joking. His expression was very serious as he stared at Thandi, who was looking aghast. She opened her mouth to speak, but Bongani wagged his finger at her to stop. "He won't let you go—not a beautiful woman like you.

And maybe you will have another baby. You never know. My first wife, she was forty when our last child was born. That made me very proud—only a strong man can make babies when his wife is forty. You can tell Samuel that too. And you can also tell him that he must stop drinking if it makes him angry. That is not good, sisi. Drinking is only good when it makes you happy."

Reverend Dlamini nodded his head, then shook his head, then frowned. He looked at Mandy and raised his eyebrows. She was flattered that he appeared to care how she reacted. It seemed to her as if he wanted to add some thoughts, but he swallowed hard and raised his head to look at the heavens instead.

It was a while before Thandi spoke. "You are right," she said finally. "I must talk to him. The trouble is, I'm afraid he'll leave me." She blew her nose and wiped her eyes. "I wasn't so clever when I was a young girl; that's why I had two babies with bad fathers. Girls are smarter today, just like you," she said, looking at Lindiwe and Mandy. Mandy felt pleased to be included in the conversation, especially when, after a moment's hesitation, Thandi leaned across and spoke in an undertone. "I'm sure you won't make the same mistakes I made. When I was young like you, I went to a clinic in Ixopo to get 'the pill.' I was very excited because everyone was talking about this wonderful thing that could stop you having babies if you didn't want them. The nurse gave me a packet with twenty-eight pills in it and explained, in English, how they worked. I didn't understand, but I was so happy to have them that I just nodded and said yes. I thought they would last me a long time. I didn't know that I had to take one every day. I thought I only needed to take one when I—you know—played. I had two babies before I discovered my mistake…"

It was both funny and sad, and Mandy didn't know whether to laugh or cry. With no hesitation, though, Lindiwe burst out laughing. She saw only the humor.

While they were still giggling, Bongani changed the subject. "I hope Joseph gets back quickly. It'll be dark soon."

"Oh, there's lots of time. Don't worry. Look, the hadedahs are still busy over there, searching for food; they haven't started flying home for the night yet," Reverend Dlamini replied.

Mpilo interrupted him. "That bird is called an ibis. That's its proper name."

Bongani grunted his reply. "You can call it an ibis if you want, but nobody will know what you're talking about. Hadedah is good enough for me. Everybody knows what hadedahs are."

Despite his shortcomings, Mandy couldn't help liking the crusty old man.

CHAPTER 9

✵

Aware of increasing anxiety among some of her fellow passengers, Mandy made a suggestion. They'd helped distract her and she could do the same for them. "I'd like to take some pictures while there's still some light," she said.

They all looked with interest at the digital camera she pulled from her backpack. Philani responded by saying, "It'll be good to think about something else. I'm hungry. All I can think about is food."

She immediately pulled a bag of peanuts from her pocket and offered to share them. "Please, help yourselves," she said to the group. There were appreciative thanks uttered and Reverend Dlamini blessed her for her kindness, adding that Jabulani was very hungry. Fueled by the goodwill, Ryan opened his backpack and pulled out some trail mix. There followed a lot of talk in Zulu, after which Bongani announced that Mandy and Ryan understood ubuntu. "You're looking after everyone, not just yourselves," he said.

By now, respect had completely replaced Mandy's earlier misgivings. She realized that her fellow travelers came with so little—just chickens, a bicycle, and stories, but they had accepted her and Ryan. She suddenly felt a part of this group.

"Let me take a photo of each of you. Who wants to go first?" she asked. They all started to laugh, but nobody wanted to be the leader. "OK, I'll choose," she said.

Eager to have a record of Jabulani, the first picture she took was of him. He looked startled as she focused the lens and pressed a button. When she examined the result, she announced that it was excellent and leaned over to show it to him; it captured the trust in his big, brown eyes. Reverend Dlamini peered at the picture as well and smiled. "You're a handsome fellow," he said in Zulu, before whispering a few more words to him.

Jabulani laughed and clapped his hands, then looked at Mandy and said, "Thank you, sisi."

"Those are the first English words he's spoken," the priest said, looking at Mandy. "I think he likes you."

"They're the *only* words he's spoken," said Bongani. "That little fellow likes listening to us talk, even if he can't understand the stories."

Lindiwe quickly said, "It's just as well he didn't understand your story, baba."

"That's very true," Mandy added, laughing.

Bongani merely grunted and took another swig of beer.

Warmed by Jabulani calling her sisi, Mandy smiled at him. He returned the smile, but quickly looked down again. She had that urge to hug him once more but she didn't want to overwhelm him. Addressing the priest, she said, "If you give me your address, I'll print it and send it to you. In fact, I can do that for everyone," she said, looking around.

This changed things; suddenly everyone wanted their picture taken. Mandy took photos and Ryan wrote down names and addresses, making notes next to each so that

Mandy would know who was who. He had to help Bongani by writing his address for him.

After a while Reverend Dlamini said, "So, where do you two come from? You're not South African; you sound different."

Ryan smiled and spoke for both of them. "We're Americans, but we've been teaching in Namibia for two years. My friend here is Mandy, and I'm Ryan," he added, extending his hand to the priest. They greeted in the African way of grasping in a handshake, quickly clasping each other's thumbs, then returning to grasp hands again. It was noticed by all the men that Ryan knew how to do this and they smiled.

"So, what were you teaching in Namibia?" asked Reverend Dlamini.

Mandy looked at Ryan and said, "Why don't you explain?"

"Sure," he replied. "We joined the Peace Corps and were sent to Namibia, to different villages," he explained. "Mandy taught English; I taught Mathematics."

The priest nodded and said, "We are lucky to get this help from you here in Africa. Thank you."

"Was it hard, my friends? Namibia is far away from America—and you were living in small villages there when you were probably used to big cities," Lindiwe asked.

Touched by another display of empathy from her, Mandy smiled at Lindiwe, happy to talk to this woman. "Yes, it was very different. I really missed having electricity and running water. In California, we're used to an easy life. The thing I missed most was the Internet though. It made me feel a bit cut off without it."

"Oh hell, the biggest difference for me was all the snakes," Ryan said. "I got used to no electricity. I even liked showering under a bucket of water hanging from a tree. But the snakes were something else...geez, there were lots of them near the house where I lived. That was a big problem when the rains came." He paused, looking around at the expectant faces. "You see, it rained so much that eventually the outside pit toilet collapsed. It'd been nice and comfortable before—not just a hole in the ground. It was a concrete seat over a deep pit. Ah, but the trouble was that the ground got so wet from all the rain that the whole thing collapsed, concrete seat and all."

Everyone laughed when Mpilo said, "I hope nobody was sitting on it at the time."

Ryan shook his head and smiled. "After that we had to go out in the fields, but we'd just planted millet seeds so we had to do our business between the rows. That was fine if you only wanted to pee," he continued, "but when you had to do something more, it meant taking a hoe to dig a hole and cover it up. It also meant squatting with your feet on one side of a row and your backside perched over the other side." His audience began to laugh again, and Mandy joined in.

"I used to wait until night time, tramping through the mud with a hoe in one hand, toilet paper and a flashlight in the other. This one time, I'd been waiting all day and was desperate to go, so I decided to do my business first and dig a hole later to cover it. I put all my stuff down and did what I had to do. But as I leaned over to pick up the toilet paper, I saw a snake curled up, resting on the ridge right underneath me."

Mandy's eyes opened wide, Lindiwe and Thandi shrieked, and the men in the group laughed more than they'd laughed all afternoon.

"That snake slept through the performance, but I'm telling you, I took off as fast as I could."

Everyone, including Mandy, hung on his every word; his storytelling was impressive. It felt good, however, when Mpilo turned to her and asked, "Have you also enjoyed being here in Africa, sisi?"

They were no longer outsiders, she realized, and that made her smile. "Yes, thank you for asking; I've loved it. But I'm especially enjoying myself sitting here, hearing all your stories." Her eyes wandered to Jabulani, who sat quietly watching her. She smiled at him; it was all she could do without language to communicate with the child.

CHAPTER 10

Philani had been sitting on a soccer ball with his legs outstretched, listening to Ryan's story. He'd been rocking back and forth, but suddenly the ball slipped and rolled away from him. Mpilo and Ryan automatically each put a foot out to stop it as Philani landed on his bottom with a thump. Smiles turned to laughs, and when they jumped up and began kicking the ball, the deserted road became an impromptu soccer field. They beckoned everyone else to join in and suddenly it was game time, with Bongani and Thandi as spectators and self-appointed referees.

The soccer match continued for half an hour, during which time Mandy was amazed by Jabulani. He dribbled the ball with skillful footwork, speeding past adults like a darting impala; she applauded when he scored three goals in quick succession. The child was laughing for the first time that afternoon and it made Mandy happy to see his exuberance. He responded to her encouragement by passing the ball to her as often as he could and she was pleased that, even without language, she'd managed to engage with the child.

Eventually, tired but happy, the players stopped to rest, each side claiming victory. As they did so, Thandi leaned over and prodded Ryan. "Your stories are better than your soccer," she said, prompting more laughter, especially from Mandy. "I'd like to hear more of them.

Tell me, my friend, have you ever seen lions? I'm an African; this place is my home, but I've never seen one."

Before Ryan had a chance to reply, Mpilo—who was still mopping his brow—spoke up. "That's because lions are endangered." When his fellow travelers looked at him in surprise, he nodded. "It's true—it's just as well we have game reserves where they're protected. They used to be all over the country, but not anymore. It's terrible. People here in Africa help hunters from overseas shoot our animals—because the foreigners have lots of cash. We can't only blame the foreigners. They couldn't do it if Africans didn't help them. And lions aren't the only endangered animals; it's the same with elephants, rhinos, giraffes... It's crazy. We can't kill our wild animals. Everything has a purpose. It's the balance of nature—but people are messing it all up."

Mandy was impressed, listening to Mpilo, and she whispered to Ryan, "This guy is passionate about wild life, isn't he?"

Ryan nodded. "Yup, and he's not shy about sharing his knowledge, either."

Mandy laughed and said softly, "Well yes, but he seems to know such a lot."

While they were whispering, Reverend Dlamini set about boiling more water. He was interested in refreshment after such a lot of exertion, and looking around at his fellow passengers, he said, "Joseph's been gone a long time. I think we could all do with more tea after that soccer game. Would you like some, Mandy?"

She was flattered to be singled out by him. "Yes please, I'd love some if there's enough."

Thandi commented, "Oh, I think Joseph's got more bags under his seat. There's plenty, don't worry. I wish he had tea leaves though; I like them better. Tea is nice and strong when you use leaves. And you know, my grandmother could tell fortunes with them."

"What do you mean?" asked Lindiwe.

"She could tell people what was going to happen when she looked at the tea leaves in the bottom of their cups."

Lindiwe frowned and shook her head. She looked at Mandy and they laughed. "Now I think she's telling stories," she said.

"No. It's true," Thandi replied. "My gogo read the leaves. She taught me how to do it too. If we had tea leaves here, I could show you."

Mpilo piped up, "I don't believe you. That's rubbish."

"Why won't you believe me? You believe that a sangoma can throw bones and tell you things, don't you?"

Mpilo shrugged. "But that's a sangoma. That's different," he said. "You're talking here about some leaves."

"I'm telling you—it's true. It works."

"Do tea leaves really taste that different from tea bags?" Mandy inquired.

"Oh yes, they're much nicer," Thandi replied.

"I'll have to take your word for it, I guess. Maybe we can break open a tea bag and you could read those leaves. What do you think?" she suggested.

"They'll be too small," Thandi replied. "We can try, though. Joseph is taking too long, so he mustn't complain if we take some of his stuff. We can pay him back, maybe."

She jumped up to search Joseph's belongings under his seat in the taxi. From where she sat, Mandy could see the meager supplies; there were a few more biscuits, a tin of pilchards, a can opener, a few slices of bread—and lo and behold, a box of tea leaves.

Philani was so excited that he jumped up and did an impromptu dance, stomping his feet and holding up his arms in triumph. Mpilo joined in while Thandi and Lindiwe began to ululate. Mandy had never seen Zulu dancing before and her eyes lit up to see Jabulani's reaction when Philani beckoned him. The boy didn't hesitate; he leapt into the air. Inspired by Jabulani's agility, Philani did a somersault while Bongani whistled and drummed a beat against his flask. Reverend Dlamini beamed with pleasure, smiling at Mandy as he boiled more water for the next round of tea—this time made with leaves.

Mandy marveled as she watched Jabulani. He was transported while he danced, and when the trio finally stopped their exertions, although the boy's brow was damp with perspiration, he was smiling. She could see how much this had lifted his spirits and when Jabulani noticed her watching him, he smiled at her again. She saw his smile grow even bigger when he was handed the bread and pilchards Reverend Dlamini had prepared for him, along with a mug of tea. He spoke to everyone in Zulu, making them all laugh, and Mpilo explained to Mandy that the boy was happy because his stomach had been crying for food, but his legs had been crying too, because they wanted to dance.

"Zulu children learn to do this when they're small," Mpilo explained to her.

"You know what," Bongani announced suddenly. "It's nice sitting here, talking. This is what matters most, not how quickly we get to Durban. Sometimes people move too fast and we forget how to talk to each other. Then there's trouble. Fighting happens because people forget about ubuntu; they don't care about one another because they don't talk. So now I'm happy that the petrol was finished."

Mandy clapped her hands and smiled as she said, "You're so right, baba. I am too." Bongani smiled at her and nodded, looking happy that she'd addressed him as baba.

"Yes," replied Reverend Dlamini. For the first time, Mandy noticed respect in his voice as he spoke to the old man. "When we were on the bus, nobody was speaking, but now we're friends, even if we don't agree about everything." These two men had disagreed strongly about everything, but they'd suddenly found commonality. Mandy was impressed.

By this time, Philani had finished his mug of tea and turned to Thandi. "Sisi, what must I do so that you can tell me what's going to happen in my life?"

Mandy noticed that his eyebrows were arched in disbelief, but she also saw that Thandi paid no attention to this. She showed him how he needed to get as much tea out of the mug as possible, then turn it around three times and tip it over. She peered at the leaves when he had done this. For a while she was silent, then her lips moved and she appeared to be counting.

Everyone listened intently when she began to speak. "I see eleven leaves here." She nodded her head and continued. "Yes. Those are the eleven cows—the lobola."

Mandy tried to conceal her amusement when Philani

groaned, "Ah no. Don't say that."

"But wait. I see you walking away from the cows, my friend. You aren't going to marry this girl."

His face broke into a smile—and so did Mandy's. "That sounds better."

"Yes, my friend. I see you with books," she continued. "You're going to finish Grade 12. And here I see you have four children—you see these four small leaves? And there's their mother; she's standing close to you. See that, two leaves stuck together? You've met her already; you're touching in the leaves. You'll get married and have lots of children; and you'll finish school."

Mandy watched as Philani's frown disappeared. "I hope you're right," he said, glancing at Lindiwe, who smiled but looked away quickly.

Nearly everyone wanted to have their leaves read after that, and Mandy watched as Thandi took the time to humor them. Lindiwe volunteered to go next, handing her mug to Thandi after following the necessary steps. As Thandi peered into it, she gasped. Everyone waited as she took her time to speak. "You have small bottles all around you; I can see them here. I think you'll have your own pharmacy one day. You'll be an important person in this place with all the bottles."

"It's a bottle store. She's going to learn how to make good utshwala," Bongani muttered.

Mandy couldn't help laughing at him—a deep belly laugh which made Bongani looked pleased with himself. Everyone else chuckled as well, amused by Bongani's quip as well as Mandy's infectious laughter.

Thandi paid no attention to them, however. "Does

anybody else want a turn?" she asked, looking around.

Ryan leaned across and whispered to Mandy, "I dare you to have a go."

"You go first."

He shrugged. "OK. I just wish I didn't have to drink this stuff, though." He swallowed the tea, trying not to show his distaste, followed instructions about emptying the mug—and then he waited.

Thandi took her time studying the leaves and Mandy wondered what she would come up with; it seemed like a lot of intelligent guess work was going on. Finally, Thandi said, "I see you working with small birds. Yes, maybe chickens." Ryan looked skeptical, but said nothing as Thandi continued. "I can see you're going to get married, but not soon. It'll take some time before you marry. You're trying to catch this girl—can you see her here?" Thandi showed him the leaves and pointed out where she saw his future wife.

Ryan raised an eyebrow and said, "She looks very small. Are you sure that's a girl and not a chicken?"

There was another outburst of laughter from the group, but Thandi slammed the enamel mug on the ground. "I'm not going to waste my time on you. You're mocking me."

The laughter stopped instantly, followed by an embarrassed silence and Ryan's apology. "I'm sorry. Please don't stop." He tried to look serious, but Thandi remained adamant.

"No. It's time for someone else."

And so, it was Mandy's turn. She went through the same procedure of turning and emptying the mug, then waited until Thandi was ready to speak. "I'm not sure what you're doing, but I see a child next to you. It's not your child, it's an African child. You're touching each other here," the fortune-teller said.

Mandy peered into the mug as Thandi pointed out what she saw: a small, dark leaf and a larger, lighter one next to it. "Can you see that?" she asked.

"Mmm," Mandy murmured, without conviction.

Bongani laughed and called out, "Can you see her getting married?"

Thandi smiled and said, "Yes, I can. There's a tall man here."

Bongani pointed at Ryan. "You must start saving. Wives are expensive, especially clever, beautiful ones."

"No, it's not Ryan she's going to marry," Thandi announced. "He's too busy chasing chickens. It's not him." Mandy was laughing at her remark, when Thandi turned towards her and murmured, "There's someone else. I can see him here; he's coming towards you. He'll be the one. You'll see."

Mandy nodded her thanks and smiled, but Ryan grunted. "She makes it up," he muttered to Mandy. "I'd be worried if I believed it."

Mandy raised her eyebrows. "I guess she didn't see any graduate school for me."

"You see what I mean. It's a load of bullshit. She just tells people what she thinks they want to hear. She's pissed off with me for laughing, so she's giving me a hard time."

Next it was Mpilo's turn to have his fortune told. As Thandi examined the mug, she nodded and said, "I see animals here; maybe they're elephants, they're very big.

And here you are with a gun. You're shooting something up in the sky. Yes, you're protecting the elephants. You're going to fight poachers."

"Hey, sisi," he exclaimed. "That's what I want to do when I finish my degree."

Mandy looked at him in surprise. Mpilo had been full of information and opinions, but he hadn't said he was a university student. She was filled with admiration, not just for Mpilo, but for all her fellow travelers' ambitions. Thandi wanted to get a promotion in the post office; Lindiwe was studying to be a pharmacist; Philani wanted to finish school; the priest had been to Fort Hare University and was looking to educate Jabulani. They all had so much to contend with, but that didn't stop them. Getting into graduate school had been difficult for her, but, by comparison, her challenge had been nothing.

Her thoughts were interrupted by Mpilo, who was explaining the dire situation of wild life on the continent. "There's big trouble with poachers. It's a huge problem. My brother, Vusi, works at Mkuze game reserve. Everything I know I've learned from him. He tells me that poachers work in teams. They fly over game reserves in micro-light planes so they can see where elephants are; sometimes they send drones. Then they radio other guys who come in quickly to kill the animals for their tusks. It used to be just elephants they wanted for the ivory, but now they want rhino horns as well. You see, some people in Asian countries think it makes them sexy—like Bongani with his pills."

Mandy smiled as the old man brushed the remark aside with a playful wave of his hand. Turning to Mpilo she said, "I bet you'll be very good at fighting poachers. It'll be a perfect job for you."

He acknowledged the compliment with a slight nod and continued to speak with passion. "It's very serious. People pay thousands of dollars for what they want, and people here in Africa get greedy. They kill these animals for them. It's got to stop, otherwise we'll lose all our wildlife."

"It's great there are people like you who will try to stop it. Good people," Mandy said.

"Wait," Thandi interrupted her sharply and looked at Mpilo. "I see something else here; I think it must be a mountain. What else could it be? It's much, much bigger than the elephants. Can you see it?" she asked, showing him the mug. "Yes. It's definitely a mountain."

Mpilo stared at the leaves. "Maybe it's Kilimanjaro. I hope so. One day, I want to go there. I want to climb it. Maybe that's what you're seeing."

This got Ryan's attention. He said, "Hey man, I also want to do that—before the glacier melts at the top."

"What do you mean?" asked Mpilo.

"Well, Kilimanjaro is the tallest mountain in Africa. It sits on the equator and it's the closest place on earth to the sun. That's why the ice is all going."

Mpilo frowned. "So? Why does that matter?" he asked. "It's still a long way from the sun. It's cold up there."

"Yes, it is, but not as cold as it once was. Global warming is causing the earth to get warmer and the ice is melting. It's nearly all gone already. That's why I want to go soon. Maybe we can go together? You too, Mandy? Why don't you come as well?"

She frowned, while Mpilo shook his head and said, "No. It costs too much money. I'll have to save for a long time. First I must finish paying for university. The ice will be gone before I get there."

Ryan stared at Mpilo and said, "I'll help you. And Mandy, think about it; it would be an amazing thing to do."

"I'll be going to grad school. I can't do it," she replied.

Ryan was not one to give up easily and she watched him turn from her to Mpilo. "OK. I'll make a deal with you then," he said to the Zulu man. "I'll help pay for you, if you help me get to the top—let's say in a year's time."

She saw Mpilo frown again. "You're joking."

"No. I'm absolutely serious. There's a lot I can learn from you, Mpilo—about wild life, about Africa."

The two men stared at one another and Mandy could almost read Mpilo's thoughts; there was no reason why he should believe this crazy American whom he'd only just met. Silence hung heavily between them as they both weighed up the situation. Finally, Ryan said, "I mean it. I'm not just making an idle offer. I would be honored if you'd agree."

Mpilo shook his head again. "You don't understand, Ryan. I've got no money and I can't take yours. I won't borrow from you either. I don't want to owe anything to anyone."

"I'd be the one indebted to you, trust me. I've listened to you speak about wildlife and I'd be picking your brains. I don't have the money now either, but I'm going back to a job. I'll save so that we can do this together. It won't cost that much; the biggest expense will be getting to Tanzania. You can fly from Durban to Nairobi and I'll meet you there, then we can catch a bus the rest of the way."

Mandy was as astonished as Mpilo was. Ryan was impulsive and generous, and he wasn't giving up on Mpilo, whose reply was slow in coming. When it did, it was measured. "I think you're crazy, but...OK, let's do it. I will pay you back one day, though, you'll see." He smiled before adding, "Maybe it was lucky we ran out of petrol after all."

CHAPTER 11

✤

Mandy grew silent as she watched Ryan. She recognized how generous he was, yet even though he'd been caring when she'd confided in him, she was filled with regret, wishing she hadn't been so forthcoming. It hadn't diminished her unhappiness telling him her troubles. Instead it had left her feeling exposed. What she really wanted was to forget about the accident, forget her guilt. Speaking about it had made all the pain resurface. Reading the tea leaves had been a distraction, but her negative feelings managed to creep back into her head, no matter how much she pushed them away.

Watching Mandy out the corners of his eyes, Ryan could see she was wrestling with demons again. The pain in her face was obvious. He wished he could help her, but he didn't know how. Lindiwe also noticed Mandy's mood change, and wondered about the American woman.

But Mpilo saw nothing of this. On a high, he was eager to talk more to his new friend. He laughed as he said to Ryan, "So do you still play soccer, or did you give it up when you came to Africa? I think you're out of practice." Addressing both the Americans, he asked if they'd been in South Africa for the World Cup soccer tournament in 2010.

Mandy, oblivious of anything but her own thoughts, was startled when Ryan nudged her. "Mpilo is talking to us," he said.

The young man was bouncing the soccer ball with one hand while looking intently at her and Ryan, repeating the question he'd just asked. It was an effort for her to concentrate on him and put her own thoughts aside, but she indicated she'd not been in South Africa then.

He nodded and continued speaking to them. "Well, even though we lost early in the tournament, it was exciting for us. We're poor people and it's hard for us to travel. But that year, we were lucky because the world came to us. We didn't need to travel. It was like a big party."

Ryan nodded. "I remember watching on TV and hearing those noise-makers everybody had. It was deafening. What do you call those things?"

"Vuvuzelas," Mpilo replied.

"Hey, I had a good business going with them," said Lindiwe, joining in the conversation. "I decorated vuvuzelas with beads, and when I couldn't do that fast enough, I started painting them with African designs. They sold as fast as the paint dried. I made good money; everybody wanted a souvenir from the World Cup." She paused and turned to Mandy, "My friend, I've got one here that I want to give you, then you'll always remember this afternoon when we had no petrol."

When Lindiwe pulled a small vuvuzela from her bag and handed the brightly decorated instrument to her, Mandy was astonished. "Oh wow," she said. At a loss for words initially, it took her a moment to say, "Thank you very much. It's so beautiful. Can I pay you for it?"

"Oh no, sisi, no. This is a gift from me to you. Whenever you look at it, you can remember me—remember all of us." The two women held each other's gaze. Then very quietly, Lindiwe added, "When I heard what you did, teaching those children in Namibia, I wanted to thank you. It's very good that you help our people. But there's something else." Lindiwe's voice was now a whisper, but her eyes didn't waver from Mandy. "I want you to be happy, sisi. Sometimes you look sad. Whatever the thing is that makes you unhappy, you must throw it away."

Mandy was astounded. Her bottom lip quivered slightly as she cradled the gift. "Thank you," she murmured. "I wish I could, but it's not that easy."

Lindiwe put out her hand and took Mandy's. The contact was comforting, and she listened as Lindiwe whispered, "My grandmother used to tell me something when I was a child. She said, 'When you're born, your life is like an empty basket that begins to fill up with stuff. Some of it *you* put in, and some of it other people put in. If you collect too many sad things, there won't be any room for happy things, so you've got to make room for them.' She's very wise, my gogo."

"But how?" Mandy replied. "How do I do that?"

"Take out the sad things, one at a time. Look at each one and say you are sorry for it, and then let it go. Better still, throw it away. Then you must be finished with it. When you've made room, you can slowly replace each sad thing with a happy thing." Lindiwe squeezed her hand, adding softly, "You can do it."

Gratitude overwhelmed Mandy and she sat speechless, clutching the vuvuzela.

Bongani, meanwhile, had been reminded of the rampant crime at the World Cup and was sharing his ideas about unruly youth. He muttered, "We must use the sjambok and whip them; it's the only way they'll learn." Looking around at everyone, he added, "I'm telling you, it was better in the old days."

Mandy, still holding her vuvuzela, began to feel uneasy as the priest looked solemnly at the old man and said, "You mustn't joke like that." Despite Reverend Dlamini being a peacemaker, it seemed like an argument might be brewing.

Bongani was having difficulty sitting up straight, but he did his best and frowned as he tried to focus. "I'm not joking, Mfundisi. It's true. When children don't listen, you must whip them with a sjambok." He raised his arm and flung it down in front of him, flicking his wrist as he did so. "I got hidings from my father when I was a boy, and I gave my children hidings too. Not too sore—not like the policemen do it. Hey, they hurt you too much."

Mandy was stunned by the old man's outburst. The thought of somebody whipping Jabulani was intolerable. She frowned and said, "Why do you think that's a good idea to beat somebody? That's cruel and unusual punishment."

"No, it's not," Bongani replied. "Like I said, you don't do it as hard as the police do it. That's cruel. But it's not unusual. It happens all the time. It should happen more."

She was pleased when the priest contradicted the old man. He might be a peacemaker, but he stood up for what he believed was right. "No. You're wrong," he said. "Let me tell you about this boy called Jacob. When he was fourteen, he was sleeping on the street; he had nowhere else to go—his parents and grandparents were dead. He began stealing because he was hungry. Soon he was in a gang. It wasn't long before those boys stole a gun and that's when Jacob grew afraid. He told them he wanted to leave the gang, but they started arguing; they didn't want to let him go. Fortunately, a policeman overheard the argument. He chased the other boys away and brought Jacob to me at the orphanage. When that child came to me, he learned what was right and wrong, but I never used a sjambok; I used kindness."

Mandy swallowed hard and murmured, "Is he still at the orphanage?"

The priest shook his head. "No, sisi. All that happened some years ago. Mrs. Liz that I told you about, she paid for Jacob to finish school—and after that she paid for him to go to university to get a degree. He's an adult now and works for a big company in Johannesburg, but he hasn't forgotten us. He sends money every month for another boy to go to school. He wants to give back to us what we gave to him. He always comes back at Christmas with presents for everybody. He's the boys' role model; they all want to make their lives better—like Jacob did."

She stared at the priest, wrestling with her emotions, and began biting her bottom lip. Filled with inner turmoil, she eventually murmured, "That's a beautiful story." The priest accepted her compliment and smiled as she continued speaking to him. "I think you are also a good role model for them. You've given them something to live for." Clutching her vuvuzela tightly, she almost choked on her words when she said, "You're a good example to us all. You're what I was really looking for when I came to Africa. I wanted to do something worthwhile. You've shown me it's possible to make a difference. Maybe all the other boys in that gang ended up badly, but you helped one boy change his life."

"Thank you, Mandy," the priest answered, touched by her praise.

She took a deep breath and swallowed hard. "I was wondering," she began—and then stopped, trying to find the right words. Everyone watched and waited as she struggled. After a few moments, she spoke again. "I was wondering whether...well, whether I can work with you for a while. You see, I've finished teaching in Namibia now and I could help Jabulani learn to speak English before I go back home."

Reverend Dlamini stared at her. "Are you serious?" When she nodded, he put his hands together, as if in prayer. "I can't believe it. I would welcome it, sisi. You are an angel that God has sent me today. You're an answer to my prayers. I cannot find words to thank you enough, Mandy."

A faint smile appeared on her face. "I have six months left before I return to California—Jabulani can learn a lot in that time." The child was watching her intently; his eyes flickered when he heard his name and he looked at the priest inquiringly. When Reverend Dlamini patted him on the shoulder and explained what Mandy had said, the boy's mouth opened wide and he covered his face in his hands. He looked up after a moment and smiled at her—and Mandy's heart was full.

She felt Lindiwe's eyes on her too. When Mandy turned, the Zulu woman nodded. "That's the way, my

friend. One thing at a time. I told you, you could do it,"
she whispered.

CHAPTER 12

"You see," Thandi shouted, "I saw it in your tea leaves. I said I saw a child with you. It was Jabulani." She began dancing while everyone else clapped. Mandy looked on, smiling, but the priest suddenly appeared concerned.

"There's one problem; I don't have room at the orphanage. It's a very small house," he said.

"Please don't worry, I don't need to stay with you," Mandy replied. "I'll find somewhere to live."

"Maybe someone at my church will give you a room. I'll ask. We'll look after you."

Ryan had listened to this exchange and, on the spur of the moment, also made a decision; before returning home, he would rather spend time here near Mandy than travel around South Africa on his own. He cleared his throat and said, "I'd like to help too. I can help the boys with Mathematics. And I can build a chicken run for those hens."

Again, Thandi cheered and shouted, "You see. I told you!"

Reverend Dlamini smiled broadly. "Truly, God has sent you both to me today. We will find places for you to stay," he said.

"Mfundisi," Mandy said hesitantly. "I wish you wouldn't say that God has sent me."

"But I believe he has sent you, for sure," he replied.

"It makes me feel uncomfortable when you say that. Please don't worry. I'll find somewhere to stay. I want to help you and Jabulani, but you see...I don't believe in God."

Ryan squeezed her shoulder and whispered, "Don't spoil things. It doesn't matter what you believe—or don't. There's no need to hurt his feelings."

Mandy pushed his hand away. This had nothing to do with him.

The priest's hearing was better than his eyesight however, and he addressed them both. "No. She's right to be honest with me."

Everyone stared at Mandy and Reverend Dlamini. Nobody said a word as the umfundisi closed his eyes, either thinking or praying. After a short while he opened them again and said, "Ryan is right. It doesn't matter what you believe or don't believe. Belief comes in many different forms."

"But I don't believe. I respect your belief in God. Please can you respect that I don't share it?" she said in exasperation. She didn't want to be working with the priest under false pretenses for six months.

Reverend Dlamini smiled and said, "But Mandy, you do believe something. You've just told me that Jabulani can learn a lot in six months. You believe you can teach him. Isn't that what you said?"

She nodded. "Yes. But I don't believe in God. That has nothing to do with what I can teach Jabulani."

Reverend Dlamini inclined his head and closed his eyes momentarily. "I think it's the Holy Spirit in you, whether you believe in it or not. It's the Holy Spirit that makes you want to help. You can't see it—just like Bongani said he can't see God. That's true; you can't. But you can see evidence that the Holy Spirit is here."

Mandy sighed, trying to contain her irritation.

"Let me explain it this way, sisi. We plant vegetables in our garden at the orphanage. We buy packets of seeds and, when we open those packets, they're all different. The carrot seeds are small, like sand; the tomato seeds are bigger; the peas are like little stones; and the squash—they're like this." He pointed to the nail on his index finger. "You see, all those things we plant, they're small—like pieces of dirt. But we have faith that if we put them in the ground and look after them properly—and even sometimes if we forget—they'll transform into plants. They grow and feed us, but they all started as tiny pieces of brown stuff. How did that happen? We can't explain how that change takes place. It's a miracle. And that's what makes me believe."

Everybody had been listening very carefully, exchanging glances, but saying nothing. Now they stared at Mandy. She relaxed and nodded. "Yes, it's a miracle, I agree. Life is a miracle. But I don't believe there's a God up there directing everything."

"That's OK, Mandy. That's why I'm telling you that belief comes in different forms—like those seeds. People's faith is different; there are Christians and Jews, Hindus and Muslims—they're all different. But they all believe in goodness, which is the Holy Spirit. Even atheists and agnostics believe in doing good deeds, don't they? In the same way, all those seeds look different but we have faith they'll grow, even though we can't explain why. There's something unseen we believe in; something we might never understand. It doesn't matter to me what you believe or don't believe. Nobody can prove their argument because it's about beliefs, not facts. What matters most is what you do, not what you believe.

"I try to teach these children how to live, not what to believe. They'll decide that for themselves. What I'm telling you is this—if we don't look after those seeds and water them, they won't grow. It's the same with children. If we don't look after them and give them a chance, they won't grow either."

Mandy nodded. "Well, I agree with that," she said, turning her gaze to Jabulani. He was watching her—and this time he didn't look away when she smiled at him. "I'm going to help you grow," she said.

He didn't understand her words, but he understood her intent. His eyes lit up and he smiled back.

CHAPTER 13

◈

Everyone settled down peacefully after hearing Reverend Dlamini's words, thinking about what he'd said. As she listened to the orchestra of crickets starting up their evening serenade, Mandy reflected on the strange afternoon. Everything had changed in a few hours. She'd befriended these strangers, heard their stories, and found an opportunity to do something worthwhile by helping this child who'd captured her heart. Ubuntu was contagious, she thought. It made her feel good. She was at peace.

Suddenly, however, the tranquility was interrupted. The hadedahs were heading home, announcing their departure with jarring cries. They'd been digging for grubs, but now that day was almost done, it was time for them to return to their roosts. Their raucous calls pierced the evening, making all the travelers look up and watch as the large birds departed. When they could no longer see them, Bongani muttered, "It's going to be dark soon. That's when tokoloshes come out and make trouble."

Mandy could see anxiety written in the old man's face.

"It's going to get cold as well. Maybe we should go back to the taxi," Thandi suggested. It was apparent to Mandy that Thandi was equally anxious.

"Yes. And we should close the door," Bongani added.

The decision was made to move and they headed

back to the Kombi with greater speed than they'd disembarked. The chickens were left on the driver's seat to make more room and Mandy tried to reassure everyone, "Joseph will be back soon and we'll get going again." Nobody seemed convinced, however, and little was said as they settled back in their seats, staring out the windows at the growing darkness.

Mandy was as anxious as the rest of them. Where was Joseph? When would they get moving again? The silence began to feel ominous to her as the minutes ticked by, so it came as a relief when Mpilo suddenly began singing Nkosi Sikelel' iAfrika—God Bless Africa. His voice was soft to begin with, but as other voices joined in, harmonizing with him, the volume grew. Mandy listened in awe. They'd told their stories and danced their dances; now they sang together to ease their worries.

While they were singing, Ryan excused himself for a bathroom break, accompanied by Mpilo. It was while he was standing behind the taxi that he noticed a telephone number written on the back of it. "What the hell!" he exclaimed. "Look at that. His number's been there the whole time; you can just see it under the dirt..."

Not sure what was happening, Mandy saw Ryan sprint back and grab his phone. She was about to ask who he was calling when she heard a voice on speaker phone say: "*Speedy Passenger Service*, Joseph speaking."

The singing stopped as Ryan shouted, "Where the hell are you? We've been waiting all afternoon for you."

Hardly daring to breathe, she heard the driver explain, "I'm sorry, but it's too hard. The petrol can, I can't tie it onto the bicycle. I tried to do it with my belt, but it won't stay on. So, I must push the bike with one hand and hold the can with the other. And this bicycle, it's got no light. Now it's dark, so I must also hold my cell phone under my arm and use it for a light, otherwise I can't see. It's very hard. But I'm nearly back to the taxi. Just wait. I'm sorry. I'll be there soon."

"Oh, sweet Jesus. Why didn't you call us to help?" said Ryan.

"I haven't got anybody's number. I'm very sorry."

"OK, no worries. I'll come and help you. Is there just one road?"

"Yes, only one. You'll see me if you come."

"Keep walking. I'm on my way."

Mandy was pleased that Mpilo volunteered to join Ryan. It was pitch dark now and she was concerned— not because of tokoloshes, but who knew what was out there?

She waited anxiously for their return, constantly scanning the road out front and checking her watch. They'd been gone a long time. When she finally saw three men appear half an hour later, she heaved a sigh of relief and jumped out the taxi to greet them while everyone else applauded from inside the Kombi. Amidst the cheering, she watched Joseph get busy pouring petrol into the tank—careful not to spill a drop of the fuel—and whispered to Ryan, "I'll be happy to get going again, but you know, I'm actually kind of glad you didn't find his number earlier."

Ryan grinned. "Well, for someone who wished we'd rented a car..."

"I know," she replied, "but we were strangers then.

We're not anymore. They have so little, yet they gave us so much. There's that word they have for it, isn't there? Ubuntu."

PART 2

Walls turned sideways are bridges.

Angela Davis

CHAPTER 14

Despite Mandy's protests, Reverend Dlamini found a place for the Americans to stay. He knew of parishioners who owned a rental property in Durban with unused servants' quarters at the bottom of the garden. These were offered to Mandy and Ryan, free of charge, in return for their help. The accommodation was basic—a small bedroom for each, a shared bathroom, and use of the kitchen in the main house.

The afternoon when they'd run out of petrol had seemed interminably long, but by contrast, the ensuing months seemed to pass in a flash for Mandy. There were hardly enough hours in the day to get everything done. She was grateful that Ryan respected the boundaries of their friendship and, for the most part, they got on well. He'd helped at the orphanage by building a chicken run, and also helped Reverend Dlamini work in the vegetable garden. He went for runs with the boys as well, but it was school holidays and they weren't interested in lessons. With time on his hands, he enjoyed the Durban beachfront where he rented a surf board. "The Indian Ocean is great; it's as warm as bath water," he told Mandy, urging her to join him.

On the few occasions when she went to the beach, it reminded her of vacations in Hawaii. She loved it, and Ryan loved her skimpy white bikini—especially when it was wet and almost transparent. Their time together there was fun, without any arguments, a bit like when they first met while training for the Peace Corps—but Mandy had a niggling sense that she was neglecting her duties at the orphanage. She brought Jabulani with her once. He was afraid of the ocean however, and refused to even paddle at the water's edge. After that, he declined any invitations to accompany her to the beach. This worried her; she felt she was letting him down. When she voiced her concern, Ryan's response was: "Mandy, live a little. You're not his mother. Don't beat yourself up about what you *should* be doing; just enjoy what you *are* doing!"

But the main focus of Mandy's attention was Jabulani. She worked almost every day with him—sometimes at the orphanage, sometimes taking him on outings. They explored together and she took delight in his enthusiasm for everything he saw. The child watched for her to arrive, running down the road to meet her; his shyness disappeared as his trust in her grew. She used some of her meager funds to buy shoes and clothing for him as he had come to the orphanage barefoot, with only the clothes he was wearing. When they ventured into Durban a few times to meet Lindiwe for lunch, his eyes opened wide at the sight of all the traffic and people, but he held Mandy's hand tightly and always had a smile on his face as he chatted happily to the two women.

"I can't believe how different he is from that day when we ran out of petrol," Lindiwe whispered to Mandy. "He never said anything then; he could barely look anyone in the eyes. I can't believe it's the same child...Whatever you're doing, it's like magic. What's the secret?"

Mandy smiled. "There's no secret. He was in shock and terribly afraid that day. His mother had just died, and then he was taken away by a stranger. He didn't know where he was going or what the hell was happening. This is who he really is, the little guy you see today. He just needed some love and security to feel sure of himself again."

"How did the priest find him?" Lindiwe asked.

"I wondered the same thing. It turns out that the farmer where Jabulani lived had connections to Marianhill Monastery. The monks there told him about Reverend Dlamini and the orphanage, so the farmer reached out to the priest for help."

"It's nice to know there are good people in the world—like you, Mandy," Lindiwe said.

The orphanage was a simple house with four bedrooms, one bathroom, and a communal room adjacent to the small kitchen. The furniture was old and minimal, but it was cozy; it felt like a home. Reverend Dlamini had the smallest bedroom, which was only big enough for his bed and a desk; the boys shared the other larger rooms in bunk beds. The common room was used for socializing and studies.

Although her focus was Jabulani, Mandy got to know the other boys during her visits. They were respectful and enjoyed talking to her whenever they could, practicing their English. Some of them even joined her doing yoga once they got over their embarrassment; Jabulani was the first to join in. She observed that each boy, including JJ, had chores to do, and they were done without any complaints. Some of the older ones had summer jobs during the six-week Christmas vacation.

She marveled at the simplicity of Christmas celebrations at the orphanage; they lasted only a few days, not all of December. The boys had so little, but they were grateful for what little they had. When she saw that they had no decorations, she and Ryan bought a fake Christmas tree that would last them in future years as well; they all enjoyed decorating it together. It was their Christmas gift to the boys. She wished she had enough money to buy gifts for them all to put under the tree, but that was not possible. The only other presents were those that Jacob brought when he returned for his annual visit.

It was obvious the boys hero-worshiped Jacob. She could see their excitement when he arrived—and when he read the lesson at their "Carols by Candlelight" service, all eyes were directed at him. He had everyone's full attention. She was happy that he paid special attention to Jabulani, carrying the child on his shoulders at times when taking some of the boys for walks. As she hiked with them, Jacob turned to her and said, "What you're giving this kid is priceless, Mandy. I can see that he cares a lot about you, but he'll come to appreciate what you're doing even more when he gets older. You know, I was also given a generous gift by an American woman. Without Mrs. Liz and Father Dlamini, my life would be very different today."

Mandy nodded. "You've made such a success of your life." She hesitated a moment before adding, "Actually, it was your story that inspired me to help Jabulani. He's going to be a success story too. I just know it."

Jabulani absorbed every word Mandy said—and smiled. He was growing daily in confidence and the bond between them grew stronger all the time.

"He's an exceptional child," she emailed her parents shortly afterwards. "I can hardly say six words in Zulu, yet here he is, in just about two months, speaking English reasonably well. He's like a sponge."

"Perhaps it's the teacher!" her mother emailed back.

"No, it's the student," she replied. "He's eager to learn—and he's smart."

Mandy and Lindiwe stayed in touch. The two women were unable to spend much time together because they were both so busy, but they called one another frequently. Of all the friends she'd known, Mandy had never had one quite like Lindiwe. She was empathetic and perceptive. Lindiwe shared news of some of their fellow passengers and laughed at Mandy's continued concerns about elder abuse. "Oh, don't worry about Bongani, he's doing fine. I saw Joseph last weekend and he says the old man travels with him regularly now, but he insists on watching Joseph fill up with petrol so he doesn't run out of it again. He'll never let Joseph forget his mistake...No doubt he's buying a steady supply of blue pills every time he comes to Durban to visit his son. Oh, and by the way, I saw Thandi when I took my grandmother to the post office to collect her pension."

"Oh yes. What's going on with Thandi?"

"You'll love this. She gave Samuel an ultimatum about his drinking, so he joined Alcoholics Anonymous. He goes to AA meetings every week now."

Mandy giggled, but Lindiwe put her hands up to stop her.

"Wait. It gets better. You haven't heard half of it. He wants to marry her, whether she has a baby or not. But now Thandi's not so sure about it anymore. She loves her job and doesn't want marriage to get in the way of it. She says she's managed without a husband all her life, so why spoil a good thing?"

Mandy put her head back and laughed her belly laugh again. She laughed so hard that she cried. When she was able to control herself, she wiped away the tears and said, "Who would have thought it? Thandi took Bongani's advice after all. Good for her."

Lindiwe loved hearing Mandy's laughter. With a twinkle in her eyes, she asked, "Have you learned to play that vuvuzela yet?"

Mandy started laughing again. "Do you want me chucked out of my lodgings? I blew it once and it gave me such a fright that now I only look at it. But I really love looking at it. It's beautiful," she added.

"It's a good idea just to look at it for the sake of your neighbors. Those things sound terrible," Lindiwe replied. "But hey, maybe you can come home with me sometime and meet my grandmother. I've told her about you; she wants to meet you. Would you do that?"

"I would love to," Mandy replied, warmed by an ever-strengthening bond of friendship with Lindiwe. It was an honor to receive an invitation like this. "And I'd love a ride in Joseph's taxi again, as long as it doesn't run out of petrol."

"That won't happen again, I'm certain; he learned a

big lesson. I have his phone number now, so we can make a plan to meet him."

"I'd like that. When Jabulani is settled in school, I'll have more free time. Let's do it then. Did I tell you that Reverend Dlamini found a school for him somewhere outside Pinetown? It was a bit of a struggle getting him into a school because Jabulani's so far behind in his learning, but the priest eventually got a school to agree. It'll be a bit of an ordeal getting him there, but I'm excited about it. The little guy is apprehensive, as you can imagine. He doesn't realize it's an opportunity for him to get an education, though. I'll go with him on his first day, to reassure him."

"He's a lucky boy to have your support, Mandy."

"I'm the lucky one. It's been wonderful watching him blossom. He seems happy—and that makes me happy too."

"It's a good thing you've done. You've given him a fine start for school."

However, when that first day of school came, it was a greater ordeal than Mandy imagined. She wasn't accustomed to catching taxis in Africa at 4:30 a.m., but such an early start was necessary to get two taxi rides. The first one was to meet the priest and pick up Jabulani in Pinetown, and the next was to travel with the child from there and get him to school, miles away, by 8 a.m. Things got worse because Ryan flaked. He'd agreed to accompany her, but when she knocked on his door at four o'clock, he shouted, "You've gotta be kidding. It's way too early."

"C'mon, Ryan. Get up."

"Forget it. I'll meet you later at that coffee shop we go

to. Jabulani doesn't need me there."

She pounded on the door. "I need you, dammit. It's still dark. Please come with me. Please."

"It'll be light soon. Use a flashlight."

She couldn't believe that he could be so disagreeable, but realizing it was wasting precious time to argue, Mandy raced off, shouting over her shoulder, "Screw you."

Keeping away from bushes that could easily conceal tsotsis, she ran in the dark with only a faint beam from her cell phone to light the way. When she arrived at the taxi rank twenty minutes later, out of breath, she was shocked to discover how crowded it was. Even at this hour, in the half-light of early morning, there were people pushing and shoving as they tried to make their way forward. Mandy clutched her tote bag tightly under her arm, wary of pickpockets on the lookout for easy targets.

Five vehicles came and left before she managed to squeeze into a seat on one heading towards Pinetown. Some passengers had children on their laps and a few women had sleeping babies tied on their backs; it was much more crowded than Joseph's taxi had been. The noise from shouts and cries was deafening, but Mandy was safely on board, without incident, and she breathed a sigh of relief as she focused her thoughts on Jabulani Jiyane. She'd begun calling him JJ—a term of endearment that was easier to pronounce than Jabulani. He'd laughed. He liked the name.

As prearranged, Reverend Dlamini met her at the Pinetown taxi rank on Anderson Road, with Jabulani at his side. The child looked smart in his school uniform— grey shorts, a white short-sleeved shirt, long grey socks that came up to his knees, and sturdy black shoes—all of which Mandy had purchased for him. She'd taught him to tie his shoe laces and how to knot the blue and gold striped tie. He looked composed until he saw Mandy; then he whispered, "I'm scared."

Before she could reassure him, Reverend Dlamini weighed in. "Jabulani, you have to go to school. It's not a choice. Look at the other boys in the house; they go to school and they don't complain." His voice was stern as he continued speaking to the child in Zulu. When the priest walked away, JJ was silent. Chastened, he withdrew his hand from Mandy's with downcast eyes.

She was furious. Didn't the priest see that JJ's needs and emotions should be considered? He wasn't just one more AIDS orphan to look after, he was a unique individual. Jabulani was just a child—and not only that, a child whose mother and father had recently died. As she retook the boy's hand, she thought: *JJ means more to me than he does to the priest. I'm the one who cares about the child's feelings. I'm the one who loves him.* And immediately a thought suddenly struck her: *Maybe there's only one thing for it—I should adopt JJ and take him back to California.*

Clasping his hand tightly, she said, "I'm going to look after you. Don't you worry." They spoke little as they traveled in the crowded taxi, but the idea went around and around in her head and the more she thought about it, the more it took root.

Jabulani was tense, but he was also brave as he sat on her lap and looked around. When she left him outside his classroom, he fought back tears and walked to the door without a backward glance. Mandy was the one who cried. She remained outside, watching other children arrive in large numbers. It seemed impossible that so many learners could fit into one room—and when she peeped through the door, she gasped. There was hardly any place for the teacher to stand. Single desks were crammed from wall to wall, occupied by two or three children instead of one. Although she knew he was in there somewhere, JJ was nowhere in sight. Appalled, she watched a man place a padlock on the outside of the door. Her heart was pounding when she confronted him.

He frowned and said, "Who are you?"

"I'm a caregiver for one of the learners in there."

"Well, I'm the principal. I'm locking the door for safety reasons."

"How can that be safe?" she said. Stress made her voice come out an octave higher. "What if there's a fire and they can't get out?"

"If there's a fire, I'll unlock the door." He hesitated a moment and added, "Sometimes the teachers don't arrive and I have to keep the learners inside, otherwise they'll be running around everywhere. We can't have that. And sometimes the teachers forget to lock the door from the inside, so it's better I do it. The teachers have phones; they can call me if there's an emergency."

"But what if someone needs to use the toilet?" Mandy asked in amazement.

"They must do that before they go inside, or wait until they come out."

With that, he turned and walked to the next classroom, where he repeated the process. Her heart sank as she watched him, but her resolve to adopt JJ grew stronger.

When she met Ryan in the coffee shop ninety minutes later, he looked at her red eyes and said, "Hey, you didn't tell me how early you were leaving. You just said you'd wake me. Don't get mad at me."

She glared at him. "This isn't about you, strangely enough. The world doesn't revolve around you, believe it or not."

He raised his eyebrows and looked away with a shrug. They placed their orders and, as they waited in line to collect them, he said, "I'm sorry about this morning. I should've come with you, I know, but I had a bit of a late night last night. Mpilo and I were out and I didn't get back until 1:30. If something else is upsetting you, though, why don't you tell me what it is?"

She blew her nose and sighed. "I can't leave JJ in that school. He'll be lost. It's so overcrowded. I've never seen anything like it. He won't learn anything there, except how to survive."

Ryan didn't reply until they were seated with their coffee at a table. He reached across to grab her hand, saying, "Knowing how to survive is an important thing for him to learn. You're getting too emotionally involved. You've done wonders teaching him to speak English, but you're getting too attached to the child."

"He needs me," she replied.

Ryan stared at her and muttered under his breath, "It's you who needs him. Two years teaching in Namibia wasn't enough to assuage your survivor guilt. You want JJ to do it."

She paid no attention to him. She didn't even hear him. And he was unprepared for what she said next.

"I'm going to adopt him. I'm taking him back to California."

"What!" he exclaimed, spilling his coffee as he slammed the mug down on the table. "You can't be serious."

Mandy didn't say anything more; she just nodded. Not blind to the difficulties of an international adoption by a single mother, she'd hoped that Ryan would be supportive. Instead he stared at her and shook his head. "You're going to take a Zulu orphan away from his home country?"

"Yup," she replied, taking a sip of her coffee.

He was cautious when he spoke, knowing she might react angrily, but he felt that she needed to keep some perspective. She was a foreigner—a single American woman, and a white one at that, with no income. "I gotta tell you, that's not in Jabulani's best interests." When he saw her eyes flash, he quickly added, "It's a very noble idea, Mandy, but it's impractical."

It was no longer of any consequence to her what he thought. Taking a deep breath, she said, "I don't agree with you. It might be difficult, but it's a good solution."

"A solution to what?" he asked. "Reverend Dlamini has provided him with a home, you've taught him English, and now he's going to school. Where's the problem?"

"If you'd seen the classroom he's in, you would understand. He's going to be fighting just to find a seat in there—how can he learn in that environment? He needs a mother—and I plan to be one for him."

"Mandy, Mandy, Mandy. You've got a big heart and I love that about you, but think about this rationally, not emotionally. Jabulani's lived most of his life in the boonies; he's never been to school before today; his parents died of AIDS and you don't even know whether he's HIV positive or not. Life isn't a Disney tale. You can't wave a magic wand by taking him to California and making everything better. Do you think that's going to make him happy?" Ryan threw up his hands in exasperation. "I don't think so; nothing could be more difficult for him. He belongs here in South Africa with his own people."

She glared at him and her chest felt tight. "For your information, he's *not* HIV positive; I've taken him to a doctor for a full checkup. He's a healthy child, physically, but not so much emotionally. He trusts me, Ryan, and I'm not going to let him down. That would break him."

She said nothing more and silence sat like a third person between them. When she stood up to leave, her blue eyes were like ice. "My mind is made up," she said, turning on her heel.

CHAPTER 15

Reverend Dlamini was digging up potatoes when his phone rang. Without glasses, he couldn't see who was calling; it took him a few moments to put down his tools and wipe his hands before he could answer. Catching his breath, he heard a familiar voice say, "Hi."

"Ryan, how are you my friend? I haven't seen you for a while. Is everything OK?"

"All good, no worries. But I wonder if you've got a few moments to speak about something."

"I've always got time for you and Mandy." There was urgency in Ryan's words and the priest wanted to sit down before he heard any more. "Can you wait a minute?" he said. "I need a drink of water; I've been working in the garden." Ryan could hear doors opening and closing and a few grunts. He waited until the priest said, "All right. What is it you want to talk about?"

"I'm sorry to disturb you, Father. It's Mandy."

The priest froze. "Oh, no. Has there been an accident? I just saw her this morning at the taxi rank when she came to fetch Jabulani for school."

"No—nothing like that."

Reverend Dlamini breathed a sigh of relief and took a sip of water. He felt responsible for the young American woman, even though she was fiercely independent. He knew that South Africa could be a dangerous place, especially for women.

"She's got it into her head that she wants to adopt Jabulani and take him back to California," Ryan said.

After what seemed an eternity, the priest replied, "I see." There were a few moments of silence before the priest started to speak once more. "I need to think about it, Ryan. That's a very big step. It wouldn't be easy for him, or for her; but then I suppose Jabulani's life isn't easy here either." He swallowed hard and said, "Actually, to tell you the truth, I worry about having him here in the orphanage. This place is supposed to be for teenage boys who've come out of state care, with nowhere else to go. Donors do it specifically for that purpose. I haven't told any of them about Jabulani. Having him here takes up a place that a teenager could have. They might not like that. They might insist he goes to a state institution, but those places are all so full."

Ryan felt anger rising in him. He'd expected the priest's support, instead of which the man was looking to protect his orphanage and his own skin. Dammit, there were other ways Mandy could help the boy. She could send him to a better school, or a private boarding school—her American dollars would go a long way in this country if she went home and found a job. She could find a South African family to adopt him.

His thoughts were interrupted by the priest asking, "What do you think?"

Ryan took a deep breath. "I don't like the idea. I think Mandy's reasons are selfish."

The priest gasped. "No, that's not a word I'd use to describe Mandy. There's nothing selfish about her. Nothing."

CHAPTER 16

Mandy was tempted to ditch her appointment. It had seemed a good idea when she'd made it, to have her hair cut and enjoy some "me" time after two years in rural Namibia. After Ryan's comments, however, she was deflated and didn't feel like sitting in front of a mirror staring at herself. She made her way there, nonetheless, and gave brief instructions to cut her hair short. She felt numb.

"Really?" Sally, the hairdresser, asked. "You're sure? How short is short?"

Mandy frowned and shrugged. "Whatever you think."

Sally thought a moment and said, "You've got beautiful blonde hair. Let's just trim the ends."

On an impulse, Mandy shook her head. "No, I want it very short. I'm tired of dealing with long hair. I haven't got the patience."

She watched without reacting as Sally set to work with her scissors. The stylist tried to make conversation, but Mandy didn't respond until asked if she had any children. "Yes. I'm adopting a little boy," she said.

"Really? I can hear you're from the States. So, you're taking a kid from here back to America?" Sally asked. "Geez, he's lucky, getting out of this place. Somebody else told me the other day about a similar thing—a Zulu kid who went to live in America with a family. Lucky little buggers. I wish somebody would take me."

Mandy's interest was piqued. "Really? Is the child happy?" she asked.

Sally stopped cutting for a moment and looked intently at Mandy. "I don't know. Do you want me to find out?"

Mandy nodded.

The stylist continued cutting in silence. When she was done, she passed Mandy a hand mirror to view her hair from all angles, but the American woman barely glanced at herself. Instead, she pressed Sally once more, "I really hope that kid's happy. Please find out for me."

Looking more like a pixie and less like a lion, Mandy emerged from the salon feeling uplifted. "Screw you, Ryan," she thought, "I'll figure out how to make this thing work on my own. I don't need your help getting JJ to America. I know now that it can be done."

After a couple of rushed taxi rides to get back to JJ's school, she was waiting when he came out of class. It was hard to find him in the sea of children all wearing the same uniform, but she picked out the red backpack slung over his shoulder and waved to get his attention. He looked right past her as he peered around, his bottom lip trembling. She tried to make her way towards him, but there were too many people blocking her way, so she shouted his name. Her voice sounded hoarse because she'd been running and JJ looked confused—until she called his name again and this time he recognized her. He ran to her and grabbed her outstretched hands.

"What happened?" he cried, sounding panicked.

"What do you mean?" Mandy frowned.

"Your hair. It's gone."

She laughed and hugged him. "I had it cut, JJ. Do you like it?"

With his lip still trembling, he frowned and shook his head

She thought, *Oh dear, he doesn't like change. Proceed with caution.* But all she said to reassure him was, "You'll get used to it and it'll grow. And now I can be more like you with short hair."

He managed a smile and continued holding her hand as they made their way to the taxi rank. It was difficult to talk in the crowded vehicle with passengers shouting and chattering, so questions were not asked about his day. The child looked too tired to speak and soon, despite the surrounding noise and discomfort, he fell asleep with his head on her shoulder.

CHAPTER 17

As Reverend Dlamini mentally replayed his telephone conversation with Ryan, his thoughts drifted between concern and dismay. Mandy had a generous heart, but he felt uneasy. He stood watching for her and Jabulani to make their way down the dirt road to the orphanage, and when he saw their figures in the distance, he hurried to meet them. The child appeared exhausted, while Mandy looked strained and quite different—it took him a moment to realize that her hair wasn't pulled back in a ponytail as usual; it was cut short.

Before either adult could say anything, however, Jabulani burst into tears. "I don't want to go back to school. I hate that place," he cried. Between sobs, he started speaking Zulu. Reverend Dlamini listened, removed the child's hand from Mandy's, and replied to him in Zulu. Still crying, the little boy nodded and ran into the house without looking back.

"What was that all about? What did you say to him?" she demanded.

"I told him it'll get better and he must be brave."

Mandy frowned. "Was that all you could say to comfort him? What did he say?"

The priest pursed his lips. "He said the teacher was rude and shouted at the children." Then he paused and added, "The boy is used to you teaching him on his own,

Mandy; now it's hard for him to be in school with lots of others. It'll be better if I take him there tomorrow."

"No," she said. "I want to do it. Please don't say that."

"Mandy, listen to me. I know you care about Jabulani, but we have to make him strong. You're letting him be weak."

"He's a child," she replied. "How can you be so tough on him?"

The priest spoke very deliberately when he replied. "He's a Zulu—not an American. Things are different here. This is a different world and life can be hard. We both want what's best for Jabulani, but I'm his guardian. I know what's necessary for him to survive here."

Mandy had a knee jerk reaction and blurted out, "Then I want to take him back to America. I can't leave him in that terrible school, without any emotional support from you. I love Jabulani; I can give him a better life."

Reverend Dlamini didn't flinch. Instead, after a moment's silence, he sighed and put his hands on her shoulders. "Calm down, Mandy. As I said, we both want what's best for him. As long as he stays with me, I will make the decisions. If you want to take him because you think you can offer him a better life, we can talk about that. But he's not a souvenir you can take home and forget after a while. It'll be a lifelong commitment. You're young, Mandy. You have your whole life ahead of you. Do you really want to be tied down to a child that's not your own?"

Her face flushed as the priest spoke. "*He* has his whole life ahead of him too. You insult me, suggesting I might forget about him. I've never been more certain of anything—I want to take care of Jabulani. I love him."

The priest closed his eyes and bowed his head in silence. After a while he looked up and said to her, "I know you're trying to help, but please be reasonable. I will take him to school tomorrow. You can pick him up at the end of the day."

She opened her mouth to speak but Reverend Dlamini put a stop to it. "If you're serious about taking him to America, you can make inquiries to see if it's even possible. I will consider it, but I'm not saying I agree. I need to think. And, of course, we need to find out what Jabulani wants to do. You know, he hasn't cried once since that day when our taxi ran out of petrol. All this time, even though his mother died, he's never cried. It's good that now he's letting his unhappiness out, instead of keeping it inside." Once more the priest paused before adding, "He's very tired—it was a long day for him. I'll go to him now. It'll be better if you leave it to me. He'll look forward to you fetching him from school tomorrow." Mandy tried to speak again, but the priest stood his ground. "Remember, I was also an orphan at his age. Trust me to deal with this."

With that, he turned and walked slowly back to the house. She stared after him, aching. More than anything she wanted to run after the child and hug him, but respecting the priest's wishes, she walked away to catch yet another taxi to her lodging.

By the time she got back there, Mandy felt drained. Eager for a quick sandwich and an early night, she made her way to the shared kitchen—but Ramona Govender wouldn't hear of her leaving. "I've made Rogan Josh; it's lamb curry. I insist you join me and a few friends for dinner—you need to show off your new hairstyle. I like it very much, by the way. It suits you." The aroma was tantalizing and the cook wouldn't take no for an answer, so Mandy sank onto the sofa with a welcome glass of chenin blanc just as the guests began to arrive.

Ramona made the introductions: "This is a colleague from work, David Malherbe...and my brother Suresh... and his girlfriend Ritu. Everyone, this is Mandy Walker, a crazy American who's saving the world, one child at a time."

There was immediate interest in Mandy and what she was doing in South Africa. Exhausted, she answered as briefly as possible, but Ramona filled them in with a fuller account—both the work Mandy had done in the Peace Corps and her current project at the orphanage. Ramona Govender enjoyed having the two Americans as neighbors. An attorney in the prestigious firm of Hulley and De Wet, with a first-class law degree and her articles completed the previous year, Ramona's ambition was to be the first Indian woman partner in the firm. She looked on track to do that.

David Malherbe was quick to seat himself next to Mandy and strike up a conversation. "I really admire the volunteerism in America," he said. "I was at high school for a year in San Diego, on an AFS exchange. Man, I was blown away by the charitable work students did there. It was required in order to graduate, as I remember."

Mandy nodded, appreciative of his comments. So often, it seemed to her, Americans were scorned for their presence and deeds; it was refreshing to receive praise. She smiled at him.

"There's such a need for that sort of thing here," he continued, "but everyone closes their eyes to it. There's a middle class of whites and blacks who don't give a damn about those left behind in poverty." He looked pained and paused a moment, before adding, "Good for you, Mandy. Two years in Namibia...That's awesome."

The compliments and wine were a combination that made Mandy immediately more relaxed. She smiled again and thanked David, feeling herself blush. God, she hated that about herself, but there was nothing she could do to stop it—and the proximity of this very good-looking man made her blush even more. He had a deep, soothing voice and the build of a rugby player—with a face like Brad Pitt. She could feel her heart rate speed up as he questioned her about her life and interests. Soon she was telling him how she'd been accepted at Berkeley to do a master's degree in English.

"So, you're not only saving the world one child at a time, you're smart as well." His look was admiring and his hazel eyes twinkled as he added, "Quite a combo... Generous, beautiful, *and* clever."

She blushed again.

"So, tell me about this child you're helping," he said, trying to put her at ease.

Mandy swallowed hard and said, "Oh, boy! I've got myself into something that's going to be a challenge." She took another sip of wine and added, "I'm going to adopt JJ."

David was not expecting this. His eyebrows shot up.

"Whoa!" he exclaimed. At a loss for words, his stare was penetrating and Mandy looked right back at him, without blinking.

The exchange was noticed by Ramona; she didn't know what had been said, but the electricity between them was obvious. She hadn't planned on being a matchmaker, but something was happening right in front of her eyes. Smiling as she placed dinner on the table, she said, "Come on, help yourselves, everybody. Sit anywhere you like. Please enjoy."

David regained his composure, making sure to sit next to Mandy again in order to continue their conversation. "It's quite an undertaking on your part, adopting a child. When are you returning to the States?"

"I don't know how long it'll take. I only decided today. I was shocked when I saw how terrible his school is. It probably sounds absurd to you," she said, slightly embarrassed.

But David didn't laugh. He smiled and replied, "Not at all. If there's anything I can do to help, please don't hesitate to ask. I'd be happy to assist with any legal work that crops up—it's the least I can do." His admiration was apparent as he spoke to her and waited for her response.

"Thank you. I appreciate your offer," she stammered.

"I mean it. Anything I can do to help."

She felt herself blushing yet again. "That's very kind of you," she said. "I'm sure there'll be lots of paperwork and I honestly don't know where to start. Probably a visit to the American Consulate."

Everyone else had been listening to this conversation. "I have a friend who works there," Suresh announced.

"Maybe he can help."

Ramona chimed in. "Strangely enough, I know a white family who brought up a Zulu child here in Durban. Their maid, Promise, had a baby that they raised as their own daughter—Annie's her name. She lived in the house with them and they paid for her to go to private school; Promise carried on living in the servant's quarters. It was bizarre, but it worked fine. Annie carried on to university and has a great job with Nedbank now."

Mandy was intrigued. It was encouraging that she wasn't alone in wanting to assist a Zulu child, especially hearing success stories like this. She was about to ask more when Suresh began to speak.

"It's weird that the mother was content to give up her child. I mean, she must've seen her every day, growing up in a different world."

"That was the point," Ramona said. "Promise knew the family would offer her daughter a life she could never give her. They even bought a flat for Annie after she graduated from university. They've emigrated to New Zealand now but Annie wouldn't go with them. She didn't want to leave Promise."

"Wow, so she still regarded Promise as her mother," remarked Ritu.

"I guess so," Ramona replied. "Blood is thicker than water in the end."

David poured himself another glass of wine and said, "Well, it's different for the child Mandy wants to adopt. He doesn't have a mother; he's an orphan. Mandy would become his mother. In time, he'd probably forget the life he had here. He's only eight years old—isn't that right?"

She nodded, feeling a weight lift from her shoulders; she *was* doing the right thing. When he reached over to clink wine glasses with her, she smiled with gratitude.

CHAPTER 18

✤

Her phone rang early next morning; it was David Malherbe. Her heart missed a beat until he said, "I've got bad news I'm afraid, Mandy."

She sat up straight on the edge of her bed, frowning.

"I've been looking into a few things for you. It seems that rules have tightened up since Madonna adopted children in Malawi. She adopted two kids in 2009 or so, and then two more a year ago, in 2017. Angelina Jolie also adopted a kid from Africa, in Ethiopia. African countries don't want this happening any more. Let me read you what a child protection specialist at the United Nations said: 'South Africa wants children to have a relationship with their familiar cultural, physical and extended family environs before looking to adoption, either within the country, or outside the country.' The long and the short of it is, you might only be able to adopt JJ if you remain in South Africa for at least five years. And, even then, it's not certain. That's from the South African side of things. I haven't researched anything from the American standpoint. There's not much point."

Mandy's hands were shaking. "That's crazy," she said, louder than she'd intended. "He's an orphan, damn it all. I'm not taking him away from his family. He doesn't have any. They all died of AIDS."

"I know, I know. I'm sorry, Mandy. I agree. You have

a lot to offer him and it doesn't make sense. But that's the law." He paused, then added, "Five years in South Africa—is that something you'd consider?"

"Oh geez, I don't know. Five years is a long time and I've got grad school next year. I need to think."

"Let's have dinner tonight and we can talk about it. Are you free?"

"Thank you, it's kind of you, but I can't manage that. I'm picking JJ up from school and we have to get a taxi back to the orphanage. I don't want to rush off immediately—I'd like to spend some time with him. It'll be late by the time I get back. I never know what the taxis will be like; they're all full at that time of day."

David stopped himself from saying what was on his mind. Taxis were generally overloaded and racing to beat other taxis. They were about as safe as standing in front of a firing squad, to his mind. Recognizing that she would not take kindly to his opinion, however, he said, "I'm going to be out Pinetown way taking a deposition this afternoon. Why don't I pick you up? If I finish early, I can be at JJ's school and give you both a lift."

The thought of a comfortable ride was appealing and Mandy accepted the offer with alacrity. When the call ended, she sat staring into space. It was ridiculous. "I want to get JJ away, sooner rather than later," she muttered, even though there was nobody else in the room. "His physical environment is shit. I can provide an environment where he can thrive, dammit all. What does it matter if it's not the culture he was born into? Every immigrant, in any country, absorbs their new environment—and children adapt much more easily than adults.

In five years' time, JJ will be a teenager; then it will be harder for him to adapt." She gave an involuntary scream of frustration, slamming her bedroom door on her way to the bathroom. When she emerged fifteen minutes later in a robe, with a towel wrapped around her head, Ryan was waiting outside, yawning.

They nodded a greeting and as he made his way into the bathroom, he turned to her. "I'm heading out of town for a while, by the way."

Mandy paused and frowned. "Oh. Where're you going?"

"To Mkuze. I'm going with Mpilo. Remember, his brother works on the game reserve there?"

"I thought Mpilo was at university."

Ryan nodded. "He is, but classes only start in March. He's invited me to go with him to Mkuze for a bit, helping his brother. I'll be gone a couple of weeks."

She took a deep breath and said, "That's a sudden decision."

He nodded. "Seems to be all the rage at the moment, making sudden decisions."

CHAPTER 19

David Malherbe had a hard time remaining patient. His client was not making sense and he regretted accepting this pro bono case. The woman was lying. How could he possibly defend her in court? The prosecution would trip her up in next to no time and he told her so, but she remained adamant that she'd been defending herself when she stabbed an old woman, although the details changed with every telling of the story. He watched as she was led back to the cells, dreading the court appearance. As he plugged Jabulani's school address into his phone, he felt relief to leave the stifling atmosphere of the prison building. He also felt despair that people were so desperate for a few bags of groceries that they would commit murder.

Poverty made life cheap and taking on pro bono cases didn't solve the problem. The apathy he encountered frustrated him, which was why he was so drawn to Mandy. He was of the firm belief that revolutions start when people are hungry—and he was very aware of the huge economic divide in South Africa. Shaking his head, he thought, *We're living on a tinder box—but maybe this American woman has the right approach, helping one child at a time.*

He texted Mandy to say where he was, feeling conspicuous in his new BMW. There were some old vehicles parked nearby, and multiple taxis causing a traffic jam in the street. As one filled up and moved on, another pulled up to take its place. It was only when numbers started to thin that he was able to spot Mandy.

People moved aside as she strode by, holding the hand of a small child. When they reached David, the boy stared at the car open-mouthed. With a little encouragement, he climbed into the back seat and continued to look around in amazement. "Is it only me sitting here?" he asked, as Mandy fastened a seat belt around him.

"Yes, just you. I'll be with you, but I'll be up front," she replied and smiled at him. "What do you think?"

His eyes opened wide as he rubbed his hands slowly over the smooth leather seats. "I can't believe it," he whispered.

She climbed into the front passenger seat and David tried to put the child at ease by asking how school had been. JJ chose not to communicate. He turned his head and looked out the window. Realizing that the child was shy, David said no more to him but turned to Mandy. "I finished my meeting early; I'm pleased I could make it here in time to give you a lift." He gestured towards the remaining taxis and added, "I don't know how you manage getting around in those things."

She smiled. "They're not so bad—and you meet some interesting people in them. That's how I met JJ."

"I wondered how that happened."

"His guardian is the priest you'll meet at the orphanage. I met Reverend Dlamini in the same taxi."

"I see. It's all starting to fit together now," he said, adding, "By the way, a quick question. Have you ever driven in Africa?"

She shook her head.

"You've never rented a car?"

"No."

He said nothing more, but an idea was taking shape in his mind. If there was a possibility of Mandy remaining in South Africa for five years, she would need to bite the bullet and drive.

The boys piled outside to see the BMW that pulled up in front of the orphanage. When JJ emerged, they laughed and cheered, rushing to peer inside the vehicle. The priest came out the door after them and his eyebrows shot up when he saw Mandy. She introduced her friend and as they shook hands, she was amused to hear David ask the priest, "Would it be OK to give the boys a ride up and down the road? They could take it in turns, four at a time. They seem very interested."

The first four were already in the car before the priest could respond. Mandy laughed at their excitement, realizing it was probably the first time most of them had been in a private car. She watched the amazement on their faces as they examined the interior, making the front seats go up and down and opening windows at the press of a button.

When the last trip had been made and they were headed out, she said to David, "I thought you'd never be able to get away."

He laughed. "I guess I'll have to do it again. Maybe I can teach the older ones to drive."

Her eyes opened wide. "Really? You'd do that? You'd trust them to drive this car? It looks brand new."

"I wouldn't go that far." He laughed. "But I have an old stick shift Ford that I was going to trade in when I bought this one. They offered me peanuts for it, so it wasn't worth it. I haven't got around to selling it yet; I'd use that to teach them. They can't take their license in an automatic car, anyway." After a slight pause, he said, "Can you drive a stick shift?"

"Kind of...I learned to drive on one, but my driving record isn't great."

He glanced at her and frowned, wondering what she meant by that, but all he said was, "Why don't we see if you can still do it this weekend? The car's just sitting in my garage, not being used. I'd be happy for you to drive it. It would make your life a lot easier."

Suddenly she felt uncomfortable. She'd only met this man a day ago and here he was offering her a car. It was one thing to accept a ride, but this was quite another matter. Seeing her stiffen, David added, "The car's perfectly safe and roadworthy, but it's about eighteen years old. I wouldn't get much for it. It's worth more for you to have it, and for those boys learn to drive in it. When you go back to the States, I'll give it to the priest—maybe I'll have to teach him too."

Feeling herself blush again, she was pleased his eyes were on the road, not on her. A nervous driver since her accident seven years ago, she felt that although taxis were a pain, at least she wasn't behind the wheel. But life would be easier with a car...

"If you don't want to, no worries."

She cleared her throat and said, "It's a generous offer. Reverend Dlamini doesn't drive, so yes, you would have to teach him. I'm not sure you should trust me, though, especially driving on the other side of the road. You might be sorry."

Turning into a parking lot, he said, "I wouldn't make the offer if I didn't trust you, Mandy. Should we give it a try on Saturday?"

She found herself smiling. Whether or not she drove the car, she wanted to see David again. "OK, if you're sure."

"Great, I'm sure. Italian or Portuguese, by the way?"

"Italian or Portuguese what?" she asked, frowning.

"Food. Remember, we're having dinner."

"Oh, yes, of course. I like them both," she replied.

"You can do better than that. You seem pretty decisive to me."

"OK then," she laughed. "Italian."

As he pulled into a parking space, he turned to her and remarked, "The funny thing is, I didn't want to go to Ramona's last night. I like her a lot and she's a great cook, so it's hard to turn down one of her curries, but it felt really awkward; I'm a partner and she's a junior in the firm. I nearly didn't go." He smiled and added, "I'm really glad I did. Discovering what you're trying to do, and what the priest is doing, has given me hope. My work always makes me see the worst in people; I needed to experience something else. I'm grateful to you."

Mandy's heart warmed. Neither of them said anything for a few seconds until David broke the silence, saying, "Come on, let's eat."

CHAPTER 20

It was 9:30 p.m. when Ryan and Mpilo reached Mkuze. Vusi, Mpilo's brother, showed them their sleeping arrangements, comprised of mats and sleeping bags in his rondavel. "Mpilo has told me all about you," he said to his American guest. "I laughed at the story about your taxi running out of petrol. Welcome to South Africa, my friend...Things don't always go as planned, but they work out somehow. And hey, you two got to meet one another. But come, it's late. I'll show you where the showers are and then let's all get to bed. It's an early start tomorrow; we need to head out at 4:45 a.m."

Ryan tried not to show his shock, but Vusi noticed his expression. "Life starts early in the bush. We're clearing out alien plants and it's best to work when the sun first comes up, while it's cool," he explained. "Tomorrow, you two will be guards, watching out for animals or snakes that come our way while we're working."

That night, Ryan's sleep was disturbed by bad dreams; he was being chased by snakes, while Mandy stood laughing at him. He awoke sweating, after seemingly only a moment of sleep, but he was quick to put Mandy and her crazy idea out of his head. It was a new day and a new adventure.

With the jeep loaded, Vusi set off with Mpilo and Ryan, followed by a truck full of workers and equipment. It was still dark when they drove away, but it wasn't long before the sky began to lighten. Trees stood silhouetted against a backdrop of grey and orange as the sun came up; impala were everywhere, unfazed by vehicles as they grazed, but alert and ready to sprint at any sign of danger. Ryan felt a thrill, riding in a game reserve with a team of rangers. Anything could happen at any moment and he was aware of the two brothers scanning the bush constantly. Soon they were driving off-road, making their way to the alien plants. As they drove, Vusi explained the importance of the eradication program. "These plants invade the area and crowd out natural vegetation. They use up precious water and upset the balance of nature, so it's important work. We chop down some of the aliens, but mostly we spray them because we have to kill them completely."

Ryan nodded. He hadn't realized just what Vusi did. He thought that Mpilo's brother was a game ranger who took tourists out on game drives, but he wasn't that at all. He was a conservationist.

"Right," Vusi said when they came to a stop, taking charge as the workers began to offload tools and set to work. "That's what we're going after today," he said, pointing out examples of the alien plants in question. "Generally, we don't have to worry about any game coming too close; the noise we make drives everything away. But it'll be good to have you guys keeping watch for us."

Ryan took up the position Vusi directed him to, sitting atop the jeep with a pair of binoculars, while Mpilo sat on top of the truck, facing the other way. Their combined view was 360 degrees, but they were close enough to talk. "All I can see are monkeys," Ryan called out. "Do they really need us to do this? What happens when we're not here?"

"They pray," Mpilo laughed.

"Well, I'm just saying, I feel kind of redundant."

"Maybe tomorrow there'll be more to do," Mpilo replied. "Vusi is being kind. I told him how much you love South Africa and he wants you to have a good time. He doesn't want you here spraying Roundup."

Once the workers had settled into a rhythm, Ryan ceased hearing their noise and began to hear bird songs instead. Peering through binoculars, he wished he knew more about South African birds; they were many and varied, with multiple bright colors. It would be an opportunity to learn about them while he was here. His thoughts were interrupted by Mpilo calling out, "So, what's going on with you and Mandy? You haven't mentioned her. I thought you were putting in some moves there. Have you given up?"

Ryan gritted his teeth. He looked over his shoulder at Mpilo and said, "I don't know, maybe I have." Suddenly, feeling a need to express his frustration, he said, "Do you know what she wants to do?"

"What?"

"Remember that orphan kid in the taxi?"

"Yeah. He didn't say much," Mpilo replied.

"Well, Mandy wants to adopt him."

"What? Take him to America?"

"Yup." This answer was met with silence until Ryan added, "She reckons she can give him a better life in California."

"Jesus," Mpilo exclaimed, "that's a big deal. He'd

become an American. He wouldn't be a Zulu anymore."

"Yup, crazy. That's the limit for me, as far as she and I are concerned."

Mpilo frowned and turned to look at Ryan. He cocked his head and said, "So you want Mandy, but you don't want a Zulu child? Is that what you're saying?"

"No. I don't want any child—Zulu or otherwise."

Mpilo began to curse, but his anger was not directed at Ryan. "Mandy mustn't do it," he said. "If I were that kid, I wouldn't want to leave my country. Nothing can make up for that loss. He belongs here, with us, his own people. I mean, you saw him dance that day at the side of the road. It made him happy. It was a Zulu dance. How can she take that away from him?"

"I agree," Ryan replied. "Trouble is, she didn't like me saying so and got really pissed off. She might be small, but she packs a big punch. She's one determined woman."

Mpilo wasn't easing up on his feelings about this. "I think she got the idea from all those movie stars. They come to Africa and think they can buy our children, just because they're famous and have lots of money. It's the fashion to come and 'save' our kids. What makes them think things are better in America?"

Now it was Ryan's turn to frown. "Mandy isn't trying to buy Jabulani. She's trying to help him." He surprised himself, leaping to her defense, but he didn't want her motives misinterpreted.

"I'm going to tell her what I think," Mpilo said. "If she wants to help the boy, she must do it here in South Africa."

"Good luck with that, mate," Ryan replied.

The following day, Vusi set another task for them. "I'm taking you to a hide overlooking Nsumo Pan. You'll be doing a game count. I want you to take notes of everything that comes to the waterhole—and if you're interested in birds, it's a good place for watching them. I'll lend you my bird book to help you, but Mpilo knows what they are. He can tell you whatever you need to know."

They followed Vusi in another official jeep, along miles of dirt roads, until they arrived at the Pan. "This is it," Vusi announced as they climbed out of their vehicles. "You're in the iSimangaliso Wetland Park; this waterhole is fed by the Mkuze River and it's a breeding ground for pelicans. Look, you can see them over there amongst the reeds and fever trees. But my friend, I'm warning you; there are hippos and crocodiles here, so stay in the hide. Don't go anywhere near the water's edge."

After Vusi left, they hadn't long to wait before visitors arrived. Two young women clambered into the hide and greeted them in hushed voices, before settling down to keep watch with binoculars and cameras. They all sat in silence, observing hippos rising and submerging in the water, snorting loudly as they did so. Pelicans swooped over them, searching for food, and a crocodile drifted by, keeping its distance from the hippos. The silence was broken when one of the women said, "I hope those hippos won't walk up the ramp into the hide."

"They stay in the water during the day to stay cool. They only come out to eat at night," Mpilo replied.

"Don't worry, you're quite safe here," Ryan added.

The taller woman spun around and looked at Ryan in surprise. "Are you American?" she asked.

"I sure am."

Her face broke into a grin. "Where are you from in the States?"

"San Francisco," he replied.

"Oh, wow. I don't believe it. I've just come back from there," she said. "I loved San Francisco."

Ryan looked at her and smiled. Why hadn't he noticed before how beautiful she was? Probably because she wore sunglasses and a big hat, both of which she'd just removed. Her dark brown hair was tied high on her head in a ponytail, and without glasses, he saw that she had enormous brown eyes that sparkled when she smiled. He quickly introduced himself and Mpilo; the women introduced themselves too. Joanna Nel was the brown haired one, and Gabby Jones the other.

"What are you doing here?" Joanna asked Ryan.

"Same as you—birdwatching and game viewing."

"You know what I mean...Why are you in South Africa?" she persisted.

"It's a long story," he began, but was cut off by Gabby.

"Can you keep your voices down?" Her tone was brusque as she settled her elbows on a ledge, trying to steady her camera. "The idea is to be quiet so that wildlife doesn't know we're here. That's why they're called hides."

Joanna rolled her eyes and mouthed, "I'm sorry," to Ryan.

He smiled and whispered, "Will you be at the main lodge tonight? We could talk then."

She nodded and he gave her a "thumbs up," before lowering his voice to a whisper and pointing out the breeding grounds Vusi had shown him moments earlier. He sounded more knowledgeable than he felt and hoped Joanna was impressed. When she and Gabby left half an hour later, she mouthed, "See you later."

"I'll be there," Ryan whispered.

As the women drove away, Mpilo laughed and turned to Ryan saying, "You really are interested in birds! Move over Mandy; make room for Joanna."

CHAPTER 21

Mandy was excited to see Lindiwe again. With the car that David had loaned her, life was much easier; she could meet her friend during lunch hour and still be back to fetch JJ when school was out. "I've got so much to tell you," she exclaimed as they sat down in a café. "But first, what's going on with Philani? Last time we spoke, you were excited because he was meeting you after work."

Lindiwe smiled. "Lots has happened since then. We see each other just about every day; he meets me after class and we go home together."

Mandy raised her eyebrows. "Ooh, that's exciting!" she said.

Lindiwe laughed. "No, it's not what you're thinking. We catch a taxi together, but he goes to his place and I go to mine. I share a rented room in a house full of people; there's nowhere we could be private. And he's in a dormitory. But I've got big news; he told the other girl he's not going to marry her."

Mandy high-fived her. "Awesome!"

"I know, even though his family had already agreed on the lobola."

"He didn't need much convincing once he met you," Mandy said.

"Well, he didn't want to pay for a wife he doesn't want, and I refuse to be his second wife. No way. I'm the only wife or no wife. His parents are angry, and so is that girl and her family. There's been big trouble."

Mandy gave her a knowing look. "So, he's asked you to marry him?"

Lindiwe looked away.

"Well?" Mandy persisted.

Lindiwe nodded, and looked down. Then she said, "We haven't told anybody else yet, so don't say anything. Not even to Ryan."

Mandy pulled a face. "Ryan would be the last person I'd tell."

"That bad, huh? But what do you want to speak to me about?"

Suddenly Mandy felt awkward. What if Lindiwe also reacted badly to her idea? She began to speak with less enthusiasm than she'd started out. "I've made a big decision, Lindiwe, and I'd like your opinion." She bit her bottom lip as her friend stared at her. Finally, she blurted out, "I'm going to adopt JJ."

Lindiwe frowned. "JJ? You mean Jabulani?"

Mandy nodded. "I want to take him back to California."

Speechless, Lindiwe stared at her, making Mandy feel uncomfortable. "Why are you looking at me like that?" she asked after a few minutes.

Lindiwe took a deep breath before she spoke. "I don't really know what to say. Does Jabulani want to do this?"

"I haven't told him. He has no concept where California is..."

"Or how different it is," Lindiwe added. "I mean, I'm an adult and I don't even know that. Is it like we see on

TV where everyone is driving around in fancy cars and living in two-story houses with big green lawns? Are the cops always speeding along freeways with their sirens screaming? Jabulani can't know what it would be like. He can't know whether he wants to live in California."

Mandy tried to be patient. "That's true, he has no way of knowing until he gets there."

"Why do you want to do this, Mandy?" Lindiwe asked.

"I love him and I can give him a better life." By now, her voice was beginning to reveal her irritation.

Lindiwe cleared her throat. "In a way, I get it; it would be good for Jabulani because you've got more money than us. But then it would be very hard for him. Nobody there would speak Zulu, or understand his culture." She smiled and tried to be lighthearted, adding, "Who would he dance with? You saw how happy he was dancing that day when we ran out of petrol. Are you going to do that with him?"

"If I have to, I will. You don't have to be Zulu to dance, you know."

"It's not the same. He would always be different and..."

"He'd have many more opportunities," Mandy interrupted her. "I can give him an education there that he won't get here. The school he's in is terrible. It's overcrowded and he's unhappy."

"It's not the only school in KwaZulu. He can transfer to something better." By now it was clear that Lindiwe had made up her mind that she did not support the proposal.

On the defensive, Mandy said, "I hear what you say, but he needs a mother and a home. That's what matters most. I don't want him to grow up in an institution."

"Then I'll adopt him—as soon as Philani and I are married. We'll give him a home and I'll be his mother."

As the two women glared at one another, Mandy thought about the vuvuzela Lindiwe had given her and felt their friendship was on the line. Finally, she said, "Thank you for your honesty. You once told me to throw away all the sad things to make sure there was enough room for happy things. Isn't that what your grandmother taught you?"

Lindiwe nodded.

"Well, I'm trying not to put anything into my basket right now. I asked you for your opinion and you've given it to me. I respect that. I can see this is a much bigger issue than I realized. But you've made something clear; I need to take JJ to California to see it for himself, before he can decide."

CHAPTER 22

✻

David Malherbe pulled up outside his parents' home to be greeted by two dogs, leaping and barking with excitement. It would be impossible for anyone to approach the house without the watchdogs announcing their arrival. His mother peered out the window and waved. "This is a nice surprise," she called, as she made her way to the front door. "Just a minute, Davey, let me find the key."

"I'd hate to see what would happen if there were an emergency here," David said, watching as she rummaged in a nearby chest of drawers, looking for a key to unlock the iron security gate.

His mother paid no attention to this remark. "Gerry," she called out. "What have you done with the key?"

His father quickly emerged from a nearby room. "Sorry, here it is. Hello, son, it's good to see you," he said, retrieving the key from his pocket and unlocking the gate. As he ushered David inside, he added, "I'm sorry we have to do this, but I don't want your grandmother wandering off. She gets lost in the house, so I hate to think what would happen if she got into the street. There are too many buggers out there, up to no good."

"I need to get another key cut then," Mrs. Malherbe said. "I'm a prisoner in my own home. I keep telling you, we need to put your mother in a place where she'll get around-the-clock care. Florence helps us on weekdays, but at nights and on weekends it's not so easy."

Dr. Malherbe sighed. "Yes, well, let's not burden David with these troubles. Come inside, my boy. Can you stay for dinner?"

"No, I can't, I'm afraid," David replied. "I just popped in because I was nearby."

"Oh, please stay for dinner," his mother urged.

"I can't, Ma," he replied. "I've got a date."

His father smiled. "It's that new car of yours. I said it would be a magnet. Come on, tell us..."

Mrs. Malherbe interrupted. "Our son is quite capable of attracting dates without a fancy car." The two men laughed and walked into the living room as she ran into the kitchen to get tea.

When they were settled, David shifted forward on his chair, leaning his elbows on his knees and banging his knuckles together. His father had seen this position before and knew his son had something important to say. "What is it? Is something troubling you?"

David looked startled. "No, no. There's no trouble. Why do you ask?"

"You've got a certain look about you that I recognize. It usually precedes an important announcement. I hope it's not trouble."

"Well, in a way you're right; it's important, but it's not trouble. I just wanted to tell you what I've done with Grandma's car," David replied. "Instead of trading it in, I'm going to donate it. I hope you don't mind."

"That's fine with me," his father replied. "Quite a good idea really. It's not worth much—your grandmother bought it when Henry Ford first built it."

Priscilla Malherbe was pouring the tea as she caught the end of this conversation. "Who'll you donate it to?" she asked.

"I've lent it to an American woman for a while. When she goes back to the USA, I'm going to donate it to a priest who runs an orphanage near Pinetown."

His mother beamed. "What a great idea. Tell us about this American woman. Who is she?"

"Just a minute," Dr. Malherbe said. "What about insurance? Is she insured? And what about the priest?"

"Hey guys, one question at a time." David laughed. "She's someone I met recently and yes, she's covered by my insurance temporarily. The priest will have to get permanent insurance, but first I'll have to teach him to drive."

Dr. Malherbe frowned. "He can't drive? How old is he, this priest?"

"About fifty, I'd say. I don't really know. Does it matter?"

"How come he can't drive?"

It was David's turn to frown. "Let's just say that he didn't grow up with all the privileges some of us have enjoyed. He didn't have the opportunity to learn before."

Dr. Malherbe put his tea cup down with a clatter. "So, he's a black. And the American woman...is she black too?"

David sighed. "Yes and no."

His mother held her breath and her tea cup rattled as she replaced it in the saucer.

David watched her reaction and deliberately left his answer hanging for a few moments. "Yes, Reverend

Dlamini is a Zulu priest. And no, she's not an African American," he said.

His mother nodded, but his father questioned him further. "Why did you choose this Zulu priest to be the recipient of the car? There are plenty of charitable organizations, rather than giving it to one individual."

"Yes, there are, but I happen to know this man and I can see the good work he's doing. His life will be made much easier if he has a car to depend on, rather than catching taxis. He can transport children where they need to go. I hope you'll come and see the orphanage; see what he's doing..."

"I would rather donate the car to the Alzheimer's Association; they could sell it and use the money for research. That strikes close to home for this family," his father persisted. "And given that it was your grandmother's car, I think that would be more appropriate."

David thought carefully about his response. There had been many family arguments and he didn't want one now. "Look, Dad, I know I should have spoken to you about this first, but I was impulsive; I've already promised the car. Grandma did give it to me, after all, so I felt free to do so. I'm sorry; of course, I understand why you would choose that charity, but perhaps if you came to see this orphanage and met Reverend Dlamini, you'd feel better."

"What in God's name did I do to deserve the sons I got? Your brother's a dubious actor with a boyfriend instead of a girlfriend—and look at you; you're almost as bad. You were a betoger at university and you're still a bleeding liberal. It's time you grew up. You haven't developed any sense. Why don't you look after your own people first? The blacks have the whole bloody country now and they're making a mess of it. Bugger them."

"Gerry, I wish you wouldn't talk like that," Mrs. Malherbe said to her husband.

"Well, it's the truth. They've had the country for almost twenty-five years and it gets worse by the day..."

David had heard these remonstrations before and had become immune to the insults and arguments. He still got angry, but discussion was pointless with his father. He came from an old Afrikaner family, and although Gerrit Malherbe had married an English woman who didn't share his beliefs, his prejudices were deeply ingrained.

"I tell you what I'll do," David said. "I'll make a donation to the Alzheimer's Association. You tell me how much you think the car is worth, and that's what I'll give them. That'll be better for everyone; they won't have the hassle of selling the car, and the priest will have his life made easier to do his good work. Does that make you happy?"

"Oh, Davey," his mother interjected. "That makes everyone happy except you. Why should you be out of pocket?"

"I can afford it, Mom, don't worry."

Dr. Malherbe grunted. "I suppose that'll work, but I still object to giving anything to..."

He was interrupted by an old lady who shuffled into the room and put her arms out to her him. "Paul," she said. "Come quickly. I saw some wild dogs outside the back door. They're trying to get inside."

Gerrit rose and said, "I'll take care of them. Don't worry." He led her out of the room, leaving David alone with his mother.

"This goes on all the time," she sighed. "She thinks her son is her husband. She's lost in a different world. I wish Gerry would listen to reason and put her into a home. There's a lovely place nearby; he could see her every day. Please help me to persuade your father."

"Mom, he's not going to listen to anything I say. You just heard what he thinks of me."

"He thinks the world of you, Davey," she replied, "but old habits die hard. It'll be good for him to see this orphanage; he needs to see African people doing good work. All he sees is corruption in the government, crime on the streets, and patients too scared to go to hospital because they've been in gunfights. Maybe you can show him something different. He's sixty-five years old; you can't expect him to change his thinking overnight, but I wish he would try."

CHAPTER 23

Ryan ignored his phone vibrating in his pocket. Joanna was sipping wine and he was drinking a beer; there was no need to speak to anyone else. She'd been waiting for him in the main lodge and had taken trouble over her appearance; her hair hung loosely about her shoulders, and she was wearing white jeans with a body-hugging red shirt. It looked good against her tanned skin, revealing a hint of cleavage. Ryan regretted not showering beforehand, but he'd been too rushed to do so.

She wanted to know why he was in Africa and he told her about working for the Peace Corps. "So, you spent two years in Namibia," she said, "and now you're heading back to the States?"

"Not just yet," he replied. "I've got a few months here still and then I'm starting a job in New York. It'll be hard to leave Africa, though." She smiled and Ryan thought it was the best smile he'd ever seen because her face lit up and her eyes twinkled. "What about you? You've heard my story. Where are you from?" he asked.

"Originally from Cape Town, but now I live in Durban," Joanna replied. "Nothing as exciting as San Francisco. I'm a freelance photographer, but I work for an advertising firm to pay the bills. We have a gig with the KZN Tourist Board, which got me a few days working here at Mkuze and the estuary."

"Nice," Ryan said. "What about Gabby?"

"She's also a photographer."

"She seems a large and in-charge kind of woman. I'm glad you could get away from her for a bit."

"She's not so bad really. I get on well with her, but her life is a bit tough at the moment. I left her having an argument on the phone with her husband."

They settled down in front of a campfire outside the lodge and she turned to Ryan, saying, "They call this bush TV, you know. You can sit here staring into the flames and forget about everything else. It's mesmerizing."

Ryan preferred to watch her face glowing in the firelight; his eyes also strayed to her cleavage. She felt him looking at her and said, "A penny for your thoughts."

"They're not worth that much," he said laughing—and quickly looked away. "My mind was a blank. I was just listening to the night sounds. What were you thinking?"

"I was thinking how strange it is to meet someone from San Francisco when I've just been there."

"Yeah, quite a coincidence. Were you working, or was it vacation?"

"A bit of both," she replied. "I had the best time. I'm already saving to go again."

"I tell you what, how about you show me around Durban, and next time you come to San Francisco, I'll show you around my city?" he suggested.

"I'd love to show you around Durban, but aren't you going to be in New York?" she asked.

He grimaced and sighed. "I'm not so sure. Africa has got into my soul—I'd rather stay here."

"That's crazy. So many South Africans are wanting

to leave, but you want to come here to live. Is that what you're saying?"

"I don't really know what I want to do." He shrugged, surprising himself with this answer, perhaps because it was a truth that he hadn't faced up to before.

Joanna instinctively reached out and touched his hand. "Sometimes things we dread turn out to be different from what we expected," she said. "You can always come back to Africa; it's not going away."

Her response exuded warmth and his hand rolled around hers, holding it firmly. He smiled at her and said, "I already have a trip planned next year. Mpilo and I are climbing Kilimanjaro together."

She didn't take her hand away and they sat for a long time, saying nothing, staring into the flames.

"Forget taxis, I've got us a ride back to Durban next week, my friend," Ryan told Mpilo as they climbed into the jeep with Vusi the next morning.

Mpilo looked at Ryan and laughed. "With that girl?" he asked.

"Sure thing. Joanna's going back next Friday and offered us a lift."

Mpilo shook his head in disbelief. "You making moves already?"

"No." Ryan's answer was terse. "Hey, if you want to catch a taxi, go right ahead."

"Don't be so touchy, my friend. I was joking."

Ryan retorted, "Well it's not like that. She works for the Tourism Board. She's coming to take more photos at the hide today."

Mpilo smiled. "What? She didn't get enough of them yesterday?"

"I guess not."

"Did you hear that? This Tourism Board woman wants more pictures of wildlife," he said, nudging Vusi. The brothers put their heads back and laughed.

As they drove through the bush, Ryan ignored them, thinking instead about the previous night. He and Joanna had gone back into the lodge when the fire had died down. They'd had a bite to eat and chatted for a long time; she was easy to be with and he'd really enjoyed her company. Suddenly he remembered he'd missed a call while he was talking to Joanna; when he glanced at his phone, he saw there was a voicemail from Mandy. He wasn't sure he wanted to hear what she had to say but resigned himself to listen.

"Hi, I've thought about what you said—and I've got lots to tell you. Nothing urgent, but call me back."

He grunted as he turned his phone off and shoved it into his pocket. She was infuriating; the last time he saw her, she nearly bit his head off. Now here she was all sweetness and charm, as if nothing had happened.

"What's eating you?" Mpilo asked. "You're attacking your phone like it just bit you."

Ryan grimaced but said nothing.

"Is Mandy giving you trouble again?"

Ryan nodded. "I can't handle it anymore. I want an uncomplicated relationship with a woman; not one where I'm always second guessing what her mood's going to be."

"Are you going to call her back?" Mpilo inquired.

Vusi chimed in. "Women can make your life miserable,

man. If it's not working, you should cut and run. It's like fishing; when your line gets tangled, there's no point in trying to sort it out. Just cut loose. There are plenty more fish out there, bro."

Ryan nodded. He would not call back. He'd say there was poor cellphone reception in the bush.

CHAPTER 24

Mandy was in a quandary. She'd taken Lindiwe's comments to heart about Jabulani. She wanted to broach the subject with him but had begun to feel unsure of herself. Nobody was giving her any encouragement. Yoga classes helped calm her anxiety until she visited her hairdresser again—and then her doubts grew worse. The stylist had news about the Zulu child in America. "It was a total disaster. He couldn't settle down and eventually they sent him back home. He got into drugs and all sorts of trouble there—and he kept running away. He wasn't happy. My client doesn't know where he is now. It's sad, but there you are. The kid shouldn't have gone to America in the first place."

This increased Mandy's anxiety even more. She tried calling Ryan, but was unable to reach him. When she returned to her lodgings, she confided her concerns to Ramona and it seemed as if the world was conspiring against her; Ramona agreed with the hairdresser. "I haven't met this child, but it would be a terrible wrench for him. He'd never hear his own language again. You'd be the only link with his past, and you've only been in his life a couple of months. It spells unhappiness to me."

This was not what Mandy wanted to hear. In desperation, she turned to David, calling to see if she could visit him at his office. It sounded urgent, so he checked his schedule and cleared some time for her before lunch.

"To what do I owe this unexpected pleasure?" he asked, smiling as she seated herself opposite him at his desk. He listened as she poured out her misgivings—and in true legal fashion, thought about what she said before giving his opinion. After due consideration, he replied, "Everything people are saying is valid, but your affection for the child is a huge factor and it's easy to see that he's very fond of you, too. Those things matter; maybe they matter the most. Why don't you take him to California for a visit, and take the priest with you? Don't say anything to the boy about staying there permanently—don't forget, we don't know how we're going to work that out. Just see how he reacts to being there."

Mandy nodded. "Great idea except for one large obstacle. Money. I can't afford their airfares and Reverend Dlamini can't either."

David leaned towards her and said, "I'll take care of that."

"What? No, definitely not," she replied. "That's out of the question."

"Why? I have miles I can use for their tickets; it's not a big deal. And I really think this will be a good first step. It won't raise any expectations on Jabulani's part, expectations that might not be met. It'll help you figure out whether he could be happy in California. And just as important, you can also see how you might cope, as well. You've been thinking solely about what's good for him, but have you thought about what's good for you? What about that master's degree you were planning to do?"

"I'm so confused," she replied, with tears welling in

her eyes. She wiped them and looked away as David got up and sat on the desk next to her. Embarrassed, Mandy stood, as if to leave, but he put his arms out to prevent her from going. Her tears were suddenly unstoppable and she buried her head in his chest. He said nothing, just held her. Eventually, when she was able to speak, she looked up at him. "You've been so kind. I don't understand why you want to help. You hardly know us."

He turned away from her and slowly walked towards a window overlooking the busy street, fifteen floors below. As he stared at the view, he said, "Come and look at all these people, Mandy." He frowned, watching crowds shove their way amongst street vendors. "They're battling to survive; most of them get up at 4 a.m. to be at work on time. Parents leave young children on their own, to get to school by themselves. That's just so there can be a bit of food on the table. It seems hopeless; they're trapped in poverty."

Mandy stood next to him, also watching the scene below. "That's exactly why I want to help JJ. But it still doesn't explain why you're doing this."

He turned his back on the window and faced her. "I've known a life of privilege—because I was born to a white family. It weighs on my conscience that I have so much, yet there are all these people who have so little—because they were born black. Much has changed since 1994 when democracy was established in South Africa; but it's a very flawed democracy. All the economic problems still exist and corruption makes things worse. I'm at a loss to know how it can all be solved. I do know this, however— if I can help one underprivileged child to have a better life, that's at least something."

"What? You want me and Jabulani to come to America for a holiday?" Reverend Dlamini asked, staring at her with his mouth agape. "We are poor people. We live a simple life. We don't take holidays like that. What are you thinking, Mandy?"

Mandy watched his face and understood his incredulity. She spoke hesitantly. "I...I think it would be good to see how he likes it there. It would just be for three weeks." When the priest still said nothing, she continued, "We could stay with my parents; they'd be happy to have you visit."

"I cannot do that, Mandy. How will we pay for tickets? It costs too much money. I don't have it."

"It wouldn't cost you anything. David Malherbe will pay."

The priest frowned. "What? Why would he do that?"

"He has his reasons and they're good ones." She didn't want to share with Reverend Dlamini what David had told her, but she had been deeply moved by his words. She felt a bond with him; they both knew about survivor guilt.

Reverend Dlamini was still frowning. He felt uncomfortable having so much money spent on a holiday when there was such a need for funds to support his orphans with rudimentary things. "Mandy, please, don't ask me to come with you. I can't leave my boys here on their own for three weeks. They also need help. If you really want to, I suppose you can take Jabulani for a holiday; but you must travel back with him. He cannot do that journey on his own. He's too small."

"I'm sure you could get someone else to come and watch things while you're away. The boys are all teenagers; they don't need you to spoon feed them. It might even be good for them to be independent. And the thing is, you're Jabulani's guardian; you need to come with him. I won't be allowed to take him without you."

He shook his head slowly as he spoke. "It doesn't feel right, but I suppose you're correct."

Mandy clapped her hands and hugged the priest. "Thank you, thank you. I'll tell David and we'll start getting your visas sorted out."

"We'll both need passports first," Reverend Dlamini said. "Nothing is simple. Passports take time to get."

"Then, the sooner we start the process, the better," she replied. "Ramona's brother knows someone who works at the American Consulate. I'm sure he can help us with the visas. I'll call Suresh."

CHAPTER 25

Basie Botha was surprised to receive an inquiry from David Malherbe about tickets to San Francisco for two passengers, Dlamini and Jiyane. He immediately called Gerrit Malherbe. "Who are these blacks your son's wanting to send to America?" he asked, calling from his travel agency.

Gerrit admitted that he had no idea. "Maybe they're clients of his."

"That son of yours has got strange ideas, Gerrit. You need to knock some sense into him. Our sons should be fighting alongside us, fighting for their volk, not fraternizing with blacks."

"He's got a lot of his British mother in him."

"Well, you should sort him out. I tell you, I'm proud of my boy, Petrus. My son is one of us—and he's got friends. They tell me the time's right for action before it's too late. We've still got muscle; let's use it. Something big is going to happen soon, you'll see." Basie dreamed of a return to apartheid. He didn't reveal his thoughts to many people because it was bad for business, but to Gerrit, he spoke openly because they had been at school together many years ago. "All I want is a piece of Africa for whites. Blacks can come and work, but they must go home at night—just like the old days."

Gerrit didn't like this talk. "Basie, you're crazy. I'm

too old to argue any more. Our people fought a good fight, but we lost. You know that as well as I do. Our ancestors trekked away long ago and found themselves a piece of Africa. For a while, everything was good until gold was discovered and the bloody British wanted it; they came and fought us and took our land after the Boer War. We got it back for a while when we became a republic, but we lost it again to the blacks in 1994. We can't win. The odds are stacked against us. Soon I'm going to be dead. My fight is over. My piece of Africa is a half-acre here in Hillcrest, and I just want some peace and quiet."

"Ag, you're a disgrace. You're not old. You're young enough to fight. We can't give up now."

"I don't want any blood on my hands. I might be retired, but I'm still a doctor. I took the Hippocratic oath to save lives, not take them. Thank you for calling me about this matter with my son; I'll find out what's going on."

He called David immediately. "Who are these black people you're wanting to send to San Francisco? Are they friends of this American woman you've met? Is she putting stupid ideas into your head?" he shouted.

David almost put the phone down on his father, but he said as calmly as he could, "The idea was mine, for reasons I don't wish to explain." But then his annoyance swelled and he added, "And just for the record, Basie bloody Botha can take his travel agency and stick it up his arse. My business is confidential."

At a loss for words, it was Gerrit Malherbe who slammed the phone down.

David was unfazed by this. He was feeling happier than he had in a long time and he wasn't going to let his father's prejudices change his mood. Mandy Walker was in his thoughts a lot. He didn't meet too many people of her caliber these days. The few moments in his office when she'd let her guard down and cried had moved him deeply; he was touched that she had turned to him for advice.

He soon received another call—this time from his mother, apologizing for his father's interference.

"You don't have to say anything," he told her. "Dad's the one who should be apologizing. But maybe it's time you met Mandy, Mom. She's a good person." He could hear his mother sighing; she'd spent a lifetime caught in the crossfire when there was an argument between her husband and sons. "I'm not sure I want to subject her to Dad, but I'd like you to meet her and understand what she's trying to do," he said.

"I'll talk to your father. He'll be OK. You know he's hot-headed sometimes. Why don't you come for lunch on Friday? It's a public holiday, but Florence will be here so we won't have to worry about Grandma disturbing the peace. I promise you, your father will be on his best behavior."

Mandy was nervous about meeting David's parents. She had no idea what to expect and was pleasantly surprised to be greeted warmly by his mother, a fine-looking woman. Tall and slender, with gray hair swept back in an elegant twist, she wore chinos with a pale blue twin set and a single strand of pearls around her neck. Mandy thought it an interesting mixture of formality and informality, and was glad she'd made an effort to dress well for the occasion herself. Instead of her regular denims and tee-shirt, she was wearing a navy blue linen skirt and a crème silk blouse.

Once Priscilla Malherbe managed to control the dogs, she unlocked the iron gate and said, "I've been looking forward to meeting you, dear. Come in. I want to hear all about the work you're doing. Please make yourselves comfortable on the verandah; I'll just tell Gerry you're here. He's in his office out in the back."

Mandy was glad of the opportunity to examine the photographs on walls as they made their way through the house. There was a picture of David in a rugby shirt, looking sweaty and dirty, but smiling at the camera. "So, you played that brutal game, huh?"

"What self-respecting South African boy wouldn't?" he replied, laughing.

A picture of two boys sitting next to each other caught her eye. She stopped to examine it, noting the similarity between the children. "You have a twin?" she asked.

He nodded. "Which one's me?"

She examined the photo again and pointed to the child facing the camera. "That one."

"How could you tell?"

"Easy. You always face things head-on. Your twin's looking at you; you're looking straight at the photographer. You're in charge."

David smiled. "Maybe Peter was looking at me like that because he thought I was an idiot!"

She laughed and asked, "Where does he live?"

"In London. He's an actor. He feels more at home there; different strokes for different folks. But let's go outside; lunch will be a braai. It's a South African way of life—what you call a barbecue in America. Actually, I think it was invented by women to get men doing the cooking; and in this case, it's me by the way, not my father. He couldn't make a piece of toast."

When they walked outside, Mandy gawked at the Malherbes' park-like garden. The verandah opened onto a vast, lush green lawn, surrounded by flower beds brimming with color. "It's so peaceful," she said, "like an oasis amidst all the craziness on the other side of the wall."

"Yup. Sadly, this country has lots of walls."

His words seemed weighted and she was about to question him when Mandy heard other voices. Turning, she saw David's parents approaching. Mrs. Malherbe was smiling as she introduced her husband, who towered over her. He was a handsome man, but his size, white hair, and mustache made him seem formidable.

"So, you're the Yankee girl?" he said. His voice was gruff.

Mandy was taken aback. She hesitated a moment before replying, "Well, I'm from the USA." Her voice was strained when she added, "It's a long time since anyone called me a girl; it makes me feel young."

As Gerrit continued staring at Mandy, his expression began to soften, and then he smiled. "When you're my age, Mandy," he replied, "every woman who doesn't have gray hair is a girl. My apologies; I can see you're a woman—and a good-looking one too. Come, let me get you something to drink. It seems my son isn't looking after you properly."

Priscilla Malherbe winked at David and her son nodded.

His father could be charming when he wanted to be. Would he keep up the façade when Mandy spoke about Jabulani? The conversation soon turned to JJ and her face lit up as she described the child, his circumstances and her plans for him. Gerrit Malherbe remained silent but began drumming his fingers on the table in front of him.

"What do you think?" Mandy asked. "I've had so much criticism from people; David is the only person who's been supportive."

"It's an amazing thing you're proposing to do, my dear," Priscilla replied quickly. "I wish you all the best with it." She looked as if she wanted to say more but changed her mind and added, "Perhaps you could come and help me get a few things ready in the kitchen, if you don't mind?"

Gerrit Malherbe had been watching his son's expression as Mandy spoke. David was smitten, it was clear to see. When the women had gone inside, the older man muttered, "How can she get such a stupid idea in that pretty head of hers? All I can say is, there'll be one less black bugger here in South Africa. Try and encourage her to adopt a few more."

CHAPTER 26

Ryan and Mpilo were ready and waiting when the two women arrived. Gabby's Mercedes SUV had more space than they were accustomed to and they looked forward to a comfortable ride. Carefully placing their bags next to all the cameras and luggage already there, Ryan remarked. "Wow, there's some serious photographic equipment here."

"We're serious about what we do," Joanna replied, laughing.

"And we're good at it," Gabby added. "Since we left Mkuze, we've been to St. Lucia and taken great photos of the estuary and the beaches. The lighting's been perfect." She seemed to be in a better frame of mind.

"Do we get to see any of them?" Ryan asked.

Joanna turned and smiled. "Not yet."

"I can wait," he said.

"We have to edit them first," she replied.

When Gabby turned on the radio, however, conversation became difficult between the front and back seats. Unused to such luxury, Ryan and Mpilo spread out, put their heads back and closed their eyes. Early mornings had taken their toll and, although he'd planned to spend the journey chatting to Joanna, Ryan dozed off, waking only as they reached Durban. The noise of traffic was jarring after the stillness of the bush—enough to wake the dead.

Gabby turned the music down and said, "Fellas, where can I drop you off? We're heading to our office in the Musgrave Centre."

Mpilo rubbed his eyes and sat up straight. "Musgrave Centre will be good. There's a taxi rank in Greyville, not too far away."

"We're close to Greyville now, we can drop you there," Joanna said, "or you can come to our office and I can run you home. I'm happy to do that."

"You can't drive me to the township, Joanna; that's too far. And don't drive to the taxi rank, Gabby; it's too busy," Mpilo replied. "I don't know what Ryan wants to do, but you can just drop me here. I can walk. Look, see all those people over there? That's where the taxi rank is."

"Oh, I think I'll take you up on that offer of a ride home, Joanna," Ryan said with a grin.

Gabby was happy not to go any further; it looked congested. She stopped the car and popped the back open for Mpilo to collect his gear. Ryan waved his friend goodbye, but just as Gabby turned the car around, he yelled, "Hang on a minute." Leaping out, he ran towards Mpilo, shouting, "Here's Vusi's bird book. Can you give it back to him?"

He'd just caught up with Mpilo when they heard the first shots. They sounded like firecrackers, but suddenly people further up the road started running in all directions—some heading straight towards them. There were screams, and more shots, and then more shots again. Joanna put her head out the window and shouted, "Quickly, get back in the car."

But they didn't hear her and Gabby wasn't waiting.

She took off at speed, away from the trouble.

Ryan could see the crowds getting closer as people stampeded. The gunshots carried on and on and he screamed at his friend to make a break for it down a side street, but when he looked around, Mpilo was heading towards the taxi rank. "What are you doing?" he shouted, his voice lost in the uproar. Ryan just made it into a side street himself, when he saw two open pick-up vans racing along Avondale Road. They were white and went by in a blur. It was difficult to see much except that there were guys with guns, sitting in the back. They were white men—and they were laughing.

Screaming and wailing continued, even when gunshots stopped. Ryan's heart was pounding as he stayed hidden behind a parked car, unsure what to do. What the hell had just happened? Thank goodness Joanna and Gabby had got away safely, but where was Mpilo? And what was he going to do without his backpack? He had no money or ID with him, and he didn't know where he was. "Shit," he groaned, sinking to the ground.

His despair was replaced by an urge to help as he heard sirens racing towards the scene; the first responders were on their way. He made his way back fast, but when he arrived at the taxi rank, he stopped dead in his tracks. Shocked, he stared at the dead bodies scattered in the street. Blood was everywhere, and wounded people, moaning in pain, were slumped next to corpses. There were taxis burning, people wailing, and children were among the dead and wounded.

His heart was pounding, and when he felt a bump on

his arm, he got such a fright that his heart almost stopped beating altogether. He spun around on high alert to discover it was Joanna. "For God's sake, what are you doing here?" he asked, putting his arm around her.

"Holy Mother of God," she cried, staring at the carnage as she leaned on him for support. "I came to see if you were OK. Gabby drove away, but I made her stop and let me out. I couldn't leave you stranded. Where's Mpilo? My God, this is horrific." She stood shell-shocked, staring uncomprehendingly for a few moments until the professional photographer took over once more. She'd been taking pictures as she ran along the street and continued to do so now at the taxi rank.

Ambulances and fire engines began arriving and paramedics were getting to work with the injured. "Where the hell does one start to help? Dammit, I wish I could see Mpilo," Ryan muttered.

Joanna said nothing as she continued photographing. However, it wasn't long before this caused a reaction. A woman, with blood pouring from her arm and a bleeding baby tied on her back, started shouting at this person photographing her misery and suffering. Other people joined in. As the mob grew nearer, Mpilo suddenly appeared. Pulling off his hoodie and grabbing another from his backpack, he threw them both at Ryan and Joanna. "Put these on and go. Don't let people see you're white. Get away from here. Go quickly," he shouted.

The urgency with which he spoke left no room for argument. Much as Ryan wanted to help, he did as Mpilo commanded and pulled Joanna away from the massacre, leaving his friend behind to assist the injured.

CHAPTER 27

Mandy listened in silence to David's mother chatting as they worked together, preparing salads. Suddenly the older woman stopped what she was doing and turned to Mandy. "My dear, there's some advice I want to give you. You know that I'm not a native-born South African, don't you?"

Mandy nodded, wondering where this was leading.

Priscilla Malherbe took a deep breath and continued. "Like you, I came here to work; I was a nurse and felt I had much to offer back in the 1970s. I didn't plan on being here for long, but then..." She shrugged and said, "I met Gerry at the hospital where I was working and we fell in love. He wouldn't move to England, so I ended up staying here."

Mandy began to feel uncomfortable. Mrs. Malherbe sensed this, but it didn't stop her. "Don't worry, I love the place and I don't regret my decision to stay. I wouldn't choose to live anywhere else in the world, but its problems are immense. They're not going to be solved in my lifetime—nor David's, probably. There's such a big discrepancy in wealth, as well as so much bigotry. This is really what I want to warn you about: be careful what you say. Not everyone has your good intentions."

Still Mandy remained silent.

"I only say this to you," Priscilla continued, "because I

can see that you want to make everything better. Don't be disappointed when you find the problems are too big for one woman to take on. My son admires you greatly and I can see why, but South Africa can break your heart..."

Much to Mandy's relief, the conversation ended when David entered the kitchen, calling out, "The meat's ready." Cheerful as he helped them carry food and plates outside, he said, "Mandy, this is the first of many braais for you if you decide to stay in South Africa for five years. I hope you like them. It's just as well you're a carnivore... No braai is complete without lamb chops, steak, and boerewors. This is the best sausage in the world, by the way."

"Will you stop talking about food and let Mandy explain to me why she's planning to stay in South Africa for five years?" Gerrit Malherbe asked.

"Oh, I'm not sure I will, but it's possible." Mandy's voice quivered slightly. David's father seemed disapproving of her, so she decided to heed Mrs. Malherbe's advice and not engage. Instead she began eating and turned the conversation back to food. "You're right, this is good sausage."

"It's a South African staple," David said, but was interrupted by a buzz from his cell phone.

As he reached for it in his pocket, his father complained, "Dammit! Can't we have a meal without that thing disturbing us?"

David stared at the text message and cursed. "Shit. All hell's broken loose." Looking stunned, he was barely audible when he announced, "There's been a shooting in Durban."

"What? Where?" Mandy and Priscilla shouted at the same time. Gerry Malherbe frowned.

"At a taxi rank near Greyville."

"Those bloody taxi-drivers and their wars. I'm telling you, the blacks will kill one another for a seat in a mini bus," Gerry Malherbe grunted.

David ignored his father. "This is big. At least forty-five people are dead; more are wounded."

They all stared at one another in shock; nobody said a word until another text buzzed on David's phone. He read it and closed his eyes before announcing, "Bystanders are saying it was white guys. They drove bakkies up to the taxis and began shooting with semi-automatic rifles. They had two vehicles and both of them got away. There's a massive manhunt going on."

Gerrit Malherbe had grown very quiet, shaking as he reached for another beer. He flinched when his wife spoke. "Why is there so much hatred and destruction in the world? Oh Gerry, this is very close to home. I can't bear it."

Mandy watched David's father get up, walk over to his wife, and put his arms around her. As he kissed her head, he said, "My liefling, we are quite safe here, I promise you." It was surprising to see the tenderness the man displayed towards his wife, who burst into tears.

"Yes, we are," she said, "but the moment we go out that gate, we aren't. Our home is safe, but it's also a prison. And what about all the people who can't stay protected behind walls and alarms? Forty-five people dead—is that what you said, Davey?"

David nodded. "I'm afraid so. At least that many."

He turned to Mandy and said, "I don't feel happy about taking you back to your place tonight. It's very isolated; it's not a good time for you to be there alone with all this happening."

"I'll be fine," she replied. "I'm probably safer there than in some crowded place—I mean, look where the shooting took place."

"But the perpetrators are on the run. They'll be looking to hide, and unfortunately, there might be people looking for revenge. Violence often begets more violence."

Priscilla Malherbe wiped her tears and apologized. "I'm sorry. I'm not usually one to break down, but it's such a shock. Mandy, I agree with David; it's a bad time to be out there. We have lots of room here; please spend the night with us. You and David should both stay. Don't you agree, Gerry?"

Dr. Malherbe nodded, his eyebrows knitted together as he spoke. "Yes, yes I do. It's a dark day. Nothing good will come of it."

CHAPTER 28

Ryan and Joanna didn't stop running until they were safely in the Musgrave Centre. Once in the deserted office, he told her about the two pick-ups he'd seen leaving the crime scene with armed men in the back. A strange look came over her. Beckoning him to follow, she headed to her cubicle and began looking at the photos she'd taken after she'd emerged from Gabby's car.

"What are you doing?" he asked.

She didn't respond, but kept going back frantically from one photo to the next. Suddenly she stopped and said, "Look at this." Frowning, she enlarged a picture as much as possible and handed her camera to Ryan. "See anything interesting?"

He examined it, but it just looked like a street scene with cars and people. "No, can't say I do."

"Here, look with a magnifying glass. Two bakkies are heading away from the taxi rank. Are those the ones you saw—the pick-ups?"

Ryan looked carefully. They were slightly blurred and small, but yes—he recognized them. His eyes opened wide and he said, "You need to text this to the police."

"Absolutely. They'll have equipment to get greater detail. They might even get the number plate on one of the bakkies. Look, it's there in the photo; it's too small for us to read."

"Joanna, you're a marvel. Let's get this into the right hands."

"I don't know where Gabby is—or anybody else—but I don't need permission. They're my photos. I'm sending them right now."

By 4 p.m., a nationwide police alert went out for a white bakkie, registered to Petrus Botha. A search at his address produced little; the vehicle wasn't there. However, an envelope with Basie Botha's name on it was discovered and when he was questioned, he admitted to being Petrus's father—but said he didn't know where his son was.

At 5 p.m., national TV made a public announcement that Petrus Botha was wanted to help with inquiries regarding a shooting in Durban.

The Malherbes did not have their television switched on—they were entertaining their son and Mandy, but David received text messages with the information.

At 5:15 p.m., Gerrit Malherbe received a phone call. "Gerrit, I need your help. Please, man—it's an emergency."

"What do you want?" Gerrit asked.

"Petrus is in trouble. He just called me. He's dumped his bakkie at the Westville Hospital to get rid of it. Now he's gone next door to the Pavilion Shopping Centre. Can you fetch him? Take him to your house for me. Don't bring him here—the police are looking for him and they're watching my place."

"Basie, I told you I don't want blood on my hands. Was your son responsible for this shooting today?"

David, Mandy, and Priscilla stopped in their tracks and stared at Gerrit, listening to his side of the conversation.

"This is war, man. He's a soldier; he needs your help. We're on the same side. The Bothas and Malherbes go back to the beginning of this country," Basie argued. By now, he had begun shouting so loudly that everyone in the room could hear him.

Gerrit Malherbe took a deep breath and exhaled slowly. His eyes were on his wife and son when he replied. "It's a war declared by one side only—yours. That doesn't make it legitimate."

"Stop bloody debating and help us."

"Answer me. Was Petrus involved in this thing today?"

Priscilla raised her eyebrows. Her husband's eyes met hers. He said nothing as Basie continued to plead with him—until Gerrit finally cut the man off. "Tell your son to turn himself in. He can't get away. And let me make it clear, I'm not getting involved in this dirty business." With that, he rang off and fell into a chair, shaking.

David walked towards his father, put his hand out to him, and said, "That took guts, Pa. I'm proud of you."

Gerrit couldn't speak. He swallowed hard and put his head in his hands.

David continued talking to him, and it seemed to Mandy that the son became the father for a moment. "I know this is difficult, but doing nothing is the same as helping. This is mass murder. If you know where he is, you have to tell the police. Did he say Petrus is at the Pavilion?"

The elder Malherbe lifted his head and slowly nodded. There were tears in his eyes when his son murmured, "I'll take care of it."

By 5:45 p.m., Petrus Botha was in custody at the Westville Police Station.

CHAPTER 29

Adrenalin was racing through Ryan and Joanna as they left her office and headed to her flat, where they could watch the news unfold on television. Memory of the carnage haunted them; neither wanted to be alone.

"I can't bear to look at those photos anymore," Joanna said, while Ryan kept scrutinizing them. "I know I can sell a lot of them, but it doesn't seem right to do that—profiting from someone else's misery."

"People need to see the terrible thing that happened. Pictures speak volumes; they're stronger than words. Think about war photographers; they provide records for posterity," Ryan said. "I think you should sell them to the highest bidder, who'll give them the greatest coverage. It'll be an opportunity for the country to see what hatred does."

"This isn't war. This is a crime scene…" she began, but was interrupted by Ryan's phone ringing.

He looked at the caller ID and said, "It's Mpilo." His hands were trembling as he hit the talk button.

Before he could say anything, he heard his friend's voice; it sounded hoarse. "Ryan, are you OK?"

"Yeah, we're good. Where are you? Are *you* OK?"

"I'm fine. I'm still at the taxi rank, helping injured people here; there are so many of them. But I need your help; Reverend Dlamini and that little boy were here today."

"What? Oh, shit!" Ryan exclaimed, his heart pounding. "Are they alive?"

"Yes, they're OK. But the boy is screaming. We can't get him to stop. The priest says they were with two other boys from the orphanage, just getting out of Joseph's taxi, when the shooting started. One of the boys, Temba, was killed. The other one, Andile, is injured. They were standing next to Jabulani. He saw everything."

"Oh Jesus. What about Mandy? Was she there? Please tell me she wasn't there too."

Watching him, Joanna saw color draining from Ryan's face.

"No, just the priest and the boys."

"Thank God." He took a deep breath and said, "So where are they now?"

"Andile has been taken to the hospital, but the priest and Jabulani are still here. Reverend Dlamini is trying to help with all these people, but we don't know what to do about the little boy."

"I'll call Mandy," Ryan replied. "Maybe he'll calm down if he's with her. Poor kid."

"No wait. It's not safe for Mandy to come here. People are very angry. She can call me and I'll bring Jabulani to her somewhere."

Ryan was shaking as he hit Mandy's number on speed dial. The phone rang and rang, before going to her voice mail. "Mandy, it's urgent; call me as soon as you get this message," he said. He began pacing as he told Joanna what had happened, explaining about the day he'd met these people when their taxi ran out of petrol. He described what Mandy had done for Jabulani, adding,

"He's an orphan. She wants to adopt him. God, where is she? Why won't she answer her phone?"

"Wait a minute. Who's Mandy?" Joanna asked.

"An American friend of mine. We were in the Peace Corps together."

"Is she your girlfriend?" Joanna asked.

He had his back to her when she asked this question, so she didn't see him bite his lip. "No, she's not," he replied, turning around to face her. Then he added. "We argue a lot. We're kind of oil and water. She's a friend, that's all."

Joanna said nothing but suddenly felt wary.

When he tried to call Mandy again a few minutes later, she suspected there was more to it than he was telling her. And when he called someone else called Ramona and asked her to check whether Mandy was in her room, she was convinced of it. Feeling so many emotions caused by what had happened in the course of one afternoon, she thought there couldn't possibly be room for jealousy—but there was. Clearly, Ryan was worried—and she presumed his concern was about this woman called Mandy.

She was correct; Ryan *was* worried. Where was Mandy? Could she have been at the taxi rank with the priest and Jabulani? Where else could she be? Ramona reported that she wasn't in her room. He checked with Lindiwe: *Is Mandy with you?* The reply came back immediately: *No.*

Eventually, when Mandy didn't return his call, he decided to text her the information he would rather have given to her in person: *JJ was at the shooting. He's with Mpilo and Dlamini.*

CHAPTER 30

Mandy ignored Ryan's phone call. She'd called him and left a message and he hadn't bothered to return her call; now he was probably back from Mkuze and needing some company. *Well, he can find it elsewhere,* she thought. She was safe in the Malherbes' home, watching the story of the shooting unfold on the news—and as every minute went by, she grew more impressed with David.

Not long after it was announced that Petrus Botha was in custody, Basie Botha phoned Dr. Malherbe again. The doctor didn't bother to leave the room to take the call and Mandy watched him as he listened to the distraught man. Finally he responded in a somber voice. "Listen Basie, I did *not* call the police, so don't call me a traitor. You were shouting so bloody loudly the police probably heard you themselves. I told you Petrus couldn't get away. I'm sorry for you, I know how you must be feeling. No matter what they do, our children are in our hearts."

Priscilla Malherbe, choking back tears, got up and held her husband's hand while her gaze fixed on a picture of her sons. Mandy watched the tenderness between the couple and her heart softened to the man; he didn't seem formidable any longer. She watched him squeeze his wife's hand as he spoke to Basie. "No, I'm sorry. If you want my son's help, you'll have to speak to him yourself; I can't do that for you. I'll text you his number and you can call him."

David frowned as his father rang off. "What does he want me for?"

Gerrit Malherbe snorted as he sent the text; it was a bitter sound. "He wants you to defend that baboon he's got for a son."

The words were hardly out of his mouth when David's phone rang. Mandy switched her gaze to him as he listened to Basie Botha. After a few minutes, he cleared his throat and said, "I'm sorry. I despise what your son has done; I cannot defend him. An attorney needs to believe in the possibility of his client's innocence to be effective; what he's done is heinous and contemptible. But I'll refer you to someone in my firm who might consider it. She's young, smart, and ambitious. Try my colleague, Ramona Govender."

There was shouting from the other end of the phone, quite audible to all in the room. "Are you out of your fucking mind? A woman? And an Indian woman at that?"

"Here's a piece of free advice, Mr. Botha. Your son will be lucky to find any lawyer to take his case. And if you don't control your temper, as well as your bad language, you'll make it worse for him. Tread carefully." He rang off and had hardly put the phone back in his pocket when it rang again.

"You bastard," Basie Botha shouted at him. "A person is innocent until proven guilty. You're not in a position to turn my son down. You have to defend him."

Mandy stared at David and marveled. He remained unruffled in the face of extreme provocation, saying calmly, "Mr. Botha, lawyers don't take the Hippocratic oath.

I don't have to defend anyone. Your son is a danger to society. He deserves to spend a long time locked up. The evidence is compelling." With that, he ended the call and blocked the caller.

Gerry and Priscilla retired to bed even earlier than was their custom. It was too painful to watch the news anymore and, after both the president and archbishop had appealed for calm, they wanted the oblivion that only sleep could offer.

When they left the room, David turned to Mandy and said, "I'm really glad you agreed to spend the night here. There are only two good things about that dark hole you're living in; the first is that it's free—and the second is that I got to meet you because of Ramona living next door."

Mandy smiled. "Free is important. I don't have any income and my savings are being depleted rapidly. I wouldn't have been able to stay and teach Jabulani if the room hadn't been free." She watched as he turned off the TV and walked towards her. Her pulse rate shot up when he sat next to her on the couch and put an arm around her shoulders.

"You know," he said, "I can't believe I only met you two weeks ago; it feels like I've known you forever." He looked at her intently and added, "I hope you'll think about staying longer in South Africa—and not just for Jabulani's sake." She blushed and her heart skipped a few beats, but she said nothing. "After today's events, that might not sound like such a good idea, but there are lots of good things about the country. Honestly."

"Oh, I know that," she replied. "Anyway, look at the shootings we have in the States; it's not as if..."

She wasn't able to finish her sentence. He gently placed a hand under her chin and drew her face towards his. She didn't resist when he started to kiss her.

They moved quickly from the living room to her bedroom, in case his grandmother took one of her nightly strolls. Her heart was pounding when he closed the door behind them, continuing to kiss her as he unbuttoned her shirt. She wanted him, she wanted him badly as they fell onto the bed, fumbling to remove their clothes. When she felt his body pressing against hers, desire had her ready to throw caution to the wind—until that little voice in her head began to scream: "What are you doing? You hardly know this man."

It took all her willpower to heed the intrusion. Pushing him away, she gasped, "No, stop David. It's too soon for this."

Her words acted like a handbrake.

He rolled away and lay on his back, breathing heavily, while she lay motionless next to him. Her heart was racing. Flushed with embarrassment, she was thankful for the darkness. They remained side by side without touching or speaking until she suddenly began to shiver uncontrollably. When he leaned over and kissed her gently on the forehead, she held her breath, overwhelmed by his tenderness. He whispered, "I'm crazy about you, Mandy," and tears began trickling down her cheeks even though she was squeezing her eyes tightly shut.

She heard him get up and leave the room. As the door closed behind him, she choked trying to call out, "Don't go." But she couldn't utter a word. Instead, she lay in bed aching for him to come back. She'd never felt this way about anyone before; he took her breath away. He was kind and generous—and she was mad about him.

Sleep didn't come easily but she was woken in the morning by a knock on the door. It opened and David appeared, smiling as if nothing had happened. He had a mug of tea for her, which he placed on the bedside table. "I don't know whether you drink this stuff or not? I couldn't find any coffee," he said.

She tried to smile. "It's perfect. I'm a tea drinker," she replied, avoiding his gaze. After an awkward pause, she murmured, "Thank you, David. Thanks for everything."

He seemed remarkably calm as he sat down on the bed next to her and said, "Thank *you*, Mandy." Hesitating a moment, he added, "I respect the call you made last night. Let's give it time..." His voice trailed off, but his eyes were twinkling when he said, "Are you going to sit up and drink this?"

She blushed. "I don't have any clothes on."

"I know that. Why do you think I brought you tea?"

That made her laugh too; he was so relaxed that it put her at ease. She reached across the bed to grab her shirt, covering herself as she sat up.

"Such modesty," he remarked, smiling as he handed her the tea.

She didn't respond. Holding the mug in one hand and clutching her silk shirt with the other, she watched his eyes stray from her face to the thin fabric covering her breasts. Her heart began to pound; she didn't need more time to know.

When he looked up at her face again, their eyes met and Mandy smiled back at him. A moment later, she let her shirt drop.

CHAPTER 31

❉

Mkuze seemed like a different world and a decade ago to Ryan and Joanna as they huddled together in her flat. They went through her photographs and kept the television on to get updates, but they were both distracted, trying to forget the horror they'd witnessed.

Ryan hadn't heard from Mandy and she wasn't returning Reverend Dlamini's calls either. When he tried to reach her again, there was still no reply. He was pacing up and down when his phone rang. In his haste to answer it, he almost dropped the phone. It wasn't Mandy however; it was Mpilo, asking to meet at Musgrave Centre. His voice was strained, explaining that he had the priest and child with him. On speaker phone, Ryan brought him up to speed with what was happening—that Joanna had taken pictures of the white bakkies and had given them to the police. One of the shooters had already been apprehended, but there were others still at large.

Mpilo coughed and said, "Can you text me those pictures?"

"OK. Joanna's sending them to you now," Ryan replied, adding, "Her flat is on Musgrave Road, right opposite the Standard Bank. Come there instead. It's near Musgrave Centre. I'll watch for you from her window; see you in a few minutes."

He bit his nails as he stood watching the street below.

It wasn't long before three figures appeared outside the bank and he rushed down to meet them. Jabulani had stopped screaming, but he was covered in blood and clinging to the priest. As soon as he looked at Ryan, he whimpered, "I want Mandy."

Ryan nodded and took the child's hand, gently leading him into Joanna's bathroom where he handed the priest a cloth and soap to clean himself, while he and Joanna cleaned the boy up as much as they could. Fortunately, he was uninjured; the blood was not his. It was from the orphan who'd been killed. The child murmured again, "I want Mandy."

"I know you want her, Jabulani. We all do. We'll find her," Ryan replied softly. He wished he could believe it as he hugged the child and carried him to Joanna's car, with Reverend Dlamini following in shocked silence.

Before he took his leave, Mpilo took Ryan aside. "My friend, there's more bad news. I told you that the priest was traveling in Joseph's taxi. Well, I'm afraid that Bongani was with him as well." He bit his bottom lip before adding, "Joseph had just filled up. A bullet hit the petrol tank and his taxi exploded. Bongani and Joseph were both killed. They were still inside."

Ryan's mouth opened wide and then he dropped his head in his hands. "No," he moaned. "I can't believe it. Not that old man and poor Joseph. No, no. No." He looked up at Mpilo and swallowed hard. "Are you sure Mandy wasn't there?"

Mpilo nodded. "I'm sure. But it's bad. I can't stay here. I must get back and help. And you must be careful; people are angry. Trouble can happen quickly. Get

Reverend Dlamini and Jabulani back to the orphanage."
He was agitated, wanting to get away. "Go now, my
friend," he said to Ryan, putting a hand on his friend's
shoulder. "Look after them. You're a good man; a good
friend. Go well." He stared hard at the American, as if he
were trying to communicate something without words.
Then, without a backward glance, he took off back to the
taxi rank.

Ryan called after him, "*You* be careful." But Mpilo
didn't acknowledge he'd heard. He began to run and was
soon lost to sight.

CHAPTER 32

Voices eventually brought them back to their surroundings and David sighed as he rolled onto his side, resting an elbow on the bed to gaze at Mandy. "I wish we could stay right here forever, instead of facing all the mayhem out there. I'm trying to keep this picture in my mind," he whispered, running his fingers lightly around her face, tracing her features. "I'm crazy about you," he said, and kissed her once more before dragging himself out the door.

Mandy stretched her arms and yawned, smiling when she noticed that the tea next to her bed had grown cold. Once dressed, she went to retrieve her phone, which had been left in the living room the night before. She felt as if she were floating as she made her way there and, despite the terrible news that surrounded them, her smile seemed a fixture—until she found her purse. It was exactly where she'd left it, but it was open, with no phone inside.

Her smile disappeared rapidly. Frowning, she checked again, emptying out all the contents. Everything else was there, but no phone. Surely there couldn't have been a burglary? That was ridiculous; she'd stayed at the Malherbes' house to be safe and they had those watch dogs that would've made a noise if there'd been burglars. Besides, Gerry and Priscilla were early risers; they would've noticed if there'd been a break-in, but they seemed unperturbed as they set about making breakfast for everyone, including Mrs. Malherbe senior. Mandy was about to tell David about her missing phone, when he introduced her to his grandmother. The old lady smiled sweetly and said, "Do I know you from somewhere, dear?"

David answered for her. "No, Grandma. This is my friend, Mandy. She's from America."

"Oh, maybe that's where I met you. I went to America once. They have good ice cream there." She carried a handbag over her arm which she clutched firmly. "I should show you my photographs," she said, opening the bag.

As she scratched around in it, Mandy suddenly saw her missing phone inside; it had an unmistakable green cover with white spots. She gasped, covering her mouth to hide her surprise, and, taking a deep breath, asked to use David's phone.

"Sure," he replied, slightly puzzled.

"I need to find mine," she explained as she dialed her number, praying that the sound wasn't muted. It wasn't. There was a distinct ring emanating from the older Mrs. Malherbe's handbag. David raised his eyebrows as he put his arms around his grandmother and winked at Mandy.

"Aren't you going to answer your phone, Grandma?" he asked.

"Oh, yes, maybe you can help me with it. It was making such a noise this morning—such a nuisance. The only way I could stop it was sticking it in here. How do you turn these things off?"

"Here, why don't you give it to me and I'll do it for you?" he said.

Mandy smiled as he took the phone and handed it to her, while distracting the old lady with the promise of eggs and bacon.

Mandy stuffed the phone into her pocket while she ate breakfast. The morning paper had been delivered and lay in the middle of the table; the pictures were graphic and she tried not to look at them, but the front page was all about the shooting. She could see images of injured children, screaming in terror and pain. It was only after she'd helped clear the table and load the dishwasher that Mandy was able to check her messages. That was when she shrieked and stood paralyzed, staring at the text message from Ryan: *JJ was at the shooting. He's with Mpilo and Dlamini.*

"What's the matter?" David asked, looking concerned.

"I've got to go," she replied. "Jabulani was at the taxi rank yesterday. I have to get to him."

"Shit. OK, I'll take you. Do you know where he is?"

She was shaking as she said, "I must phone Ryan. He'll know. Or Reverend Dlamini." She saw that she'd missed calls from both of them earlier in the morning; their messages simply asked her to call back with no other details.

David wasn't sure who Ryan was, but he said, "Well, call them, Mandy. Let's find out."

She was obviously in shock and trembling so much she could hardly speak when Ryan answered his phone. "Mandy," he said; his relief was almost palpable. "Where in God's name are you?"

"Never mind that. Where's Jabulani?"

"He's fine. He's back at the orphanage with the priest. Mpilo got them safely away and we drove them back home. I've been worried sick about you."

She began to breathe more calmly, but it didn't all add

up. "How did you and Mpilo drive them?"

"A friend helped us—Joanna. She's got a car."

"And Jabulani wasn't hurt?" she asked again. "Please tell me the truth."

"Mandy, he's fine. But he's had a hell of a shock. One of the other boys from the orphanage was killed. Jabulani saw it happen."

She closed her eyes and dropped her head, stifling a sob. Ryan's words hit her like a body blow.

"And I'm afraid that's not all, our friends Bongani and Joseph were also killed."

"Oh no. My God, no," she wailed.

"Listen, Mandy, I don't know where you are," he continued, "but come back here and we can go to the orphanage together. My friend Joanna has offered to drive us there."

"Thanks, but I can get there by myself. That'll be quicker."

She ended the call immediately and called Reverend Dlamini. His voice sounded strained when he said, "Thank goodness you've called, Mandy. Jabulani's been asking for you. Please come as soon as you can."

"I'm on my way."

David drove at speed, familiar with the road to the orphanage. They drove in silence. It was clear to Mandy that now, more than ever, she needed to get JJ away and take him to California. The pictures in the paper were imprinted on her brain, children screaming and blood everywhere. It was only as they arrived at the orphanage that she turned to David and said, "Thank you. Thank you for your support."

He turned off the ignition and took her hand, saying, "Whatever you want or need, you have only to ask me."

She nodded and jumped out the car with David close behind, racing inside to find Jabulani. The child ran towards her, flinging himself into her arms. He clung to her, begging, "Don't leave me, Mandy. I want to stay with you."

She crouched to hug him and whispered in his ear, "I'm taking you with me, JJ. You're safe now."

Reverend Dlamini and the other boys stared at her, their eyes red from crying. They were seated close to one another, all of them wanting to be near the priest. Still holding Jabulani, she looked towards them and said, "I'm so sorry, so sorry. It's very hard to lose a friend; it hurts badly. Trust me, I know how you're feeling. You just can't believe it's true."

Reverend Dlamini nodded. "We keep thinking Temba will suddenly walk through the door again." Some of the boys began speaking in Zulu. The priest listened and shook his head. "No, I'm sure. It's true. I was there. I saw it happen. Andile is going to be OK. He'll come back to us, but Temba...he's gone, he's dead." He was trying hard not to cry, but he couldn't stop the tears which began to pour down his face. Trying to regain his composure, he got up and excused himself as Jabulani buried his head in Mandy's chest. She could feel his sobs.

A hand touched her shoulder and she turned to see David watching her. Slowly she stood up, holding Jabulani in her arms. "I'm going to take him home," she said. "He wants to come with me."

David nodded. "But you can't take him to that hell-hole of yours, Mandy. There's barely room in it for you, let alone a child as well. You can both stay at my place; I have a flat in Durban and there's room for us all until you've figured out what you're going to do." She stared at him, confused, saying nothing. So much had happened so quickly that she was having difficulty processing it all. His voice was gentle as he said, "Come. Bring the child."

Reverend Dlamini returned with his tears wiped away. He overheard David's offer and added his encouragement to Mandy. "It'll be best to get Jabulani away from here. I wish all the boys had that option, but we'll get through this together. We've all dealt with suffering before and we'll do it again. We don't have a choice—but little Jabulani, he does—thank God." He hesitated a moment and added, "I'm very sorry, Mandy, but you realize I can't leave these boys now; I cannot come with you to America. I'm sure you understand. You can take Jabulani if it's possible to do so without me accompanying you, but you'll have to bring him back after his visit." He put his arms out to the child, who let go of Mandy to embrace the priest. They spoke in Zulu before JJ turned and walked back to Mandy.

"I'll get his things for you," Reverend Dlamini said. "He doesn't have much; just his school uniform and the other clothes you bought him. I've applied for his passport; it should be here in six to eight weeks. I'll let you know when it arrives."

As he walked away, Mandy frowned. "That's two months! I don't want to wait that long."

David cleared his throat. "We can try and expedite it.

I'll do my best. And the tourist visa won't take long after that." His heart was heavy as he said this; he'd only just found her and didn't want her to go. She seemed so small and vulnerable, standing there with the child. He wanted to protect her *and* the boy.

CHAPTER 33

After dropping the priest and child back at the orphanage, Joanna drove Ryan back to his lodging. Neither of them wanted to be alone after such trauma, so when Ryan invited her in, she happily accepted the offer. Emotionally and physically exhausted, Joanna barely said a word as she collapsed on his bed, falling asleep almost immediately.

She lay curled up on her side, like a child, and Ryan stood watching her for a while, marveling how uncomplicated she was. She was warm-hearted and spontaneous, so different from Mandy—and much easier to be around. Despite the horror of the day, she'd stayed calm and shown great fortitude, and as he watched her breathing deeply, he felt again like he had around the fire at Mkuze—at peace. He smiled, glad she was here with him. So as not to disturb her, he put his sleeping bag on the floor and soon he was sound asleep as well.

They were awakened in the morning by voices coming from next door. Ryan ran outside and Joanna heard him shouting, "The least you could've done was return my call." With a sinking feeling, she knew it was Mandy. Although he denied it, she felt sure that he had feelings for this person. Curiosity got the better of her and she walked out to see.

A man, a woman, and a child stood staring at Ryan,

saying nothing. The woman was undoubtedly Mandy, and Joanna felt a stab of jealousy again. How could she compete with this blonde pixie? As she watched however, the man—who was extremely handsome and composed—put an arm around the woman and said, "I think Mandy's had more important things on her mind than returning calls."

Ryan stopped in his tracks and looked the man up and down. "Who the hell are you?" he asked.

"I'm David Malherbe." Glaring at the stranger, he clenched his jaw before adding, "And who the hell are you?"

Ryan frowned at him. "I'm a friend of Mandy's, Ryan Thompson." Then, turning his attention to Mandy once more, Ryan said, "Would you mind explaining what's going on?"

She spoke for the first time and Joanna heard a soft American accent. "I'm moving out, Ryan. David's offered me and JJ a place to stay while we wait for his passport. JJ's coming back to California with me."

"Goddammit, Mandy," Ryan exploded. "We've been through all that. It's a terrible idea. The kid's a Zulu. He needs to stay here where he belongs."

"He belongs with me," she replied. "He wants to be with me and that's what matters. I don't care what you think."

As they glared at one another, Joanna stepped forward and said, "Excuse me, but we haven't met either—I'm Joanna Nel. I've heard what you're doing and I think it's awesome. Good luck." Then she turned to Ryan and said just one word, "Cheers." There was nothing else to say.

As she walked away, Ryan strode after her. "Wait, Joanna. Let me explain," he called.

She carried on walking and said over her shoulder, "You have explained, but I don't believe you." Suddenly she stopped and turned to face him. "Stop fooling yourself. And stop trying to fool me."

At a loss for words, Ryan watched her go and began kicking stones. Mandy had seen this impatient gesture many times. She glanced at David, who nodded and turned his back to give the two Americans a moment alone. Mandy walked towards Ryan and said softly, "Go after her."

He shrugged and said, "I can't deal with it right now. There's too much going on." Then he added, "I like your hair, by the way."

Her hands shot up to her head. "I'd forgotten about it; glad you like it." She'd seen him explode before and then just as quickly, the anger would subside. She hoped this would be the case again. "Who is she?" she said, gesturing towards Joanna's departing car.

"I met her at Mkuze. We were together at that taxi rank yesterday," he said. "We were nearly caught in the shooting—just a few more minutes and we would've been target practice for those bastards." He raised his eyebrows and said, "Joanna was awesome; she's a photographer. She caught the perpetrators on camera and the police used her pictures to make an arrest."

Mandy grabbed his hands. "That's great, Ryan, but I couldn't bear it if anything had happened to you. I lost one good friend when Michelle died; I can't lose another."

His mouth twitched. "I always hoped we could be

more than that." They stared at one another until he said, "Are you really going?"

She nodded. "I'm moving into David's flat. I just came to get my stuff."

"What? You're moving in with this guy?" he said. "What the fuck? When did you meet him? I've only been gone two weeks."

"A lot has happened in that time. Everything has changed."

Ryan stared at her open-mouthed for a few moments. "Excuse me!" he exclaimed when he'd regathered his wits. "Aren't you the one who said that relationships grow, they don't just explode? Geez, this is an explosion if ever I saw one."

She blushed and looked away. When she turned back to face him, she replied, "I guess I was wrong. I've never felt this way before. I didn't realize that with the right person, a relationship *can* explode. I'm sorry, Ryan."

He stood watching her walk away and realized in that moment that he felt no regret. He was actually relieved. He'd been attracted by her good looks—he couldn't keep his eyes off her when they first met. But that wasn't enough. They'd had some good times but it wasn't working between them; long term, they could never make one another happy. Vusi was right; it was like fishing. The time had come to cut loose. He watched as she grabbed two duffel bags, climbed into an old car parked outside her room, and drove away with Jabulani. Without even a backward glance, she was gone.

Seeking company, he wandered over to Ramona's kitchen. She was happy to see him and made a pot of coffee, settling down for a chat. He'd hardly had a chance to tell her what'd happened when there was a text from her brother: *There's an angry mob on the rampage in Durban. Be careful.*

They turned on the TV to watch continuing news flashes—pictures of cars on fire, and crowds hurling rocks at cars. Ryan's thoughts flew immediately to Joanna and Mandy, out on the roads, and then he thought about Mpilo. Glancing at Ramona, he mumbled, "He was afraid this would happen. He tried to warn me."

"Who?" she asked.

"My friend Mpilo. We were at the shooting. I think he knew there were going to be vigilante groups seeking revenge. Shit, I hope he's not involved in it."

"I don't know who he is, but you'd better hope not," Ramona remarked. "You can bet the police will crack down big time. This situation is getting out of hand fast."

Ryan watched her as she got up and poured herself another coffee, but he wasn't really seeing her. He was remembering the bloody scene and the fear in Jabulani's eyes. Maybe Mandy was right about the child after all. It was only after she'd spoken to him a third time that he heard Ramona offering him another cup of coffee. Frowning, he shook his head while reaching for his phone; he had to try and reach Mpilo. There was no reply, however. It went straight to voicemail. He got up and began pacing up and down, unsure what to do.

As if she could read his mind, she said, "Just sit tight. He knows how to get hold of you, I presume. You can't go out looking for him; where would you start?"

He stopped pacing, standing instead at the window and

staring into the garden. Suddenly he saw movement near his room. A figure emerged on the path. It was Joanna. She began banging on his door, calling his name. Without a word to Ramona, he charged out and as soon as she saw him, Joanna ran to him. "Thank God you're here," she cried. "Come quickly. I need your help." Without any explanation, she led him to her car and opened the back door. Sprawled across the seat in a pool of blood was Mpilo. He lay there, unconscious.

By this time, Ramona had appeared to find out what was happening. "Is this your friend?" she asked.

Ryan nodded and quickly introduced Joanna, who explained that she'd only just got home when Mpilo arrived at her door, bleeding profusely from his left leg. She tried to tie a tourniquet around it and managed to get him to her car, but he wouldn't let her take him to the hospital. "He said it would be dangerous. He's lost a lot of blood and there's a bullet in his leg; we need to get it out," she added. "He got really upset when I spoke about hospital; he wanted you. I could see him drifting in and out of consciousness in the rearview mirror, so I tried to keep talking as I drove. I didn't want him to pass out. My God, he's lost so much blood. He collapsed about five minutes ago and stopped responding."

Ramona cleared her throat and took charge. "This is tricky. Without medical attention, he'll be in trouble, but if he goes to the hospital, it sounds like he'll be in trouble too. Let me phone a co-worker. His father's a doctor. I'll see if we can take Mpilo there."

Ryan watched as she made a call. She was pleading, and he overheard her say, "OK, please try. Call me back.

It's really urgent."

Turning to them, she explained, "My colleague's father has retired; he's not sure his dad will agree to help." She was biting her bottom lip as she added, "It's not exactly kosher to extract a bullet from someone without reporting it to the police." Ryan's heart sank. But a moment later, her phone rang and she said, "Right, we'll meet you there."

Punching an address into her phone, Ramona jumped into the front seat next to Joanna and gave directions, while Ryan sat in the back, placing the wounded man's head on his lap. Mpilo opened his eyes for a moment, registering Ryan's presence. A fleeting smile crossed his face as he murmured, "I tried to tell them not to do it." Then he lost consciousness again.

CHAPTER 34

✤

The child was calmer by Mandy's side, although every now and again, he shuddered involuntarily. He seemed particularly nervous every time they stopped at a traffic light. They avoided the Greyville area, but there was a strange eeriness in the streets as they followed David to Morningside. It was a relief to arrive there without incident.

When David opened the door to his flat, Mandy couldn't believe her eyes; it was spacious, with a beautiful view of Durban from its 7th floor position. "Wow, how come you have such a huge apartment all to yourself?" she said, holding Jabulani's hand tightly. The child was wide-eyed, but silent.

"It was my grandmother's," he replied. "Yeah, you're right, it *is* a lot for one person. That's why I'm glad I'll have company now." He smiled and put an arm around her as he ushered her inside. Jabulani clutched her hand even more tightly—his palm was sweating.

At that moment, David's phone rang. He saw that it was a call from Ramona and excused himself, but Mandy was too busy exploring with JJ to notice. David seemed to make a couple of calls before apologizing profusely that he needed to head out for a short while.

"I'll be fine," she assured him. "It'll give me a chance to settle JJ. Please, don't worry about us."

"I'll be back as soon as I can," he promised.

David cursed. The last thing he wanted was to get involved helping some guy with a bullet in his leg. More than anything, he wanted to help Mandy and Jabulani settle into his flat; he hadn't even had a chance to show them around. He'd expected a blast from his father for requesting assistance and was stunned when he agreed to do so. "Unlike you, I *did* take the Hippocratic oath," his father said. "I don't have a choice. And fortunately, I've still got all the medical equipment I need in my old office out in the back."

David was thankful that Mandy was unfazed, and thought that perhaps it was better she and JJ had some time alone. The child was in shock; the only person who could help him was Mandy. As he raced to join Ramona at his parents' home, David's thoughts were jumping all over the place; thoughts of Mandy were interlaced with his concern over the chaos unleashed in Durban. He kept thinking how he didn't want Mandy to return to America just yet, but he had a sinking feeling that it would happen soon.

Meeting Joanna's car at his parents' gate, he punched in the access code and they entered the property quickly before the gates closed behind them. As he silenced the dogs, he felt his pulse rate quicken when he recognized Ryan; neither of them said anything as they lifted Mpilo and carried him to the doctor's office at the back of the house. When they'd placed him on the examination table, they watched in silence as Dr. Malherbe took a look at the injury and grunted. "I don't want to know anything about how this happened, do you hear me? But we can't let the poor bugger bleed to death." He examined him further before adding, "I'll fix him up and then I don't want to see him again—or hear anything more about it. Is that understood? I don't want to know who he is, or anything else." He looked at each of them in turn and waited for them to acknowledge what he'd said, before he set to work. Priscilla worked as his assistant and shooed them out into the waiting room.

As his mother closed the door on them, David stood transfixed. Twice within 24 hours, he'd been surprised by his father showing unexpected humanity and integrity. While everyone else thanked him, heaping praise on Dr. Malherbe, he listened and nodded. It felt good to be proud of his dad for a change—perhaps the old guy had a heart after all. Why did he have to hide it?

He walked out into the garden, followed by Ryan, who called out, "I'm sorry about what happened earlier. I was a bit surprised by...you know...seeing Mandy moving out with you." He took a deep breath and added, "I'm not sure what's going on between you, but she means a lot to me. Don't mess with her."

David had his phone in hand, about to call Mandy. He stopped, turned around and walked towards Ryan. When he was close enough to look him in the eyes, he said, "She means a lot to me too, mate."

The two men glowered at one another, sizing each other up, until Ryan muttered, "I appreciate your Dad's help with Mpilo."

David nodded. "He's retired, but he's a good doctor.

Your friend's in excellent hands." With that, he turned and walked to his car, leaving Ryan to rejoin the others in the waiting room.

Joanna had been watching the exchange through the window. She sat down when she saw Ryan returning, pretending to read a magazine. He positioned himself next to her and said, "I wonder how long we're going to be waiting here?"

She shrugged and frowned. "What are you going to do with Mpilo? Where will you take him?"

Ryan put his face in his hands and groaned. "Oh shit, I hadn't thought about that."

"He's going to need someone to look after him," she added.

After a few seconds, he looked up and said, "I know. Mandy."

"What? Mandy won't do it," Ramona responded. "She's looking after that child."

"Yeah, but she's moved out of her room. Mpilo can stay in it and *I'll* look after him. He'll be safe from the police there too. He can't go back to his place in the township; it would be dangerous."

"Didn't he say something about trying to stop the crowd?" Ramona asked. "That's a good defense. If Mpilo needs it, I'll defend him. My God, that's better than that dumbass Petrus Botha who asked for my help; no way would I help him. But it'll be better if Mpilo escapes prosecution in the first place and doesn't need any defense at all, don't you think? That's a brilliant idea of yours, Ryan."

Joanna reached across and took his hand, holding it in both of hers. "You're a loyal friend; Mpilo is very lucky," she said. In a whisper, she added, "So is Mandy."

Ryan raised his eyebrows, then beckoned Joanna to follow him outside. Once the door shut behind them, he put his hands on her shoulders and said, "Joanna, there's nothing between me and Mandy, I promise you. We were in the Peace Corps together and we traveled together, that's it. It doesn't work that way with us. She's a friend; nothing else." He slipped his arms around her and pulled her close. "But I think *we* are good for each other."

Swallowing hard, she murmured, "I'm sorry. Could you repeat that, please?"

He wiped the hair out of her eyes and said, "I think we're good for each other."

When she said nothing, he said, "What would I have done without you today? You had me snared already at Mkuze, sitting next to the fire. We didn't even need to talk much—it was just good being there together. It was magic. And if that wasn't enough, today you came and rescued me. And then your photographs caught the perpetrators. You're an amazing woman. I hope I'm as good for you as you are for me."

Mpilo regained consciousness, but it was three hours before Dr. Malherbe considered him safe to leave. Entrusting him to Ryan, he said, "This guy is very lucky the bullet lodged in his leg, not in his torso, and it came out cleanly without too much damage. I've cleaned the wound and given him antibiotics, but he's weak and needs to drink lots of fluids. He clearly lost a lot of blood and his body is in shock. Are you going to look after him?"

"Yes, sir," Ryan replied, and added, "I'm very grateful for your help. I don't know what happened to him, but he's a good friend of mine. He was probably caught in cross-fire somewhere. He was an innocent bystander, I'm sure of it."

The doctor grunted again. "They all say that—*it wasn't me, it wasn't my fault*. If I had one rand for every time I've heard that, I'd be on a luxury cruise somewhere, not sitting around patching up stupid buggers who get themselves into trouble with the police." He stopped and frowned. "Are you an American?" he asked.

"Yes, sir. I am."

"I thought so. I seem to be surrounded by Yanks at the moment. We had some American girl staying here last night. She's got her eye on my son."

Ryan felt himself begin to boil. He didn't appreciate being called a Yank, but he didn't want to engage in a discussion with this man. They owed the doctor a lot; he knew it would be best to leave before he lost his temper and said something he might regret.

Dr. Malherbe refused payment and shooed them all away. Mpilo was able to limp to the car with Ryan and Joanna supporting him. He was weak, but as he fastened his seat belt, he said, "You guys saved my life. Thank you. People were going crazy. I thought I was going to die."

"You'll be OK now," Ryan reassured him. "I'm taking you back to my place until you're stronger. Don't try and talk. There'll be time enough when you're better."

Mpilo nodded, but he was eager to make something clear. "I tried to stop people from rioting, Ryan.

Everybody was going mad at the taxi rank. Some guy saw my phone, that picture Joanna sent of the bakkies, and he went wild. That's all it took to get everybody going crazy. Nothing could stop them. They attacked the first white car they found and everything else they could lay their hands on. Somebody in one of the cars started shooting and that's how this happened," he said, pointing to his leg. "Too many people have died. I'm lucky I wasn't one of them, my brother."

CHAPTER 35

✤

It wasn't just JJ who was bewildered and traumatized. Mandy put her arms around the little boy and held him close, struggling with the knowledge that Bongani and Joseph were dead. Deep-seated nightmares came flooding back that she didn't want to revisit. Life was so fragile. It was hard to grasp that the *Speedy Passenger Service* was no more, but she was filled with gratitude that JJ and the priest had been spared. If they'd been slower leaving the taxi—if they'd been stuck in the back corner—they would also be dead. She tried to hide her emotions from the child, displaying only her relief that he was with her. As she hugged him, she said, "We're going to stay here now, JJ. You and me. You'll be safe here, I promise. I'm not going to let anything, or anyone, hurt you."

The child stared at her, dry-eyed, and whispered again, "Don't leave me."

Mandy continued hugging him and as he clung to her, she knew she would never give up on him. Whatever she needed to do to keep him with her, she would make sure it happened. He was in her care now and she would never let him down.

She soon realized that there were many adjustments for JJ. For starters, it was difficult for him to accept sleeping alone in a bedroom; he was used to being surrounded by others. The priest had got him accustomed to sleeping in a bed instead of on the floor, but he cried at the thought of being alone. She spent the first week sleeping in the same room as him, gradually weaning him to sleep with the door open and a nightlight on, reassuring him that she was in the bedroom next door. He was also afraid of heights; he didn't want to look out the window at the ground below. The lift was also an ordeal. After a few days, she coaxed him to look down with no fear and he grew excited to press the buttons in the lift, learning his numbers very quickly and recognizing *G* for ground floor. But Reverend Dlamini had not warned her about Jabulani's aversion to bathing. On the farm where he grew up, the child had been accustomed to standing next to a bucket of water and washing himself with his hands. The priest had obviously allowed him to continue doing this at the orphanage. Immersing himself in water was something JJ was not prepared to do. With great determination, he resisted her efforts to get him into a bath, standing firmly against the wall and shaking his head. She cajoled and bribed. Nothing worked. The best she could do, for days on end, was let him stand next to the bath and dip a cloth into the water to wash himself.

Finally, David made a suggestion. "Why don't you get into the bath first. Maybe he'll agree to climb in with you?"

She blushed. "I don't feel comfortable doing that," she replied.

"Ah, that modesty again," he laughed. "He's eight years old, Mandy. What's the big deal? I'm sure he's seen naked women on the farm where he grew up. Nudity doesn't bother him—it's water that's the problem. You should give it a try."

"Why don't you do it?" she said.

"If that's an invitation to climb into the bath with you—sure."

She smiled. "You know what I mean."

"Well, OK. I'm heading to the shower now; let him come with me," David said.

Jabulani followed David to the bathroom and watched as he turned on the water. "Look, JJ. It's like rain, except it's warm. You know what rain's like, don't you?" David asked, not sure what he was doing, but following his instincts. The child nodded, although he kept his distance. Inspiration came to David and he started stomping, first with one foot, then with the other—and Jabulani started to giggle. David could see that the child recognized the beginnings of a Zulu dance as the boy began to stomp as well. When David undressed, and stomped into the shower, he beckoned JJ to follow. Without hesitation, Jabulani laughed and ran to join him. It soon became a game with a lot of noise. There was plenty of water on the floor when they emerged with towels around their waists, but they were clean and smiling.

It wasn't certain how long JJ's passport and visa would take, but there was one thing Mandy was sure about— she wouldn't return him to the school they both hated. Her hope was that by expediting the passport service, it would be just weeks before they'd leave for the USA and so she began teaching Jabulani at home.

When the violence subsided in town, Mandy deemed it safe to venture out once again. On one of their walks, they were drawn by the sound of children's laughter and discovered a small school called Bridges. Attached to an Anglican church and run by a retired teacher, the school provided education for children of domestic workers. Further investigation revealed there were thirty children, divided into four groups according to their ages, taught by four teachers. It took no time for Mandy to volunteer her help in return for Jabulani attending the school; her offer was readily accepted when his situation was explained. JJ had been starved of playmates his own age and adjusted easily to the small group of children. Before long, he was able to write his name and sound out words, eager to catch up with everyone else. He was a very bright child.

At the end of each day, Mandy found herself waiting for David's return from work, listening for his key in the door. A little voice kept telling her she'd be returning to California soon and this relationship would only complicate matters; but she no longer listened to the voice. Lulled by happiness, she stopped worrying about the future. Cocooned in this comfortable world, she was able to forget what lay just beyond it. She called Ryan a couple of times to find out about Mpilo and considered visiting them, but because of her concern for JJ and protecting him from any more trauma, she opted not to do so. The child had stopped having nightmares and was conquering many fears in the secure environment she'd created; she wanted to maintain that stability.

Lindiwe came to visit one afternoon. They met at Bridges, where Jabulani was excited to show her his school and introduce her to his new friends. "This is very nice," she told the child as he beamed with pleasure. "Can you show me some of your work?"

He ran to his cubby and pulled out a ream of papers where he'd been practicing his writing. When he spoke to her in Zulu, she laughed and clapped her hands. As they walked up the hill to David's flat, she said to Mandy, "I'm very pleased to see his school and his work. I was scared that he was becoming a white boy with a black skin, but he's still a Zulu. That's good."

Mandy said nothing in reply, but she was smarting. Her discomfort increased when they entered the flat and JJ ran to show Lindiwe his bedroom. Her eyes opened wide and she said, "You have this room all to yourself?"

He nodded, his enthusiasm apparent when he jumped on the bed, laughing.

Mandy noticed her friend stiffen as she looked at the surroundings, and when they stood in the kitchen drinking tea, Lindiwe said, "You're very lucky, Mandy. You have everything."

Mandy took a deep breath. Something was eating at Lindiwe. "I am lucky, I know, but it's not mine," she responded. "The flat belonged to David's grandmother. He inherited it from her."

"Just like the car he gave you," Lindiwe added.

"Yeah, that's not mine either. He's lent it to me. I own none of it. In fact, I've got very little money left. It's time I went back home so I can start earning again."

"You don't have to own it to enjoy it," Lindiwe said, walking to the window and admiring the view. "Look at that. I can't believe you wake up every day and see that view of Durban." Turning to face Mandy, she added, "You know what I see when I wake up? My view of

Durban is latrines and water pumps, people pushing and shoving to get to taxis first, and mangy dogs looking for scraps of food. It'll be a long time before Philani and I can afford a place of our own. David's lucky his grandmother owned this; my grandmother lives in a hut in the country with no running water or electricity."

Clenching her jaw, Mandy held back her words. Lindiwe had always been so positive that this criticism came as a shock to her. On the day they'd met, it had seemed possible to build a friendship, but their differences were getting in the way now. "None of this is my fault," Mandy said. Her voice was very soft as she spoke. "All I've tried to do is help. Generations of inequality haven't been caused by me personally."

"You will never understand what it's like for us, Mandy. We are poor people. You say you don't have any money, but look where you're living and the car you're driving. You can go back to America and get more money from your parents; they'll give you some. When we've got no money, we live on the streets and look for food in rubbish bins."

Conversation between them was impossible after this. Fortunately, Jabulani didn't understand what passed between them and chatted happily—in English to Mandy, and Zulu to Lindiwe.

When it was time for Lindiwe to leave, Mandy offered to drive her home, but the offer was refused. "It wouldn't be safe for you where I live."

"Let me at least drive you to the taxi rank," Mandy said.

"No. Jabulani will be reminded of what happened

at Greyville if you take me to the taxi rank. I'm used to walking; stay here and keep him safe. That's best." She hugged Jabulani and closed the door behind her.

Looking down from the window, they watched Lindiwe walk away. Mandy's tread was heavy as she went into her bedroom and held the vuvuzela that Lindiwe had given her. "Why are you so angry with me?" she said softly, overcome with a sense of loss.

Six months came and went before Mandy's cocoon came to an end. She was plunged back into reality by a phone call from Father Dlamini. He had good news; the passports and visas had arrived. Furthermore, because Andile and the other boys in the orphanage were doing better, a priest from a nearby parish had agreed to stay with them while Reverend Dlamini went to America. He could keep his promise after all, to accompany JJ to California.

It was what she'd been waiting for, but her heart sank.

There was a sense of gloom that night as they lay on the living room floor, deep in thought, listening to music. David turned to her after some time and said, "You know that I don't want you to leave, don't you?" He was leaning on one elbow watching her. "JJ has settled down at Bridges. He's learning so quickly. He's happy; we're happy. Why don't you stay?"

"Don't tempt me," she said, rolling to face him.

"Why not, Mandy? Why's it such a bad idea?"

She sat up and said, "Because I can't work here. All I can do is volunteer. My savings are rock bottom and

I can't ask my parents for money; I'm twenty-five years old, not exactly a child. And I can't depend on you to subsidize me either, like you have been doing. I live here free and drive your car. No, David, I have to go home and I'm taking JJ with me."

He loved the fire in her; he'd seen it the first day they'd met at Ramona's. That was what had attracted him, not to mention the beautiful packaging. He reached across and traced the outline of her face. "I think you're forgetting something, though. He only has a tourist visa. You can't keep him there, Mandy."

She clenched her jaw. "Once I have him there, I'll work to change his status. It happens all the time."

"But it's not only his immigration status in the States. It's the adoption process. It can't be done like that. It would be a crime. You could be charged with abduction, or child trafficking, by the South African authorities."

As she stared at him in surprise, he reached over and pulled her down towards him, whispering, "Why don't you marry me?"

Stunned, she lay in his arms, saying nothing, not sure if she'd heard him correctly. After a while he said again, "Will you, Mandy? Will you marry me?" He was no longer whispering; he was hoping for an answer.

She wanted to shout out, "Yes, please," but she couldn't bring herself to do it. She'd only known him just over six months; it was too soon to make such a big decision. She said nothing.

He didn't press the matter. Instead he continued stroking her face and said, "Think about it. I won't rush you."

This evoked a reaction from her at last. "You've been

so kind to me," she said.

"You mean everything to me, Mandy. I can't bear to think of life without you."

He was about to say something more, but she stopped him, suddenly blurting out, "Do you love me, though? You've never said so. You've never once said the 'L' word."

He shook his head in disbelief. "Mandy, I've *shown* you how much I love you, haven't I? That's what matters most."

She nodded. "But I'd like to hear it as well. Say the words."

"OK then. Mandy Walker, I love you." He pulled her towards him again and said, "There, now that I've said it—does that make a difference?"

As she smiled and leaned over to kiss him, he asked, "Is that a yes, then?"

She sighed and sat up again, biting her lip. "If only it were that easy. Marriage is a big step. There are so many complications."

"Name them," he said, lying outstretched. "Every problem has a solution, and as I see it, the biggest problem is whether or not you want to marry me."

She sighed. "The biggest problem is that I'm American and you're South African. We live on different continents. One of us will have to move."

"OK," he replied. "There you are. You've just said what the solution is."

"And you know I come as a package with Jabulani, don't you?" David didn't have a chance to answer before she added, "The thing is, we haven't known one another very long to make such a commitment. If it weren't for the arrival of these passports, we could've had longer getting to know one another. We shouldn't make a decision like this just because it's convenient." He wanted to contradict her but she stopped him. "You know I've been totally happy here with you these past months, but it can't go on like this forever."

"It can," he said. "Just because the passports have arrived doesn't mean you have to leave."

"You're forgetting that I'm going to graduate school in the fall, in California."

David took a deep breath and got up. He walked across the room to the window and stared out at the city lights, at a loss for words. His fear was that if she went back to the States she would never come back, and he knew that he didn't want to leave South Africa. She was right. It was complicated. Loving one another wasn't enough.

CHAPTER 36

Mandy called Lindiwe to tell her that she was returning home, taking Jabulani and the priest with her to California. The silence was so long that Mandy wondered if the call had been disconnected. "Are you still there?" she asked.

"Yes, I'm here. I don't know what to say, that's all."

"It's just a vacation. He's coming back."

"You're sure about that? This is where his roots and his ancestors are. He belongs here with us."

Mandy was frustrated to hear Lindiwe speak like this—the same woman who had argued with Bongani about adapting to change instead of being stuck in old traditions. Mandy expected her to be more open and was tempted to remind her friend of that conversation, but it seemed so long ago and she felt emotionally exhausted. "I was hoping I could see you before I leave next week," she said simply, trying to reach out to Lindiwe.

"Sorry Mandy, I haven't got time. I must go home to see my grandmother. She's not well."

"Oh, I'm sorry," Mandy replied. "I hope she gets better soon."

The call ended abruptly, leaving Mandy feeling empty and miserable. Lindiwe had given her the brush-off; she knew it.

Preoccupied with looking after Mpilo, Ryan had reached out to Mandy a few times, but she was so busy with Jabulani that they hadn't really spoken much in the last three months. That wasn't a bad thing, he'd decided. He got on really well with Joanna; there was no friction or angst like there'd been with Mandy. It was peaceful and they had fun together; he was happier than he'd been in a long time. She was adventurous too, eager to climb Kilimanjaro with him. They spent hours talking about it with Mpilo, which helped the patient set his sights on a positive goal as he recuperated.

Ryan was pleased that his friend was well enough to attend university by the time classes started. He persuaded Mpilo to remain in the room instead of returning to the township; it was a much easier commute and a quieter place to study. He laughed when Mpilo said, "Are you trying to turn me into a white boy? What's Vusi gonna say?"

But Vusi was happy—especially that Mpilo wasn't imprisoned after the Greyville incidents. Ryan was touched to receive a phone call from Vusi, thanking him. "Now you're a brother," he said. "When you save someone's life, you're joined forever."

Life was going along smoothly, so Ryan was surprised when out of the blue, he got a text from Mandy: *Travel docs in order. Leaving next week. Please call me.*

He phoned immediately and they arranged to meet for lunch. It was strange seeing her again. She looked different. It wasn't just the haircut; it was something else intangible. "Are you excited to be going home?" he asked as they sat down.

She shrugged. "I'm nervous," she replied. "There's so much at stake. When are you going back? I thought you had to start your job in New York soon?"

"It's been postponed until next year."

"Oh. Are you seeing Joanna?" she asked.

He nodded. "Yeah. It's all good." He didn't really want to discuss this with Mandy, but it seemed polite to ask after her relationship. "How are things with David?"

She blushed and said, "He's asked me to marry him."

"Jesus!" Ryan exclaimed. "That was quick. Is he after a green card or something?"

"Oh, screw you, Ryan. You always manage to press my buttons. Actually, he wants me to stay here."

He raised his eyebrows, but said nothing.

"I haven't said yes. I'm thinking about it. But I want JJ to see California."

"So, you're still going ahead with your plan to adopt him?"

"More than ever. I love that little boy."

"Do you love David?" he asked.

She looked down at the table, pushing food back and forth across the plate. "Yes, I do," she replied finally. Looking up at him, she said, "I love him very much, but I need to go home and see how I feel being back there. It's been so long. He'll never leave South Africa, and I don't know whether I want to leave California."

Ryan reached across and took hold of her hands. "It would've been much easier if you'd fallen in love with me instead, wouldn't it? But you're a smart woman, Mandy. You'll figure out what to do. You've been chasing happiness for a long time. Don't let it get away from you now."

CHAPTER 37

The priest looked away as Mandy said her goodbyes to David at the airport. She choked back tears when he whispered, "I love you. Did you hear that? I love you. If you come back, I'll be waiting."

As he held her, she closed her eyes tightly. There was so much she wanted to say, but she couldn't find the words. In the end, she just whispered, "I heard you, and I love you too." When she walked away, the pain was almost physical.

The flights to San Francisco seemed interminable and exhausting. It helped that she had to concentrate on helping her travel companions who had never flown before; it took her mind off her emotions. Passport control and security were nightmares; she tried to hide her embarrassment when the priest was uncertain what to do. The man's hands were shaking as he handed over his passport to be stamped and he was bewildered going through a security scanner. He was shocked to have his hand luggage inspected, but he followed her instructions and made no comments.

JJ slept well on the flight from South Africa to Heathrow, and was alert on the last leg of the journey to San Francisco. Gazing out the window, his delight was infectious as he gawked at the clouds. "We're inside them," he told Mandy. He marveled when they flew over Greenland and he saw icebergs; he'd never even seen snow before, let alone mountains of ice.

She figured that arrival in the United States could be tricky and opted to stay in the foreign passport line with the two of them. It was just as well. They were interrogated by an immigration officer who wanted to know exactly what the purpose of their visit was, how long they would be staying, and where they would be traveling. Jabulani was so tired that he started to whimper, which made the official suspicious. Mandy's stomach was churning when the man began drumming his fingers as he stared at them. She began to sweat and hoped he wouldn't notice.

"What proof do you have that you're his legal guardian?" he asked the priest.

Reverend Dlamini produced the document with his name on it, as well as Jabulani's birth certificate and his parents' death certificates. Mandy could see that his hand was trembling.

The officer scrutinized the papers for a long while, saying nothing, before turning to Mandy. "Why are you travelling with them?"

Her voice was shaky as she answered. "I was impressed by the work that the priest does. Someone in South Africa sponsored him to come and see similar work here in California."

"That doesn't answer my question, ma'am. Why are you travelling with them?"

She frowned and said, "They're my friends. I wanted to travel with them; they're going to be staying with my parents."

The immigration official grunted. "And what work do

you do?" he asked Reverend Dlamini, peering at him over the top of his spectacles.

"I'm a priest. I look after an orphanage, sir."

The immigration official pursed his lips and frowned. "So, why is the boy here?"

Mandy swallowed hard. "He was recently bereaved. He's grown very attached to his guardian, now. It seemed a way of bringing some happiness to him, giving him a trip to San Francisco. It would have been frightening to be left behind when he'd just lost his mother. The person who sponsored the priest agreed to sponsor Jabulani as well. As I said, my parents have offered them accommodation in their home."

"Where do your parents live?" he asked.

"In the South Bay, in Los Gatos."

"What about you? Are you back to stay? You've been gone a long time."

"I was working in the Peace Corps for two years. I'm back now."

The official eyed her, and then stared at the priest and Jabulani. "You're not planning to keep these individuals here, are you?" he said, turning back to Mandy.

She frowned again. "Of course not. They're Zulus. They don't want to live here. They're visiting."

"Hmm, we'll be checking up on that. They leave when?" he asked.

Reverend Dlamini, who had left Mandy to do most of the talking, produced their return tickets dated in three weeks' time. The official nodded and smacked the tickets down on the counter, saying, "Don't miss your flight." Then he turned to Mandy and said, "Welcome home."

She breathed a sigh of relief when they exited the security doors into the arrivals hall. The worst was behind them. When she saw her parents, Mandy completely forgot the anxious moments. She ran to meet Dennis and Janet Walker whom she hadn't seen for over two years. Janet and Mandy were sometimes mistaken for sisters; they had the same energy and smile. Her father, a big man with a gruff voice, was more reticent. He watched the women embrace before putting his arms around Mandy in a bear hug. Introductions were made and Mr. Walker took charge of getting the suitcases into the trunk while everyone else climbed into the SUV. There was so much to tell, but it had to wait because all three passengers fell asleep during the hour-long ride home, waking only when the car stopped and the garage door opened.

When they'd taken all the luggage out of the car, Dennis Walker turned to JJ and said, "Would you like to close the garage, young man?" Jabulani stared and said nothing. "Here, press this button and see what happens," he urged the child.

Jabulani reached out and pressed it—and jumped as the door closed at his touch. He looked at the older man and smiled, saying, "Can I do it again?"

Father Dlamini was impressed to see that Jabulani was comfortable taking a shower and congratulated Mandy on this breakthrough. "I can't take the credit," she told him. "It was David's coaxing. And he's fine sleeping in a room on his own now, although he'll be sharing with you while you're here with him."

The priest looked startled. "You've done wonders,

Mandy. But what you just said, what do you mean by that?"

"What did I just say?"

"You said he'll be sharing with me while I'm here with him. Does that mean you're planning to keep him? You're expecting me to go back without him?"

They were standing in the hallway outside the bedrooms and Mandy didn't want this conversation to be overheard by her parents or JJ.

"Let's talk about it tomorrow," she said. "We're all exhausted."

The priest stared at her and spoke very slowly. "If that's what you've been planning to do, you've been deceiving me. I'd rather talk about it now."

She frowned and led him into her bedroom, closing the door behind them and speaking in a whisper. "We spoke about this, about me adopting Jabulani. Why are you so accusatory now? We agreed he needed to come to California and see it before he could choose what he wanted to do. I hope he'll like it. If he does, it makes sense for him to stay. Why waste money on another airfare? Why are you so surprised?"

"You said he was coming—*we* were coming—for a holiday."

"It *is* a holiday, a vacation." Hiding her annoyance, she clasped the priest's hands and said, "I promise you, if he wants to go back with you, I won't try and stop him. I want what's best for him, what will make him happy."

Reverend Dlamini nodded and went to his own bedroom, leaving Mandy frustrated. It wasn't the first time he'd made unfair judgments about her. Tired as she was, she couldn't sleep but lay in bed, staring at her old room without really seeing anything. She didn't know what she was doing anymore, but she knew she was missing David terribly. She texted him to say they'd arrived safely and received a smiley face emoji and a heart in return. Eventually sleep came to her, but it was fitful, and when jetlag had her awake again at 4:30 a.m., she tiptoed downstairs to make a cup of tea. Not long after the clock struck five, she heard the newspaper arrive with a thud, landing at the top of the drive with a deft toss from the delivery van. She smiled at the familiar household routine; soon the birds would start singing and her father would be down to make tea. Meantime, she would sit and read the paper, reveling in the solitude.

Sure enough, her father arrived as anticipated and she followed him back upstairs to her parents' bedroom so they could have tea together. She sat cross-legged on their bed and they began to chat.

"Thank you for having my friends to stay," Mandy said.

"Of course," her mother replied. "You know your friends are always welcome."

"I appreciate that a lot. There are so many orphans in South Africa. It's tragic. They're mostly AIDS orphans." Seeing her mother's worried expression, Mandy quickly added, "It's OK. JJ's perfectly healthy; he's not HIV positive. But his life has been difficult."

"What will become of him? Will he continue living with the priest?" her father asked.

Her voice was soft as she said, "Unless someone adopts him."

"Is that likely if there are so many orphans?" Mr. Walker said.

Mandy shrugged. "It's possible." She took another sip of tea and added, "*I* would do it if I could." She was expecting some reaction from her parents, but there was none. She saw them look at one another in that infuriating way they had of communicating silently, but not a word was said and their expressions gave no indication of their feelings.

Her mother finally said, "The priest seems very nice. I was intrigued when you befriended him; I had the feeling that you'd gone off religion."

Mandy pressed her lips together as she looked at her mother. "I have, but that doesn't mean I can't be friends with someone who is religious. I don't eat pickles and you do, but I still care about you," she said, laughing.

"I take your point," her mother smiled. "Maybe you'll change your mind..."

"About pickles?"

They both laughed and Mandy said, "You know, Reverend Dlamini is an amazing man. He was imprisoned on Robben Island during apartheid days; he was there with Nelson Mandela." Her parents were taken aback and she quickly added, "The day I met him at the side of the road, he told us about it. Mandela was a mentor to him." She paused and added, "He knows I'm a nonbeliever and accepts that. He says he's more interested in what I do than what I believe. That was what drew me to him; I really respect that."

Her parents stared at her until her mother finally said, "I'm humbled to think that I have such a man staying in my house. What an honor."

"Do you think he would come and talk at the Rotary Club?" her father asked.

Mandy shook her head. "No, and for God's sake, please don't ask him. He's a very humble person. He would hate that attention. I shouldn't have told you."

"OK," Dennis Walker replied. "I won't say a word."

They sat in silence, drinking their tea until her mother said, "It's lovely to have you back, Mandy. Your stay in Africa seemed like forever and we missed you so, but I can see that it was a wonderful experience for you. You're glowing. And I love your hair short like that, by the way. The pictures you texted didn't do it justice."

"Thanks, Mom. I'm not quite sure what to do next, but I'm happy."

"Grad school, surely?" her father said.

"I guess so." She paused before adding, "Life is a bit of a question mark at the moment. It took me a long time, but I've finally made peace with myself, thanks to meeting Father Dlamini and JJ. Something happened that day; it's hard to explain exactly what. It was a chance meeting, in the middle of nowhere, and it changed everything."

Suddenly her phone vibrated in her pocket and she blushed when she saw it was David calling her. Grabbing it, she said, "Hi, no, not at all. I've been awake for hours. I was going to call you, but I thought you'd still be at work." Excusing herself from her parents with a wave, she slipped back to her bedroom, leaving them looking at one another again with raised eyebrows.

David wanted to know about Jabulani's reactions and Mandy explained that so far, he'd reacted only to a garage door opener. "Reverend Dlamini also hasn't said much. I think he's concentrating so that he knows what to do on the way back."

"So, you won't be coming with him, then?" David asked.

"I've only just got home and I need a job. I can't afford a bus ride let alone a plane ticket."

"I know, I'm sorry. Forget about all of that. Just enjoy being back with your family and showing your guests the sights. I'm kind of jealous."

"You can come too."

"You never know, I just might," he said.

That first morning, Mandy was inundated with phone calls from friends, welcoming her home. She had fun chatting to them again and made plans to meet once her guests had left. It was good to be home, where she belonged.

Deciding to take it easy on day one, Mandy took her visitors to downtown Los Gatos. It was an easy stroll from the house and Reverend Dlamini kept commenting on how open all the houses and gardens were. Mandy smiled when he said, "I don't see any burglar bars or fences. And people have benches outside on their lawns. Look at this; every house has them. Don't they get stolen?" He looked puzzled.

"No, that's not really a problem here. But I never see anyone sitting on them, mind you. People are mostly gone all day. There's no time to sit outside and chat."

The priest shook his head. "That's too bad. These houses are beautiful. You live in a lovely town, Mandy."

As they walked along the main street, Mandy noticed

a few stares. JJ was dressed in regular clothes—shorts, a T-shirt, and running shoes; but Father Dlamini wasn't wearing his clerical collar. He wore a bright, multi-colored kaftan, like Nelson Mandela's. She wondered whether he was aware of the looks he was getting. He and Jabulani, for their part, stared at the shops and restaurants, especially fascinated by the nail parlors. Eventually, after they'd passed the third one, Reverend Dlamini said, "Don't people cut their own nails here?"

Mandy laughed. It was fun looking at things through his eyes and she made a suggestion. "How about we get a burger for a real taste of America?"

The burger and fries were smothered in pickles, ketchup, and mustard, and were followed by the biggest ice creams JJ and the priest had ever seen. There were so many flavors that Jabulani had a hard time choosing. He slowly went from one end of the counter to the other and finally settled on rocky road. When Mandy suggested he could have another scoop on top with a different flavor, his eyes opened wide.

"Really?" he asked. Mandy nodded and JJ was quicker to make a choice the second time around. "Chocolate chip," he said, smiling.

"Any toppings?" the server asked.

When Jabulani looked inquiringly at Mandy, she explained, "You can put some of these things on top; sprinkles, marshmallows, gummy bears..."

She wasn't able to finish. Reverend Dlamini shook his head and said, "No, that's enough. He'll get a stomach ache if he eats all that."

Jabulani looked disappointed but accepted the decision

and ate the ice cream cone with relish, as evidenced by the remains of it around his mouth. When he'd finished, Mandy asked, "How was that?"

He smiled and said, "Good."

"I'm glad. Welcome to America," she said, and JJ laughed.

"I like America," he told her.

She took a photo of him and texted it to David, before putting her arms around the child and hugging him, then wiping his face clean. He looked up and said, "Why did that girl who gave me the ice cream have green hair?"

"I don't know. She thinks it looks nice, I suppose," Mandy replied.

"I think it looks funny."

The priest frowned. "I agree with you Jabulani, but it's better not to say that. Keep your opinions to yourself, otherwise people will think you're rude." After a moment, he rubbed his forehead and added, "I'm enjoying seeing your town, Mandy. I'd like to see where you went to school. Can we do that?"

"Of course," she responded. "It's just down the road. We can walk there now, if Jabulani isn't too tired."

The child had been energized by the sugar surge. He took Mandy's hand and said, "I want to see everything."

It wasn't far until they came to the impressive building with an expansive lawn in front of it. It was lunchtime when they got there. Students attending summer school were milling around; some were stretched out on the grass, some strolled over the road to buy food at a convenience store, and others took off in cars. A group stopped and stared at the priest; one of them said, "Cool, man. I need a shirt like that. Where'd you get it?"

The priest looked away, embarrassed.

Mandy laughed and told the student, "It comes from Africa. You'll have to go there to get one."

Reverend Dlamini smiled but continued to look perplexed as he gazed around. "Don't they wear uniforms? And do they drive to school?"

"Some do," she replied. "There's a big parking lot behind this building."

"Did you drive?" he asked.

"No. I walked; it wasn't that far, as you see. But lots of my friends had cars."

"They had their own cars?" he asked in amazement.

"Some of them." Mandy looked down at her feet and murmured, "I was kind of jealous. They got them for their sixteenth birthdays. I didn't. I felt left out."

"Hey," he replied. "I'm glad your parents didn't do that, give you a car for your sixteenth birthday. You were still a child."

"I didn't think so at the time, but maybe I was." As she and Reverend Dlamini moved to a nearby bench, leaving JJ stretched out on the grass, she turned to the priest saying, "I've never told you about the terrible thing I once did." He looked at her in surprise, but said nothing. She hesitated and looked down at the ground. "It happened when I was seventeen. I was driving my Mom's car too fast. I had an accident and..." She swallowed hard before speaking the words that were so hard for her to say. "My best friend died. I killed her."

He reached across and took her hand in his. At first, he did nothing but watch her; then he closed his eyes as if in prayer. After a while he said, "Now I understand, Mandy. I always knew there was something that caused you great pain; I didn't know what it was. You've suffered a lot because of that, I can see. I'm very sorry." He squeezed her hand and said, "But you didn't kill your friend; you mustn't think like that. Nobody intends for accidents to happen."

Mandy said nothing as she wiped a tear from her cheek.

"We have to learn to forgive. That means forgiving yourself, too," he said. Still holding her hand, he added, "Let's stay sitting here for a while. I need to rest."

As they watched students gathering in groups, Jabulani moved closer to them. He turned to Mandy and said, "Look at that guy sitting by himself. He looks sad. Doesn't he have any friends?"

"I don't know, JJ. Maybe he's new and doesn't know anybody yet. Remember how hard it was when you first went to school? You didn't know anyone either."

She had no answer when he said, "But we all talked to one another. How can he make friends if nobody talks to him? Is it because he's black, like me?"

Reverend Dlamini decided to keep a journal while he was in California. The boys at the orphanage would want to know all about his trip when he returned. At the end of the first day, he wrote:

Mr. and Mrs. Walker are very kind. Their home is much bigger than the orphanage. It's got three bedrooms and three bathrooms as well. All the houses here are made of wood, not bricks, and when you knock on the walls, it sounds like a drum. (I had to stop Jabulani beating a tune on the wall in our bedroom.) My bed is big enough for two people, and so is Jabulani's. I had to stop him jumping on the bed, too. But it's good to see him laughing. He's happy.

Today was interesting. We walked to Los Gatos and had lunch in town. It was too much food; one hamburger would have been enough for all three of us and then we had huge ice creams as well. We also went to see Mandy's old high school. There were no taxis there because students have their own cars.

CHAPTER 38

Waking early gave Mandy an opportunity to have a morning chat with her parents. They were curious to know how the previous day had turned out because everyone had been too tired to speak the previous evening when her parents got home from work. Their inquiries had received monosyllabic answers. Mandy described JJ's reactions at the high school to them. "I didn't think he'd notice people's color; he's never said anything before. I was surprised that I'd never thought about it myself."

"Why don't you take them somewhere with more diversity?" her father said. "I could take them to see Bellarmine. My old high school has a more diverse population."

"And it's Catholic. I'm sure Reverend Dlamini would like that. That's a great idea," Janet Walker added.

"Yes, with your mother working there in the library, and me as an alum, I'm sure I could organize for him to meet some of the Jesuit priests. They'd be interested to talk to him, I bet."

Mandy nodded, thinking ahead that it would be a good fit for JJ when he reached high school.

"And maybe we can drive up together and show them Berkeley, if the priest is interested in seeing where you're going to grad school," her father added.

"Great. We could come home through San Francisco.

Do some sightseeing." She hesitated before adding, "I'm not all that sure about grad school anymore, by the way."

"Why on earth not?" her mother asked.

Mandy shrugged. "My heart's not in it. And I need a job; I'm flat broke."

"We'll help you. That shouldn't be a problem."

"Thanks, Mom. I just don't know if that's what I want to do anymore. I know it's not what you want to hear; I'm sorry. I haven't decided for sure, though," she said. Before either of her parents could question her further, she asked, "As a matter of interest, did you ever think it strange, the homogenous student body at my high school?"

Her mother shrugged and said, "Not really."

"We just wanted you to go to a good school. That's why we moved to a good school district. If Bellarmine wasn't boys only, we would've sent you there. Diversity didn't come into it," her father said.

"But diversity is part of education. Learning to be with people who are different and finding the things you have in common, rather than seeing only differences—that's what education should aim for," she replied.

"So, do you think we should start busing into Los Gatos?" he asked. His tone was sharp.

Mandy replied with a knee-jerk reaction. "I don't know what I think, but I have a horrible fear that when I adopt JJ, he'll be the only black kid in the school."

There was a gasp from Janet Walker. "Mandy, no," she cried. "What are you thinking?"

Her father's face looked thunderous. "Good God. Is this why you're changing your mind about grad school? I can't believe it. You're 25 years old. You have a bright future ahead of you. Adopting him would be an albatross around your neck. And, apart from anything else, how could you afford it? You've just said you're flat broke."

"JJ has his whole life ahead of him too. And if he stays at the school he was at, his future will be bleak. He's a very intelligent child; I can offer him something much better."

"At what cost to yourself, Mandy?" her father said. He was now red in the face.

She was saved from answering as her phone began to ring; David was calling and she hastily excused herself. Back in her own room, her heart beat faster when she heard him say, "Hi gorgeous, I'm missing you."

He wanted to know what she'd been doing and she relayed Jabulani's observations, as well as the discussion with her parents that had just taken place. When she described their reactions, he said, "Give them time. You can't expect to throw something like that at them and not get kickback. Keep your cool. Every problem generally has a solution. I think I've said that to you before."

"I can't see what it is, though. I don't know what to do."

"The answer is obvious, but you'll have to figure it out yourself. I'm just saying, there are excellent private schools in South Africa, and grad school programs too," he added, laughing.

She smiled, listening to his calm voice of reason. "You know, you're still the only person who hasn't shot me down in flames for wanting to adopt JJ. Thank you."

"I love that kid as much as you do," he said. "I'm missing *him* too, although there's a lot less water on the bathroom floor since he's been gone."

Dennis Walker felt helpless. "She'll live to regret this," he declared, "and what's more, I'm not going to support her and that boy. If Mandy goes ahead with this crazy idea of adopting him, she'll be on her own financially."

Janet Walker tried to calm him. "There's nothing to be gained by putting your oar in," she said. "You know only too well it'll make no difference to her plans; it'll only end up alienating her. Anyway, we don't know for certain it's going to happen. Please, keep your thoughts to yourself."

Dennis glared at her. "I saw from the way you reacted that you don't like the idea either."

"You're right, I don't, but it's her life and her decision, not ours. And I don't like the idea of losing our daughter, either. If he's going to be our grandson, we might as well try and have a good relationship with him," she added.

"That child is not my flesh and blood. He'll never be my grandson." Her husband was sitting on the edge of their bed and he dropped his head in his hands, covering his eyes.

Not sure if he was weeping or not, she moved slowly and sat next to him. Putting a hand on his knee, she said, "If he were a white child, born in America, would you feel differently?"

He shook his head, without looking up.

"Remember Dennis, Mandy's the only child we have. Think of it differently; think that we'll have another child to love," she continued. Dennis Walker shook his head again, but she hadn't finished speaking her mind. "Don't forget how much he's suffered; he lost both his parents.

He has no family. He loves our daughter and feels secure with her. And she clearly loves him."

Dennis held his wife's hands and said, "You're a much better person than I am."

Putting her arms around him, she whispered, "Have faith. Our daughter is a good, strong woman. Be proud of her."

True to his word, Dennis Walker contacted Bellarmine, where Reverend Dlamini was well-received by members of the faculty and given a tour of the campus by Father O'Connor. The Zulu priest was impressed with everything he saw; the chapel, the boys-only environment, the library where Mrs. Walker worked, the facilities—and the graciousness of the Jesuit priests. When he was told that every student needed to complete 25 hours of community service each year in order to graduate, he was even more impressed. Each year had a different emphasis, but by the time they finished high school, each boy needed to have 100 hours of service.

"What sort of work do they do?" he asked.

"All sorts of things. Our motto is 'Men for others.' They do tutoring at schools where students need help learning English; they help them with their homework too. They also work in soup kitchens, taking meals to sick and elderly people. Things like that," Father O'Connor replied.

Father Dlamini's impressions were all favorable, until he saw the car park. There were just as many vehicles at this school as there'd been at the high school in Los Gatos.

Noting Reverend Dlamini's frown, Father O'Connor

explained, "The boys come from great distances. Many come by train or bus, but there isn't very good public transport here. They need cars."

Reverend Dlamini thought of the many kilometers children walk to school in Africa, but he said nothing. That evening, he wrote in his journal:

I wish my boys in the orphanage had opportunities like the students I saw today. I can't help thinking of young Joseph Hlangani; how hard he worked to get his taxi, only to lose everything to a bullet. He had determination and ambition, but little education, and fewer opportunities. He deserved better. I can see that Jabulani must get a good education.

CHAPTER 39

While Father Dlamini was visiting Bellarmine, Mandy took the opportunity to reach out to friends again. She was impatient to see them all, but a chat would have to suffice until she had more time. Cassie, Michelle's older sister, was different, however. Mandy wanted her to meet Jabulani.

"Thanks for your emails," Cassie said when Mandy called her. "I didn't phone because I didn't want to intrude. I know you're busy."

"Don't be ridiculous. We have so much to catch up on. Can you come over sometime? I want you to meet JJ." Mandy swallowed hard before adding, "I'm going to adopt him, Cass."

"What? Bring him here permanently?"

"Yes. He's an orphan. You have to come and meet him; you'll see why I love him."

"Wow, Mandy." She paused and Mandy anticipated criticism might be forthcoming. But Cassie said, "I'm at a seminar in Seattle for a month, unfortunately. How long will your visitors be with you?"

"The priest is here for three weeks. My plan is to try and keep JJ here and not send him back."

Cassie choked on her words as she tried to speak, but she cleared her throat and said, "Mandy, be careful of ICE. They don't treat things like that kindly. They take their immigration enforcement duties seriously and age doesn't deter them from sticking a kid into detention to await deportation."

Her words were like a bucket of cold water being thrown at Mandy. She shivered and said, "I know it's going to be difficult, but I'll figure it out somehow. I want to do this. I want to look after this child."

"All right then, but be careful. Don't get into trouble with the law. I guess I'll meet him when I get back into town. Can't wait to see you again, and meet JJ. Welcome home, my dear friend. Gotta go now."

The next few days were unseasonably hot, so Mandy chose to relax next to the pool at the country club with her guests. Father Dlamini didn't have a bathing suit and declined the offer to borrow one from her father, but they purchased one for JJ. The priest looked uncomfortable as he sat under an umbrella, dressed in another bright kaftan and shorts. When Mandy emerged from the changing room in a bikini, he avoided looking at her altogether for a while.

She entered their names in the register, then took JJ's hand. At first, the child was reluctant to get into the water and sat on the steps, getting only his feet wet, but he watched carefully as Mandy swam some laps. He smiled then and said, "How do you do that?"

"My mom taught me to swim when I was a child. Would you like me to teach you?"

Before he could answer, two other children arrived and jumped into the pool. They were about the same age as him and he watched them diving for colored rings.

Mandy sat down next to Jabulani on the steps and said, "I think you'd be a good swimmer. You're a good runner, and a very good dancer. Swimming is like that in a way; you have to use those strong arms and legs of yours. I think you would learn very quickly because you're clever as well as strong. Do you want to give it a try?"

He nodded and walked down the steps with her until his feet were touching the bottom of the pool in the shallow end. "It's nice," he said, but his eyes opened very wide.

The other children stopped and watched. "Don't you know how to swim?" the boy asked.

JJ said nothing but kept his eyes on Mandy. She wished that the other kids would go away, but they were intrigued. Acknowledging them with a smile, Mandy then turned away and said, "Come, JJ, I'm going to hold you under your back. I want you to float with your arms out to your side, like this."

She was reminded of how brave he'd been on his first day at school as he showed the same resolve now, following her instructions without flinching. Before long, she was able to remove her hands, leaving him floating by himself. He didn't realize she wasn't holding him until he saw her standing further away and immediately started to sink. When his feet came into contact with the floor, he gasped and frowned. "You said you'd hold me," he said.

"I did hold you. But you've been doing it by yourself for ages." She gave him a high five and he laughed.

"Does he want to play with me and my sister?" the boy shouted.

Mandy smiled. "Why don't you ask him? His name is

JJ. What are your names?"

"I'm Josh. My sister's Erin. Do you want to play, JJ?" he asked.

Jabulani shrugged. "I can't swim," he said.

"Well, we can still play if you want to. Throw these rings for us and we'll dive for them. OK? You can try and get them too, if you like."

As Mandy sat at the side of the pool watching the three children, she and Reverend Dlamini exchanged glances. JJ tried at first to grab the rings with his toes, but Josh stopped him. "No, you have to go down head first. Hold your breath like this and push yourself down."

When JJ struggled, and came up empty handed, Erin said, "Keep your eyes open. You won't find them otherwise." His next attempt was successful and all three children high-fived one another. Mandy felt a sense of relief, seeing the children's reactions.

Suddenly a voice called out, "Josh, Erin, come here please." A tall, blond woman sat down at the other side of the pool. She pulled a magazine out of a bag, put on her sunglasses, and began covering herself with lotion. When the children got to her, Mandy overheard her say, "I told you not to get in until I could watch you—and you haven't put any sunscreen on. You know you're not allowed to swim without it." As she started applying it, she added, "Who's that boy you're playing with?" Then she dropped her voice and spoke to them in undertones.

Mandy watched, saying nothing. When Josh and Erin were suitably covered in sun screen, they picked up their toys and jumped into the deep end of the pool, leaving JJ all by himself. Mandy thought for a moment before walking over to the woman. "Excuse me," she said. "Do you mind if my guest plays with your children? He's come all the way from South Africa."

The woman put her magazine down and looked at Mandy. "I'm sorry, I didn't get your name."

"I'm Mandy Walker. JJ and his guardian are friends of mine. They're visiting."

"Oh, I see. Well then, I'm happy to meet you—and your friends." She called out to her children, "You can play with that little boy if you want to. He's this gal's guest." Her smile was stiff as she picked up her magazine and turned away from Mandy.

The incident went unnoticed by Jabulani, but Reverend Dlamini saw it all. Mandy was now the one feeling uncomfortable as she sat down next to him. When the silence seemed to be expanding between them, she said quietly, "I'm sorry."

"It's OK, Mandy. It's not your fault. I know all about prejudice. It hurts. But look. You see that her children and Jabulani don't notice any difference—except that Jabulani can't swim," he added with a slight laugh. The priest paused a moment before saying, "My friend Nelson Mandela, he said that we're taught to hate; we aren't born that way. What we just saw proves it. That should give us hope; we have to stop hatred from developing."

Father Dlamini wrote in his journal that night:

We spent today at a swimming pool. It was the first time Jabulani and I have seen one. Jabulani was very brave, but I wasn't. He stayed in the shallow end and played with some other children. He's not afraid to try anything. There was a woman who made me feel uncomfortable about being there. It was awkward, but Mandy smoothed things over. She had a very polite way of dealing with the situation.

CHAPTER 40

Adoption wasn't discussed again because there weren't any more early morning chats with her parents; Mandy pretended to sleep later but she was really lying awake, worrying. She felt saddened by her parents' disapproval, yet she loved JJ and wasn't going to give up on him. But would he want to stay with her in California? And then there was David; she loved him too, but how could they resolve living on different continents? California was her home.

Her confused thoughts were interrupted by a text message: *Tough case. Working late. I'll call tomorrow. Hugs.* Tears welled in her eyes and as she rolled over, she began to sob into her pillow. Life felt incomplete without David.

She tried to conceal her red eyes but her mother noticed. When they were alone, she put her arms around Mandy and said, "What's troubling you, darling?"

Mandy shrugged. "Nothing. I'm just tired."

Her mother frowned. "How about we get lunch together? You've been away so long and now you're back, I'm hardly seeing you at all."

Part of Mandy wanted to collapse into her mother's arms and offload all her worries, but instead she recoiled. She needed to figure things out herself without any maternal advice. Pulling away, she said, "Mom, I can't leave Father Dlamini and JJ. I'm too busy at the moment. I need to focus on them; I don't have the bandwidth for anything else."

Her mother gave a half-smile that showed no amusement, only wistfulness. "Mandy, I'm your mother. Don't shut me out," she said. "Your father would be happy taking them to his office and showing them around today. It'll be interesting for them. I get off work early; it's a half day at school. I have to rush now, but please let's meet for lunch."

There was no escaping it for Mandy.

"Let's have some wine to celebrate," her mother said, as they settled at a table and placed their orders

"What are we celebrating?" Mandy asked.

"Us. You and me. Mother and daughter having lunch together. It's been a long time."

As they clinked glasses, Janet opened the conversation by saying, "What an amazing experience you've had the last two years. I'm so proud of you."

Looking into her glass, Mandy swirled the wine around and said, "I loved being in Africa, despite the violence."

"I was really worried after those shootings in Durban, especially when you said you knew people who were killed. That was terrible."

"JJ and the priest were there, you know," Mandy said. "They were standing next to someone who was shot. And the taxi behind them went up in flames. People we knew were trapped inside."

Mrs. Walker inhaled sharply.

"Yup," Mandy continued. "For JJ, it seemed to be even more traumatic than his parents' death."

"Oh, that poor child," her mother replied. "Witnessing such violence for anyone would be terrifying, but a child is so defenseless; it would be even worse. That poor little boy; he's so young, but he's experienced so much trauma."

"That's why I want to take care of him," Mandy said. "He needs me."

There was nothing her mother could say. They sat in silence staring at one another, until Mandy decided to take the plunge and confide. "I met someone in South Africa, Mom. He means a lot to me."

Janet Walker smiled and said, "I thought that might be the case. Is that why you were crying this morning?"

Tears welled in Mandy's eyes again and she looked away. Taking a deep breath, she replied, "I suppose so. It's complicated."

Her mother frowned. "Why?"

"Well, he's South African. His roots there go deep. I doubt he would leave and I don't know that I want to live there. Much as I love Africa, this is my home."

"Is it this person who's been calling you?"

Mandy nodded. She looked up and said, "His name is David Malherbe. He's asked me to marry him."

Her mother held her breath.

"I haven't given him an answer," Mandy added quickly. "I don't know what to do."

"Does he know you want to adopt JJ?"

Mandy nodded. "He's the only person who under-stands; he's very supportive. God, remember Ryan, that guy I traveled with? He got really angry when I told him what I wanted to do."

Mrs. Walker sipped her wine. "Maybe he was jealous?"

"No. He's opinionated, that's all. We clash on everything."

Her mother smiled. "They say that some people come into our lives as lessons, and some as blessings."

Mandy laughed. "Well, Ryan's a lesson on what I don't want in a relationship." She took a few sips of wine and then put her glass down. "But how do I know David's the right person? I mean, for a while I thought Ryan was pretty cool. I was really excited about traveling around South Africa with him, but it didn't take long before he irritated the heck out of me. We just didn't think the same way about things. How do I know it won't be like that with David too?"

Her mother smiled. "It's the biggest decision you'll ever make and you have to be honest with yourself. Make a choice with good intentions. After that, make it right; it isn't right automatically. There'll be problems; nothing's perfect. You make your happiness." She took another sip of wine and said, "The wonderful thing about marriage is that someone's always got your back; it sounds like David definitely has yours. Your decision hinges on whether you're prepared to have his. It's a commitment, for better or worse."

With furrowed brow, Mandy said to her mother. "Can I ask you something?" When her mom nodded, she said, "Did you have any doubts when you married Dad? Did you have any regrets afterwards?"

Her mother raised her eyebrows and smiled. "Those are probing questions." She shook her head and said, "Honestly, I just knew I wanted to spend the rest of my life with him. I could hardly face the world when he was deployed to Bosnia, and yet distance drew us closer in a way. I was pregnant with you. I was terrified he wouldn't come back. I was thankful when he got sent home because he was injured, but he was suffering from PTSD as well. That was the hardest part. The nightmares and anxiety—and his guilt that he'd survived when so many friends didn't. But he got help and we made it through the dark times."

Mandy stared at her mother; it was the first time she'd spoken so openly about these difficulties. She'd never considered that her father might have suffered survivor guilt after the Bosnian War; he always seemed so sure of himself. But before she could say anything, her mother added, "And to answer your question, no, I never had any doubts or regrets. I just wanted him to get better."

Suddenly Janet Walker's expression changed and she began to laugh. "Before your father, there was someone else who asked me to marry him—a nice guy. He checked all the boxes, but I guess the chemistry wasn't right. I knew the answer was 'no' when I thought about the 'in sickness and in health' bit of the marriage vows. The thought of looking after him sick was a complete turn-off. I knew I couldn't do that. It was different with your father..."

Mandy laughed as well and as they clinked their glasses together, she said, "Thank you for that perspective. It was helpful; I can relate to everything you've said."

Janet Walker reached across the table and put her hand on Mandy's. "When you love someone, it's not just duty. It's easy to put their needs right up there with your own. That's what love is."

Reverend Dlamini wrote in his journal that night:

Jabulani and I went to work with Mr. Walker today. He has a big office in San Jose, on the tenth floor, with windows all around. You can see the city below and the mountains all around. San Jose is in a valley they call Silicon Valley. Mr. Walker tells me it's very important because it's the high-tech capital of the world. He is a very kind man and he's sending me home with a laptop computer for the orphanage. I hope we can figure out how to use it.

CHAPTER 41

When Mandy arrived home, there was a message on the answering machine for her: *This is Beverley Wiseman. I got your number in the club directory. Josh would like JJ to come to his birthday party. He's turning eight.* She left details and her number for Mandy to call back.

"Wow," Mandy exclaimed. "I did *not* see that coming." She had mixed feelings as she relayed the message to Jabulani and Reverend Dlamini. It was hard to believe that the woman had made such a turn around. The priest applauded Mandy again for the way she'd dealt with the situation at the pool, and JJ was excited; he wanted to go to the party. That was the thing that worried her. He'd never been to a birthday party before. Would he feel ill at ease? She dismissed any misgivings and accepted the invitation on his behalf. JJ had handled so many different things in the past few months, what was one more?

Her concern was put aside as they spent the next day sightseeing. They piled into her mother's SUV with her parents, heading along busy freeways as they made their way to Berkeley. Father Dlamini sat in the front next to Mr. Walker, watching traffic speeding by in multiple lanes. He turned and said, "This is just like the roads at home. Everybody goes too fast. Mandy's friend wants to teach me to drive, you know, but I'm afraid to do it."

"Which friend is that?" Dennis Walker asked.

"David. He's been very good to all of us, especially Mandy and Jabulani."

Seated in the middle of the back seat, Mandy was trying to listen to the conversation in the front, but JJ was chatting about everything he saw and asking questions, so it was difficult. However, she managed to hear her father say, "Tell me about this man." Fortunately, the child saw a police car with a flashing light just then and watched it in silence.

"Mr. Walker, you know there are some people in the world that you immediately feel a connection with. He's one of those people. When he walked into our orphanage with Mandy, the boys loved him straight away. He understands them and he's very sympathetic. He's going to teach them all to drive, and he's giving us the car he was lending Mandy."

She hadn't told her parents about that. Her father glanced at her in the rearview mirror and raised his eyebrows. "I didn't know you had a car there," he said.

"Oh, it wasn't for long. It was an old car that belonged to his grandmother. I drove it for the last few months I was there," she replied. She was willing Father Dlamini to stop talking about David, but he was unstoppable.

"David Malherbe gives me hope for our future," he continued. "Too many people with money, whites and blacks, don't even notice what poor people's lives are like. And some people just shrug their shoulders; they say the problem's too big to solve and so they do nothing. But David's different. He's a lawyer; he helps people free of charge if they need it. I was complaining once about the problems in our country with so many poor people, and he said to me, 'Reverend Dlamini, if you can't feed a hundred people, you can at least feed one.' I've never forgotten that. That's what he and Mandy are doing for Jabulani; looking after one."

"So, David's helping Jabulani too?" Mr. Walker asked.

"Oh yes. Didn't you know? Jabulani's been living with them. It's David who paid for us to come here."

"I see," Dennis replied. When he met Mandy's eyes in the rearview mirror, his brows were arched in surprise.

The freeway led them away from the bay on the east side, through green hills. Oak trees and horses made the scene look bucolic, except for traffic racing by. When they emerged from the hills to flat terrain again, the green disappeared and was replaced by new housing developments as far as the eye could see—with billboards lining the freeway, advertising everything from insurance to iPhones. Before long, though, the freeway was barricaded by solid walls and they could see nothing. Father Dlamini was relieved when they finally took an off-ramp, although soon he stared in shock. All he'd seen of California thus far were big homes with spacious gardens and luxury cars. What he saw now was not like that at all.

Small houses, close together, had burglar bars on their windows and they were surrounded by concrete and weeds. There were no green lawns or gardens. Cars were parked everywhere—in the street, on the sidewalks, in driveways and in front yards. They were mostly old cars, many with people working on them. There was old furniture sitting in some of the yards, piled high with junk. The shops on street corners had graffiti painted on their walls and there were lots of young men outside, standing around smoking. He also noticed people living under a bridge with all their belongings in shopping carts. The priest said nothing but took everything in.

Jabulani noticed as well and he looked happy. With bright eyes, he turned to Mandy and asked, "Do they speak Zulu?"

It was hard not to smile, but she said, "No, JJ. I don't think they do."

He was visibly disappointed as he turned away and looked out the window again. After that, he grew very quiet, asking only once how much longer before they would be there.

"Not long now, maybe fifteen minutes."

Finding parking was difficult when they arrived in Berkeley, but it was a relief to get out the car when they did so. As they walked through the university's impressive gates and she saw the Campanile, Mandy felt her pulse quicken. It was an extremely competitive campus and she knew she'd done well to get accepted here; it was exciting feeling the buzz of student life again. Perhaps this was what she wanted after all.

As they walked around, her father put his arm around her and said, "I wouldn't pass this up too quickly, Mandy. You worked hard to earn a place here. It's a life-changing opportunity. Think carefully." She turned to say something, but he stopped her. "Your mother told me about David's proposal. He sounds like a good man; maybe this should be a test. Two years might seem like a long time, but it's the blink of an eye over a lifetime. And don't worry about money; I'll happily pay the tuition for you." He gave her shoulder a squeeze and said nothing more.

She was about to answer her father when she noticed Father Dlamini stopped in front of a notice board, reading it intently. She froze. He was peering at a large photo of two girls holding cardboard signs that read, *"Don't shoot."* Underneath was a description of the police shooting of Michael Brown in Ferguson in 2014. Another poster was pasted on the board that read in bold letters: *"Black Lives Matter."*

"What's this? What does it mean, 'Black Lives Matter?'" he asked her.

She took a deep breath and said, "It's a movement that started amongst African Americans. A policeman was acquitted of shooting a black teenager and people were angry. There've been lots of protests about police brutality."

Reverend Dlamini drew a deep breath and said, "Brutality towards black people?"

Mandy nodded.

He raised his eyebrows and said, "That's what used to happen in South Africa during apartheid. We didn't know if we'd get home when we were stopped by the police."

Another notice caught his eye and he read it out loud: *Police officers killed 1,129 people in 2017.* He shook his head and moved to another board displaying information about gun violence and school shootings: *Between 2000 and 2008, an average of 30,288 people per year died of gunshot injuries in the USA. We have, on average, one school shooting a week in the United States. Should teachers be armed with guns in classrooms? Come to a meeting tomorrow and join the debate.* The time and place were given underneath.

Turning to Mandy, he said, "So it's not just in South

Africa where this happens." When she shook her head, he said, "That place where we were driving, when Jabulani asked if they spoke Zulu..." He frowned and leaned forward as he asked, "Do black people live separately from white people here? I wanted to ask you in the car, but I didn't want to say anything in front of your parents and the child."

Mandy rubbed her forehead as she thought how to answer. Finally, she said, "Some areas have more African Americans in them than others. But people can live wherever they want to; it's not like apartheid or anything."

He was frowning as he listened to her. "So, it's a question of money, not the law. Is that what you're saying?"

She nodded. "I guess so."

He shook his head and said, "I thought it would be better than this in America. I thought it would be safer for Jabulani." Suddenly he turned abruptly and faced her. His voice was filled with pain as he said, "It's no different. People like us are poor. All those young men on the street corners—why weren't they working? Haven't they got jobs? There were homeless people there too. I saw them under a bridge. And all these school shootings," he said, pointing to the billboard. "It's just as violent here as it is in South Africa. This isn't the place for Jabulani, Mandy. I'm sorry. He'll be better at home; you heard how he asked if people spoke Zulu. We're his people. We'll look after him. I know you love him and you've helped him a lot. You can still help him, but he must come back home with me."

Mandy was speechless. Suddenly the buzz of Berkeley was no longer appealing. She wanted to scream. This was not why she'd brought him here; she wanted him to see the university campus and what it had to offer, not students' notice boards full of protests and complaints. Couldn't he open his eyes and look around at everything else, at the diverse student population? One look at his face told her that he could not.

Fortunately, her parents carried the day. Their enthusiasm as they drove the visitors over the Golden Gate Bridge and showed them the sights of San Francisco compensated for her unhappiness—which she tried hard to conceal. Father Dlamini was also quiet, but JJ enjoyed everything he saw. A ride on a cable car made him laugh, and he loved the touristy things at Fisherman's Wharf. When he saw curvy Lombard Street, he wanted to run all the way down and then back up again, but the more enthusiastic he was, the more she wanted to weep. He should be the one to decide where his future lay, not the priest. And besides, Jabulani wouldn't be growing up in poverty; he would be growing up with her.

After eating dinner in the Ferry Building and exploring the shops there, they headed back south to Los Gatos. JJ was asleep before they got home and Mandy carried him straight to bed, before excusing herself and going to her room. She wanted to be alone. Her solitude was interrupted, however, by a knock on the door. Her mom appeared and put her arms around Mandy, saying, "Did something happen?"

Mandy buried her head in her hands and sobbed, "Reverend Dlamini won't let JJ leave South Africa."

Janet Walker stroked her child's head and hugged her, saying nothing except, "I'm sorry."

When eventually Mandy was all cried out, she sat up and murmured, "I thought it would be a good idea for him to see some diversity, but all he could see was negative stuff. He didn't even notice the diversity of the student body at Berkeley and what that means for the future; he was too busy reading about gun violence in other parts of the country. It's made him blind to what I can offer JJ; what America can offer the child. All Reverend Dlamini sees is what he wants to see." She coughed and said, "I'm not giving up. I don't care what he says."

The next day when Mandy took JJ to a toy store to buy a birthday present for Josh, the child looked around in amazement. Other than a soccer ball, the only toys he'd owned were ones he and his friends had made themselves, using scraps of wire and wood. When an assistant asked JJ what he liked to play with, he hid behind Mandy and said nothing. This filled her with remorse; she'd never bought any toys for him. He was so undemanding and grateful for any small kindness; it hadn't crossed her mind to do so. But she remembered that at Bridges school, he'd enjoyed the "building" corner. So, they purchased two Lego sets; one for Josh and one for JJ. The rest of the day was spent figuring out how to put together a plane, and wrapping the birthday gift.

Reverend Dlamini and Mandy hardly spoke to one another. He wrote in his journal:

It isn't about Mandy's wishes, but Jabulani's needs. The boy's a Zulu. Our people endured a long struggle; our victory didn't come easily. It doesn't make sense for him to grow up in America now. We have problems at home, but this place does too. There's more chance of Jabulani having a good future in South Africa amongst his own people, than growing up here amongst strangers. He needs us and we need him. He's a clever child. If she helps him get a good education in South Africa, he can be whatever he wants to be. If he stays in America, he'll be part of a minority group. Just because America once had a black president doesn't mean there's no more racism.

CHAPTER 42

Mandy could see the excitement in JJ's face as they set off to the birthday party. She explained there would probably be games and activities, as well as a cake with eight candles on it that Josh would blow out while they all sang to him. She taught JJ how to sing "Happy Birthday" and they practiced all the way to the party. When they arrived, he placed his gift on a table with all the others and looked around in astonishment.

Front and center of the play area was a large bouncy house, a rental that had been inflated for the occasion. It was filled with children running, jumping, shouting, and laughing. JJ had never seen anything like it and smiled when he saw kids scrambling to climb inside. Alongside the bouncy house was a petting zoo with farm animals. JJ headed there, but Josh dragged him off to play in a pick-up soccer game. He didn't have a chance to feel shy or nervous because immediately he was chosen to be on Josh's team and the game got going. JJ's footwork made him an instant star, even when the opposition had two people marking him. Soon he was laughing and scoring goals and other children came to watch his prowess. Everyone wanted to play with him.

"We want a turn with JJ on our side," the other team shouted.

"No. It's my birthday and I want him on my team,"

Josh responded.

"JJ, you're a rock star," one of the party helpers shouted. She was a teenage girl, hired to assist with the children.

When the soccer stopped, Jabulani went to check out the sheep and goats. He immediately had a following who wanted to hear him speak because they knew he was a visitor from Africa. "When's your birthday, JJ? Are you going to have a party?" asked one of Erin's friends.

Jabulani pretended he didn't hear her as he patted the sheep, but the little girl persisted with her question. This time JJ turned to face her with a shrug. "I don't know," he replied.

She started to giggle and said, "You don't know when your birthday is? You must know. Everybody knows that. Mine's next week; I'm going to be seven." She and Erin began to laugh as they discussed her party. JJ, however, thought they were laughing at him. He left the petting zoo and went to find Mandy.

"Can we go now?" he asked.

She looked at his furrowed brow and was concerned. "No, JJ. We have to wait until Josh has cut the cake and opened his presents. What's the matter? Why do you want to leave?"

He began grinding his molars and turned away.

"Have you been in the bouncy house?" she asked.

He shook his head. "I don't want to do that," he replied. Then he turned to her and said, "When's my birthday?"

"It's on October 30th. You'll be nine. Would you like to have a party as well? Is that the problem?"

He shook his head. "No." Then he looked at her and

spoke so softly that she needed to bend down to hear him. "Why do you know when my birthday is, but I don't?"

She took his hand and they walked back to the now deserted petting zoo. "I know because I saw a copy of your birth certificate."

"What's that?"

"It's a piece of paper that says when and where you were born, and who your parents were. Remember, we needed that to get your passport. That's how I know when your birthday is." He was still grinding his teeth as he stared at the sheep. "I don't know why you didn't know; I guess it wasn't very important," Mandy continued. "You and your friends didn't make a big deal of birthdays, did you?"

He shook his head. "But that girl said everyone knows when their birthday is," he said. "She laughed at me."

"Oh, I see," Mandy replied. "Well, now you do know when yours is, but what difference does it make? You're still the same Jabulani Jiyane you were before—and the best soccer player I know," she added, smiling.

"Why did she laugh at me?"

Mandy took both his hands and said, "Maybe she was laughing at something else?"

"No. She laughed because I didn't know when my birthday was."

"Well, if she did, shame on her. That was very rude. The thing is, JJ, birthdays are big events here, but they aren't where you come from. That doesn't mean that they're right and you're wrong, or the other way around; it's just different."

He walked away from her, returning to the sheep and

whispering in its ear again. Mandy was curious to know what he was saying but refrained from asking. His pride was hurt and he was embarrassed, she could see that; she hoped her explanation had helped.

Suddenly the children began to gather around a table with shrieks of "cake, cake," so Mandy took JJ's hand and led him back to the patio. His eyes opened wide when he saw the spread of food and drinks, but when the cake was carried out, he gaped. It was enormous—the size of his suitcase, decorated with little soccer balls and goalposts on top of it, and surrounded by candles. He joined in singing "Happy Birthday" as Josh blew out the candles, but he could hardly wait to sink his teeth into a slice of cake. His smile returned and with his spirits restored, he happily accepted a second helping.

There were so many gifts piled high that they completely covered the table. The birthday boy ripped off wrapping paper and pulled out boxes so fast that he barely looked at the gift before grabbing the next parcel. His mother kept reminding him to say thank you while everyone laughed at his eagerness to keep opening. When he opened the gift that JJ had given him, Josh remarked, "Oh, more Lego. Thanks. I've got this one already."

Mandy spoke up quickly and said, "There's a gift receipt there. You can exchange it."

As Mrs. Wiseman thanked them and apologized, Josh was already opening the next present without so much as glancing at JJ. Jabulani watched a moment longer and then returned to the petting zoo, unnoticed by anybody other than Mandy.

He was very silent as they drove home. Mandy asked whether he'd enjoyed himself, but JJ looked away and said nothing. The moment they walked in the door, he ran upstairs to his bedroom, closed the door, and threw himself onto his bed. When Mandy knocked on the door and entered, he buried his face in his pillow. She stroked his head and told him again what a good soccer player he was, and how everyone had loved playing with him, but he was inconsolable. Eventually, she went to her own bedroom and retrieved an old teddy bear from her closet. She took it to him and said, "This was my bear. His name's Charlie. He was given to me when I was eight years old and I would like you to have him now. You see, whenever I was sad, I used to tell Charlie about it. He always understood what I was saying and made me feel better. He's a very wise bear. I loved him very much."

JJ rolled over to examine the brown stuffed toy. His cheeks were wet as he reached out and took the teddy bear from Mandy.

"Say hello to him," she said.

He glanced at her and said, "Can he speak Zulu?"

She nodded and smiled. "Only a little bit, though. You'll have to teach him."

While JJ was at the party, Father Dlamini went with Mandy's mother to the Episcopal church she sometimes attended. Even though he was a Catholic priest, he smiled and told Mrs. Walker that he didn't think God would mind, adding, "Mandy told me that she doesn't believe in God at all."

"I know," Mrs. Walker replied, frowning. "She was

baptized and confirmed and all that...she was brought up as an Episcopalian. I think that's like the Anglican church in your country."

"Yes, that's right." He paused before adding, "Those sacraments are important in the church, but they don't make you a Christian, you know." He scratched his brow and added, "It's like saying Jabulani went into a swimming pool, so now he's a swimmer."

Janet Walker laughed and said, "Well, let me put it this way; Mandy used to believe, but she lost her faith after a tragic car accident. It's sad, because that's just when you need to keep your faith, when you're going through difficult times."

Father Dlamini nodded and said, "Mandy and I talked about religion and she was very honest with me. I told her that it doesn't matter to me what you believe. What matters most is what you *do*, not what you *believe*."

Janet Walker was curious to know how Mandy had reacted. She glanced at him and raised that question.

"She didn't change her mind about God, but I think she was pleased that I saw the Holy Spirit in her."

After JJ had gone to sleep, Reverend Dlamini removed the journal from his suitcase and wrote:

Jabulani was very quiet after the party; maybe it's because we go home next week. He was having nightmares last night and I heard him crying in his sleep. Mandy's also been quiet. I think she's angry, but that's too bad. Jabulani must come home with me. The immigration official said there'd be big trouble if we don't return.

I've been anxious about what's right for him, so when I went to church this morning, I prayed for guidance. I put everything in God's hands. His answer came to me clearly in a reading from Corinthians: 'Three things will last forever: faith, hope and love. But the greatest of these is love.' God was telling me that there is nothing more important than love; that's what matters most—not culture, not language, not even country. Love is everything; it never fails.

Even though I care greatly for Jabulani, maybe he needs a mother's love; maybe that is more important. He and Mandy love each other deeply, so who am I to deny them happiness? I must listen to God. If the boy wants to come and live here with her, I won't stand in his way. I will tell her that. But he must come home first because she mustn't break the law.

The priest at Mrs. Walker's church was a very nice man. He wants me to speak to his parishioners about our orphanage; he thinks there might be funding in an outreach program to sponsor a boy's schooling. God works in mysterious ways!

CHAPTER 43

Sleep was eluding Mandy as JJ's departure grew closer. She wanted to confront Reverend Dlamini, but he didn't meet her eyes and avoided being alone with her. Resentful, she tried not to let her feelings show; she didn't want to spoil things for JJ.

Monday, the day following the party, dawned bright and sunny; it was a perfect day to show Jabulani the Pacific Ocean. Her parents asked to be included in the outing; they, too, were conscious that time was short with the South African visitors. They took time off work and as they drove over the hill on the winding highway, Mandy pointed out redwood trees to JJ, explaining that they had lived a long time—some were more than 2000 years old. That was lost on him until the priest said, "They were here before Jesus was a baby, Jabulani. That's how old they are."

Mandy noticed that this statement seemed to make sense to him. He began to speak earnestly in Zulu to the priest, who listened and nodded, but said nothing at first. She was eager to know what he'd said, but Reverend Dlamini offered no translation, replying to Jabulani in just a few Zulu words.

When they arrived in Santa Cruz, they parked on the wharf and strolled along to see the sea lions. JJ was fascinated by the creatures sunning themselves on the beams below the pier and laughed at the barking sounds they made. "They sound like dogs," he said to Mandy, "and look, they float in the water. I can do that now too." He saw seagulls strutting around and ran to chase them, laughing as they took flight. He stopped and stared, however, when he saw a pelican sitting on a rail. It was the strangest bird he'd ever seen and Mandy smiled to see his joy, reflecting how much happier he was here than at the party.

Reverend Dlamini's voice interrupted her thoughts suddenly and she was startled when she turned around and saw him standing right behind her.

"I have something important to tell you, Mandy," he said.

He'd approached so quietly that she'd been unaware of his presence. Immediately she felt tense, but he appeared not to notice how tightly she gripped the railing.

Her voice was strained when she replied. "What is it?" She couldn't bring herself to look at him.

He took a deep breath and said, "I've given the matter a lot of thought and I've finally made a decision. You have my permission to adopt Jabulani."

She gasped and spun around to look at him. "What? Are you serious?"

He nodded.

They stood in silence as Mandy absorbed this information.

Before she could speak further, he added, "But there are some conditions."

She held her breath and waited for him to continue. "First, he must agree. I'm sure he'll want to live with you, but he might not want to live in America. If he wants to stay in South Africa, you must respect that wish. Then it will be up to you; you will have a choice to make, whether *you* wish to live in South Africa or not."

Mandy nodded as she thought about this. "Fair enough. So, what other conditions are there?"

"Two more. Everything must be done legally, whatever the law in both countries requires. That means he must return to South Africa with me now and you start the process from there." She frowned and was about to say something, but he stopped her. "That's not negotiable, Mandy."

She frowned and said, "But the process will take years."

He remained resolute. "Jabulani cannot start life here on the wrong side of the law. You can always help him in South Africa, you know, whether you're there or not. You can send him to a better school and he can carry on living with me in the orphanage. I will persuade my sponsors to allow that. And now that we'll have a car, I'll be able to drive him to school; no more taxis."

She looked away with her heart pounding. "What's the last condition?"

"He told me in the car that you never say prayers with him. He wanted to know why. If you adopt him, he needs to continue having a religious education. If *you* can't do it, then he must go to Sunday school. Somebody else will have to do it."

Mandy spun around and said, "But you told me it doesn't matter what someone believes; it's more important what they do. The love I give JJ would be the lesson he'd need. You said yourself that you teach the children at the orphanage how to live, not what to believe."

"That's true. I tell them about God, but I don't tell them they have to believe in him. They listen to me and they watch how I behave, and I trust they will find their own way, asking their own questions. But they have to have something to question in the first place, just like you did. Your mother told me that you had a religious education. The love you give JJ is a very good lesson about how to live, Mandy. You set a fine example, but it doesn't teach him about faith and belief. If he's wondering why you don't pray, then he's got questions that need to be answered."

"I can give him answers, but I can't be a hypocrite," she muttered, before taking a deep breath and stopping herself from having any further outburst. Instead she said simply, "Thank you for reconsidering the whole question of adoption. I appreciate how difficult it's been for you. It's up to JJ now, I suppose."

She gritted her teeth when Reverend Dlamini replied, "And God. It's in his hands."

When they got home, there were messages on the answering machine for Reverend Dlamini and Jabulani. The rector at the Episcopal church had called to say he was unable to organize a meeting on such short notice, with only two days before Reverend Dlamini's departure. He had, however, spoken to the vestry and they'd agreed to sponsor one boy at the orphanage the following year. He asked whether Mandy would talk to them about her work with Jabulani, as well as the priest's work at the orphanage. This could be done after the South Africans left.

Reverend Dlamini was overjoyed at the news—and relieved that he would not have to address all those people. Mandy agreed to the request. "I'm happy to do it," she said, adding with a grin, "as long as I don't have to pray!"

He smiled, but said nothing.

The message for Jabulani was from Josh, asking if he could come and play the next day; he wanted to see JJ again before he left. When Mandy relayed the message to him, the child shook his head. "I want to be with you."

"And I want to be with you too, JJ," she replied, putting her arms around him. "I want to go and have another ice cream with you."

David's case had been a long and difficult one, and communication with Mandy had been brief—just the odd email. The time difference made it difficult to phone one another, so Mandy was delighted to get a text from him next morning: *Case over, good result. Call me when you're awake.*

Her heart was racing when he answered on the first ring. "How are you?" he asked. "It's been too long. I'm sorry, I've been working day and night; the case has been a bear, but we won."

"Congratulations," she said. "Now you can breathe again."

"For now. There's always the next one, but yes—I'm taking a bit of a breather."

"I'm pleased to hear that," she said, adding quickly, "Why don't you come and visit me over here, then? You said you might."

He was silent for a moment before he answered. "Will

you come back with me, if I come?" When she said nothing, he said, "I'll buy the ticket."

She said nothing, but her head was reeling with thoughts.

"Mandy, why you are so afraid of commitment?" he asked, breaking the silence.

"I'm not. But..."

"But what? We love each other. We share interests and ideals. We're happy when we're together and sad when we're not. What more can we ask?"

"OK, I'll ask you this—would you come and live in America?"

There was silence. After a few seconds, Mandy repeated her question. Only then did he say, "If that's what it takes for you to marry me, I'll do it. If you won't come here, I'll come there."

She was astonished. She'd thrown the question out as a test, never expecting that response.

David continued, "I recognize that one of us will have to move. It's a really tough choice and I've been presumptuous asking you to do it; it could just as well be me. I can requalify and write the bar exam over there." Silence hung between them once more until David eventually said, "On the other hand, if you agree to live here, I'll never stand in your way to return as often as you wish. That would be a prenuptial agreement."

She was stunned.

"I love you Mandy. I want you in my life—whatever it takes."

Just then, her bedroom door opened and Jabulani came in, a teddy bear under his arm. She beckoned him and as he snuggled next to her, she said, "Do you want to say 'hi' to David?"

The child's face lit up and he grabbed the phone. "Hello," he said, but he had the phone upside down. She showed him how to hold it properly and his eyes were wide as he heard David's voice. Then they began to fill with tears. He could hardly speak when David asked him if he was enjoying himself.

"It's nice," he said. "But I miss you. I want to come home."

Mandy lay in bed that night, staring at the ceiling. *I've been such a fool, she thought. I was so sure I could make it work; that JJ would be happy to live in California. I didn't really consider that he wouldn't want to be here with me.* She was numb as she thought back over the past few months. *I tried so hard to make the impossible happen, but I'm swimming against the tide. Cassie warned me about the dangers of ICE, that Immigration Enforcement would have no qualms locking Jabulani up before deporting him. It makes me go cold thinking about that. And everyone else warned me how hard it would be for Jabulani to leave his culture and adapt to mine. I ignored them all. But JJ's words to David, "I want to come home," hit me hard. What a chilly dose of reality that was.*

Tears of remorse trickled down her face. How stubborn she'd been, refusing to consider anything but her own ideas. Ultimately it had to be about what JJ wanted, not what she wanted. And he wanted to return home. She rolled over, buried her head in her pillow, and sobbed.

CHAPTER 44

As they cleared the breakfast dishes next morning, Father Dlamini said to Mandy, "We need to speak to Jabulani together about this adoption thing, don't you think?"

She was bent over, loading the dishwasher. Taken by surprise, she almost dropped the plate in her hands. Straightening, she looked at him and said, "Right now?"

The priest nodded. "He's having nightmares, like he did after the taxi shooting. I've heard him whimpering in his sleep the last few nights. He doesn't know what's going to happen to him and he's afraid of losing you, Mandy."

Tears sprang to her eyes as she closed the dishwasher —she couldn't bear to think of the child so torn. "OK. Let's sit in the garden and talk. He's old enough to understand—and now that he's been here, he knows enough to make a choice."

The discussion stopped at that moment because Jabulani walked into the kitchen with his glass and plate to put in the dishwasher. He turned to Mandy and said, "When can we get ice cream?"

"You've just finished breakfast!" She laughed and took his hand to lead him outside, beckoning the priest to follow. "We'll go downtown later; first we have to pack your suitcase—but before we do that, Father Dlamini and I want to talk to you about something."

The child hesitated. "Have I done something wrong?" he asked, his eyes opened wide as he looked up at her.

She sat down on a bench and patted the seat next to her, indicating that he should sit there. Father Dlamini sat on a chair opposite them and listened as Mandy spoke to the boy. "No, JJ, not at all. You've done everything perfectly. You've done nothing wrong." She smiled as the concern disappeared from his face. "You and I, we love each other very much, don't we?"

He nodded.

"Well, I would like to become your mother." His face broke into a smile, the likes of which she'd never seen before. "Would you like me to be your mom, JJ?"

He nodded again. "And will David be my dad?"

Mandy felt herself blushing.

Reverend Dlamini spoke up. "You can't ask that question, Jabulani. Mandy can only speak for herself."

The child looked the other way and said, "Sorry."

"It's OK. The thing is JJ, do you think..." She stopped, at a loss for words. The child was waiting to hear what she would say next and began to look anxious again.

Reverend Dlamini interrupted. "Jabulani, Mandy wants to adopt you. That's what they call it when somebody who isn't the person who gave birth to you becomes your mother. I can see that you are very happy with Mandy and you are very lucky that she wants to take care of you. But Mandy lives here in America, not in South Africa. Either you will have to come to America, or she will have to consider moving to South Africa."

JJ clapped his hands and jumped up to dance, pulling Mandy to join him as he kicked his legs high and whistled.

"I'm going to teach you how to do a Zulu dance," he said.

Mandy was smiling as she followed his steps and said, "Now you're the teacher, I see."

The priest watched with amusement for a few moments, before interrupting them. "So, Jabulani, do want to live in California?"

JJ had just landed a somersault and was down on his haunches when he heard these words. He stopped and stared at Mandy. "Aren't you coming back to South Africa with me tomorrow?"

Short of breath from the exertion, she was panting as she said, "Not tomorrow, JJ."

He frowned as he dropped to sit on the ground. "But you said you're my mother now."

Reverend Dlamini spoke up. "Not yet. She'll have to sign some papers first. But do you want to live here or in South Africa, Jabulani? That's what you have to decide."

The child looked from Mandy to the priest, then back again at Mandy. "I want to live in that place with you and David, where we were before."

That night, Reverend Dlamini wrote in his journal:

I'm sad to be leaving Mandy and her family tomorrow, but I'm glad I've had this opportunity to see what good, generous people there are here in America. Young people do so much good work, like Mandy and Ryan. At school, they're taught to volunteer their time helping others. We should be doing that in our schools too, but it's difficult when many learners are so poor. It's hard to help others

270

when you're struggling to survive yourself.

Before she went to bed that night, Mandy texted David: *Can you talk?*

In response, her phone rang immediately. "What's up?" he asked.

"I just wanted to chat to you. I feel miserable about JJ leaving tomorrow."

"I know. I've been thinking about you and how sad you must be. I'll pick them up at the airport—please tell the priest that. But I've got some news for you," he replied. "I hope it'll cheer you up."

"What is it?"

"I've bought a ticket to San Francisco. I'm arriving next week."

"What?" she shrieked.

"Yup. You've met my parents, for better or worse; and now it's time I met yours."

Her ensuing tears were a mixture of pain and joy—for the goodbyes and the hellos. As he listened to her crying, he said, "I was hoping to cheer you up."

"You did," she replied between sobs, "you've made me very happy."

"It doesn't sound like it," he said—but there was laughter in his voice.

When she'd gained control of her emotions, she told him about the conversation with JJ. It felt awkward repeating all that the child had said, but David pressed her to tell him what had transpired. On hearing the boy's words, he said, "Well, I have to say a big thank you to him." He hesitated a moment before asking, "Has that helped you make up your mind?" When she didn't answer, he continued, "We can send him to a good school here. We can raise him together, Mandy. And you can get your master's degree here too. Please say you'll marry me." When there was still no answer, he said, "Mandy, are you still there?"

"Yes, but not for long. I'd like to go back to South Africa with you. And yes, I will marry you."

As they prepared to leave for the airport, JJ clung to Mandy. "Why can't you come back with me?" he pleaded. "I want to be with you, Mandy."

She hugged the child and whispered, "We'll be together again soon, but you must go back today and I'll come and get you when I get back to South Africa. It won't be long. Can you keep a secret?"

He looked at her with teary eyes and nodded.

"Do you promise you won't say anything to anyone?"

Again, he nodded.

"David and I are going to get married. He's coming here to meet my parents, and then I'm coming back to South Africa with him. We'll be together then—always."

Jabulani began to smile. "When will you come back?" he asked.

"In a few weeks' time. You must go to the orphanage with Reverend Dlamini until David and I come and fetch you. Then you'll come and live with us."

JJ wiped his tears and whispered, "I'm happy now. I'll keep your secret."

Mandy winked at him. "You see, the thing is, I haven't told my parents yet. It's going to be sad for them that I'm going so far away again."

The child nodded. He understood the pain of loss and separation.

Reverend Dlamini finished a last-minute check of his bedroom and Mandy helped him carry their suitcases to the car. The laptop computer was safely stored in his carry-on luggage with instructions handwritten by Mandy. Dennis Walker insisted on driving to the airport and Mandy was grateful for the support as she sat in the back next to JJ, holding his hand. He was much calmer now that he knew what lay ahead, that Mandy would be returning. With the teddy bear under one arm, he wore his brave face again. He even managed a smile as he took the priest's hand and waved goodbye at the airport. It was Reverend Dlamini and Mandy who had tears in their eyes.

CHAPTER 45

Dennis and Janet Walker were surprised that Mandy had let Jabulani go back to South Africa without putting up a fight. "I wasn't sure how it would end up, but I didn't think it would be like this," Mr. Walker said. "I was certain that little boy was going to be a permanent fixture in our house."

"No, I knew that wouldn't be the case—not immediately, anyway. It might still happen. She loves that child a lot, but I think there's something going on that we're not aware of. I have a feeling..." When her husband gave her a quizzical look, Janet arched an eyebrow and said, "A mother just knows these things."

That night, they were in bed, reading, when the phone rang. It was an anonymous caller from an unknown number with an international prefix of 27. "That's South Africa, I believe," said Dennis. "It's probably for Mandy. You answer and I'll give her a shout?"

She put a restraining hand on his arm and said, "Why don't *you* answer it? Maybe it's for you."

He frowned. "I don't know anyone there except Reverend Dlamini and I know it's not him. He's on a plane right now."

"Just answer it," she insisted.

He frowned and ran his fingers through his hair. "This is ridiculous," he said.

"Just answer it," she said again.

The phone was on its tenth ring when he picked up the receiver.

A voice, different from anything he'd heard before, said, "Is that Mr. Walker?" It sounded almost like an English accent, but not quite.

"It is. How can I help you?" he replied.

"This is David Malherbe here. We haven't met, but I'm a friend of your daughter's—from Durban."

"Oh yes, she's told us about you. Let me give her a call."

"No, don't do that. It's you I'm calling. I hope you don't mind, but I'm coming to San Francisco next week to see her—and to meet you."

Dennis raised his eyebrows and said, "I see." Open-mouthed, he turned to his wife, who was gesturing for him to put the phone on speaker. He responded to her request, listening as this stranger continued speaking. "Sir, I'm phoning to ask your permission to marry Mandy."

Dennis Walker felt his chest constrict. After a moment of stunned silence, he slowly exhaled. His words were drawn out when he responded. "Oh...I see."

Even though he knew that marriage had been discussed between his daughter and this man, he was taken aback. Regaining his composure, he said, "Well, yes. Yes, of course...I appreciate you calling." At a loss for further words, he glanced at his wife. She was smiling, encouraging him to say something more, but he was too surprised to think of anything he could add. Finally, he murmured, "I'm not sure it would make any difference to Mandy what I say. If she wants to marry you, she will—with or without my permission."

"Well, I suppose it would be more accurate to say that I'm asking for your blessing, then," David laughed.

Dennis was drawn to this unknown man, impressed by such courtesy and respect, but it raised questions about the future that were less agreeable to him. When the call ended, his voice was shaky as he turned to his wife and said, "I suppose this means she's going back to South Africa. We're losing her, Janet."

"We're not losing her, for heaven's sake. Pull yourself together," she replied. "This is a time to rejoice, not mourn."

"I can't rejoice at losing my daughter." His emotion was apparent by the way he barked his response.

Janet didn't flinch. She stared at him and said, "Think back to the night of her accident, when a policeman came to our door and asked if we had a daughter called Mandy?"

Dennis frowned. "Why on earth are you bringing that up now?"

"Think about it. Remember how he talked in the past tense, as if he were also reporting Mandy's death when he told us that Michelle had died? Remember our relief when he said Mandy was still alive? But then, when we saw her bleeding and broken in the hospital, we thought we would lose her as she teetered between life and death—and there was nothing we could do except pray. All those hours we waited by her bedside, while she lay unconscious, I begged God to spare her. I kept telling him how young she was and how much she still had to live for." Mrs. Walker's eyes were moist as she recalled the pain of that night. "She was spared, Dennis. They were dark days, but we didn't lose her. And we never will."

She took his hands in hers and paused a moment before adding, "I have to tell you, I'm overjoyed to see Mandy with purpose again. For so long she couldn't find her way, no matter how hard she tried—but she's got it figured out now. She's found a soul mate and she's got something to live for. What more can we ask?" As her husband continued to stare at her, Janet added, "I know she took a different road from what we expected, but she's following her heart. I promise you, there's plenty of room in her heart for us, as well as David and Jabulani."

CHAPTER 46

The following week was a whirlwind of catching up with friends. Mandy was torn between spending time with them, or with her parents, and as each day went by she began to feel more anxiety about the decision she'd made. She didn't doubt David, not at all, but she doubted her will to leave this place she called home. Her roots were just as deep here as David's were in South Africa, and if it weren't for Jabulani, she would've been happy for David to be the one relocating.

When Cassie got back to Los Gatos, they went out for dinner and over a glass of wine, she expressed her feelings. "I can't say this to anyone but you," Mandy told her, "but I'm having a really hard time accepting that I'll be leaving. I'm going crazy thinking about it. I love David and Jabulani, but I love California too; my home, my parents, my friends. I'll miss all of that, and I'll miss you, Cassie. I kind of resent that I have to be the one to uproot." She sighed as she took another sip of wine. "I'm sorry you didn't get to meet JJ, because that would help you understand," she added, pulling out her cell phone to show Cassie the latest pictures of him.

Cassie laughed and said, "Soon you'll be showing me his school reports and soccer trophies! But yes, I can see how appealing he is. Can't he be persuaded to change his mind? He's only eight. Why is he dictating your future?"

"It's the law that's dictating things, not JJ. I'm sure he would adjust to living here with me and David, but the law doesn't permit it."

"Well, there you are then," Cassie replied. "The decision's been made for you. Stop torturing yourself with second-guessing everything. These are the facts: you want to marry David, you want to adopt JJ, you can only do it if you live in South Africa. Case closed. You have to stop that little voice you've told me about, the one that always pops advice and criticism into your head. It's not your conscience this time, Mandy. It's self-pity."

Mandy gulped and looked away, fighting back tears. She said nothing as Cassie continued speaking. "I'm sorry, that sounds harsh, but it had to be said. You've chosen the road you're going to take. Get on with it now and look forward, not backward." She reached across and took Mandy's hand. "It's not the first time I've given you advice, and our friendship not only survived, it grew stronger. We care about each other and that will never change; you are my dearest friend. We can Facetime every day. Anyway, I'm just saying, I've always wanted to visit South Africa!"

Mandy's spirits lifted the moment David entered the arrivals' hall. His smile when he saw her made her pulse race and as they hugged one another, she knew that Cassie was right. The place she wanted to be more than anywhere else was right there in his arms.

Her parents were charmed by him—even her Dad whom she thought might be a harder nut to crack than her Mom. As they sat watching a 49ers' game on TV, with her father explaining the rules of American football, she could see that both of them were at ease in one another's company. Afterwards, her Dad was keen to know all about rugby, looking with admiration as David described the intricacies of the sport. She accompanied them for games of golf and tennis at the club and knew that her father was in seventh heaven. David had definitely received the stamp of approval.

"I feel bad that I'm not sight-seeing more with you," Mandy said. "Perhaps we should go to Yosemite."

"No, Mandy. I've been there when I lived in San Diego; I'm sure there'll be other times to go again. And I've spent lots of time in San Francisco as well, so don't bother about it. Right now, I'm here to see you and meet your parents."

She reached up and kissed him on the cheek. "Well, have you ever been to Point Lobos?"

He shook his head.

"It's a beautiful park, one of my favorite places. I'd like you to see it."

"Then I'd like to see it with you. Let's do it."

They made a plan to borrow her mom's car, making their way over the hill and driving down the coast to the small town of Carmel. It was difficult to find parking, so they headed to the beach for a walk. "My God, it's magnificent," David said as he stared at the turquoise water and white sand. "It looks inviting. What a pity I know the water's so damn cold."

It felt good to hear his praise and when they arrived at Point Lobos State Park, a few miles farther down the coast, she was even happier to hear his comments as they hiked the trails. They watched seals swimming in a small cove, and birds diving into the water or swooping into their nests. "You should see this in spring," Mandy said. She was glowing as she pointed to the hillside alongside them. "Wildflowers are everywhere as far as the eye can see; they're like a carpet, they're so thick and colorful." But as she spoke, the thought struck her that she might never see springtime here again, and she quickly looked away.

David noticed the changed expression on her face. He stood behind her, looking at the hillside with her, and put his arms around her. "I promise you, we'll come back to see them as often as you wish."

Tears began to trickle down her cheeks and as she wiped them away, she murmured, "Thank you for understanding."

He held her close and whispered, "I understand completely, and I appreciate the sacrifice you're making. I'm humbled by it all. I can see how much you love California and I can see why you do. If it were possible to adopt Jabulani and bring him here, I would happily do it." He cleared his throat and said, "You know Mandy, we could support him in South Africa by sending him to a private boarding school; Reverend Dlamini could oversee things there for us. We could live here and bring him over to join us for vacations. I've told you before; I'll write the bar exam here and start over. The most important things for me are that we're together and that you are happy. Why don't we do it that way?"

Amazed, she turned and stared at him. The sound of the ocean seemed louder than she ever remembered as waves crashed below them, drowning out the cries of gulls. Closing her eyes, she tried to reign in her thoughts that were racing wild. She'd only been home a short while and was loathe to leave again so soon. It felt as if David was throwing out a safety line to her. It was tempting to grab it. But... she had made promises to JJ, and what sort of life would that be, seeing one another once or twice a year? It flew in the face of everything she'd been trying to establish with the child. Yet, on the other hand, she could stay in her beloved California—and she could go to grad school in the fall.

Her conflict was very apparent to David who felt a rush of compassion. "I'll do whatever you want, Mandy. It's your decision."

She opened her eyes and looked at him, seeing something more clearly than ever before. It was something that spoke much louder than words, a look that was filled with love. In that moment, the cloud lifted and her thoughts stopped racing. She smiled at him and said, "I couldn't do that to Jabulani—and I won't do that to you. I think you have wildflowers in South Africa, don't you?"

Cassie came over for dinner to meet David and they hit it off immediately. She was considering law school and had questions about that, as well as South Africa. He answered openly, expressing his concerns—but also his hopes. Mandy's parents joined in with their own questions. David reassured them all. "I know you're concerned about Mandy's safety. She's lived more than two years in Africa already, so it's not the unknown for her. She knows what precautions to take and I'll be watching out for her, don't you worry. She won't be catching taxis anymore, I hope."

"Definitely not," Mandy replied. "You'll have to come and see for yourselves. It's not as dangerous as everyone thinks."

When Cassie was helping Mandy in the kitchen, she whispered, "What a catch, my friend. I'd follow him to the ends of the earth if I were you. Does he have a brother, by any chance?"

Mandy chuckled and said, "Yup, an identical twin." When Cassie raised her eyebrows, Mandy said quickly, "He's taken, I'm afraid."

"Dammit. It would've been perfect. We could've both lived in Durban with matching hunks!"

"No, I'm afraid not. Firstly, his brother lives in London. Secondly, he's gay. But don't look so disappointed; maybe you'll meet someone else at our wedding. I'm hoping you'll be my bridesmaid."

Cassie dropped the dishtowel she was holding and put her arms around Mandy. "I'd be honored."

CHAPTER 47

✳

Ramona threw a party to celebrate Mandy's return and forthcoming marriage. Everyone the American woman had known since arriving in Durban was there, but the person most anxious to see her was Ryan. "Hey you," he said, hugging her before standing back to stare in admiration. "Yup, you're as beautiful as ever. Who would've thought a taxi running out of gas would change your world so much, huh?"

She nodded. "It seems such a long time ago since that happened, but it's just been a year." Cocking her head to one side, she asked, "How about you? What's happened with that girl you met?"

"Joanna? She's over there talking to Ramona's brother." He smiled and said, "Things are good between us. When I go back to New York to start my job, she's coming with me."

"To stay?"

"Let's just say she's coming for a long visit. We'll see how things go. But it's going to be hellishly hard leaving South Africa," he added, frowning. "I think I'll be back one of these days."

Their conversation was interrupted by Mpilo's arrival. "Mandy, my friend," he said. "You're coming back to live in this crazy country of ours, I hear."

"I am—and I'm happy to see you looking so well."

He nodded. "Your future father-in-law saved my life," he replied. "He said he never wants to see me again but now he'll have to. I'll be at your wedding."

Mandy smiled and said, "He's got a strange way of thinking but his heart's in the right place. He kind of..."

Mpilo nodded as her voice trailed off. "We're the rainbow nation, my friend. He's one of the colors of the rainbow!"

"Actually, he's all bark and no bite. We would've been lost without him if he hadn't helped Mpilo," Ryan said.

"Hey, I was lucky. And by the way, you've still got time to join us when we climb Kilimanjaro, you know," Mpilo added.

She laughed. "Not a chance. Are you two still planning to go?" she asked, looking from one to the other.

"Hell, yes. We're going next month, before Ryan goes to New York," Mpilo answered. "That girlfriend of his is coming too; Joanna's taking photographs and we're writing blogs. She found a travel magazine to sponsor us so we don't have to save any money at all. The magazine is paying for everything."

"Oh, my goodness, that's fantastic," she said. Looking at Ryan, she asked, "So, things are serious with Joanna, huh?" She gave him a friendly jab in the arm as she spoke.

He nodded and smiled. "Yup."

"I'm happy for you," she added.

He looked at her in silence for a moment before replying, "Thanks, Mandy. Thanks for everything. Things have worked out well for me and Joanna and I wish you and David all the happiness you deserve, I really do. You deserve lots of it. Good luck." He gave her one last hug and turned to find Joanna.

As he walked away, Lindiwe and Philani arrived to greet Mandy. There was a moment when neither woman said anything, but their differences were quickly put aside as Mandy reached out to her friend. "How are you?"

Lindiwe was biting her bottom lip and suddenly her words came out in a rush. "Philani and I got married last month. I wanted to text you in America to tell you, but then I heard you were coming back so I decided to wait and tell you in person." When she saw the astonishment on Mandy's face, she explained, "We got married in a hurry because my grandmother is very sick. She wanted to see me married before she joins the ancestors. I wish you could've been there."

She was so apologetic that Mandy felt sorry for her. "I understand. You don't have to apologize. Honestly. Congratulations, the two of you; I'm happy for you both but I'm sorry about your grandmother," she said, taking Lindiwe's hands in her own. "I really hoped to meet her."

"She's still hanging onto life and she wants to meet you too. I told her all about what you're doing; I also told her that we had some bad feelings." Mandy stiffened, taken aback by Lindiwe's forthrightness, until her friend offered an explanation. "After she heard all I had to say, she reminded me about the basket I was born with. She said I'd let it fill up with jealousy and it was taking away the space for love." Lindiwe paused and took Mandy's hands. "She was right. I'm sorry, Mandy."

Mandy's eyes filled with tears. Overcome, she put her arms around her friend and hugged her. "I'm sorry too," she replied. "Your friendship means a lot to me, Lindiwe."

Mandy was grateful for her parents' understanding and support. She knew it was a sadness for them that she was moving to South Africa permanently, but they'd welcomed David and made the wedding possible. Gerry and Priscilla Malherbe, for their part, were delighted to provide the venue in their garden. Preparations had been hectic, but they were finally done.

"I'm excited for our wedding tomorrow," Mandy confided to David, "but does it sound ungrateful to say I'll be glad when it's all over? It's been fun staying in a hotel with my parents, and they're raving about the country, but I can't wait for it to be 'us' again. JJ was good about going back to the orphanage until after the wedding, but I worry about him."

"It won't be long. And don't worry, I've been looking into some good schools for him—but in the meantime, Reverend Dlamini is driving like a pro, getting our boy to Bridges every day. My grandmother would be amazed to see her car doing so many miles. It's probably done as many in the last year as it did all the years she owned it. She hasn't forgotten you're an American. That made a big impression on her. She still talks about American ice cream." He paused and added more seriously, "My brother is also a fan of yours, by the way."

Mandy had met him the previous day when he arrived from London; he was very like David, but quieter. "It was an anxious moment when Pete walked into the house, unannounced; he didn't want me to tell our folks beforehand. I wasn't so sure it was a good idea. My mom is OK with him being gay, but my dad—well, not so much. But to his credit, he immediately put his arms around Pete."

"Surprises are fun. I love them," Mandy said.

David grinned. "Just as well. You might be in for a big one."

"What do you mean by that?" she asked.

"You'll have to wait and see, won't you? Otherwise it wouldn't be a surprise." Before she could ask anything more, he smiled and said, "You've been a civilizing influence on my father. He was intolerant of dissent when we were growing up."

"He has a much gentler nature than you give him credit for."

"You wouldn't have thought so if you'd been his kid. Honestly, I never believed he'd accept Peter being gay. Whether he'll accept Pete's partner is another matter." He shrugged and added, "But then, I didn't think my Dad would ever entertain black people in his home."

"Oh, come on, that's not fair. He gives medical attention to anyone who needs it, regardless of race," Mandy reminded him.

"That's a duty—very different from befriending black people. But now he thinks Reverend Dlamini is 'one of nature's gentlemen.' I couldn't believe my ears. He's been to visit the orphanage and has even offered to help when they need a doctor. Can you believe it?"

"Actually, I can. And I think it's fantastic," she replied.

"His change of heart is in large part thanks to you, Mandy Walker. You made him see things differently."

"Your father's a good man, he was just a product of a different era. Now he's able to think outside the box he grew up in. You should be proud of him." She sighed and added, "Unfortunately, lots of people stay trapped in their boxes."

Mandy watched in the mirror as her mother and bridesmaids, Cassie and Lindiwe, made final adjustments to her ivory dress and veil, before leaving to take their places outside for the ceremony. She could feel her heart pounding as they walked away; this was it. There was no turning back. Her father, sensing her nervousness, whispered, "You look beautiful, Mandy." Then he kissed her forehead and took her arm, saying, "Come, it's time."

Everything was a blur when they stepped outside into the garden. She saw David at the flower-bedecked arch, with Jabulani standing there as well. JJ was the ring bearer. Peter, the best man, stood to one side and Reverend Dlamini, prayer book in hand, stood beaming in front of the make-shift altar. Her bridesmaids, also wearing ivory dresses, stood waiting for her too. As she waited for the processional music to start, her father restrained her, whispering, "Hang on. Just a second, Mandy."

Surprised, she stood still, wondering why he was holding her back. Then she saw why; the boys from the orphanage—dressed in new clothes bought for the occasion by Dr. Malherbe—rose and stood in front of the priest. She saw Mpilo join them, and then Ryan moved to stand in front of them all. He smiled at her before turning to face the boys with raised arms, like a conductor, waiting for complete silence. At a signal from him, their voices began to soar as they started singing Nkosi Sikelel' iAfrica.

Overcome with emotion, she listened to their perfect harmony—never before had music sounded as beautiful to her. It was the best wedding gift imaginable; a national anthem that was now to be hers, sung by Reverend Dlamini's boys. This was their surprise for her. She listened in awe as they sang all the verses with gusto, and when the anthem ended, they quickly returned to their seats in well-rehearsed fashion.

On cue, a string quartet began playing Pachelbel's Canon in D. She was trembling when Dennis Walker took her hand and said, "Now, my beloved daughter, we can go. David's waiting for you."

All her tension disappeared as she began walking up the aisle on her father's arm; the knot in her stomach was replaced by a calm sense of well-being. Everything was perfect; the music, the flowers, the people, Jabulani living up to his name—happiness. And there was David...

His eyes met hers and they spoke all the words he didn't need to say.

NOTE FROM THE AUTHOR

"We believe that the combination of multiple voices in harmony, to create something more beautiful than the sum of its parts, is an extraordinary, effective tool for helping people learn to talk to each other again" (The King's Singers, 2019).

The King's Singers are a British a cappella ensemble. I was fortunate to hear them in concert at Stanford University, singing "Nkosi Sikelel' iAfrika"—the South African national anthem. Undoubtedly the characters in ROADS AND BRIDGES would agree with their belief in the power of music.

GLOSSARY

Ag.................................*an expression of frustration or disgust*

Baba..........................*father or old man*

Bakkie.......................*a pick-up van*

Betoger.....................*a protester*

Braai.........................*barbecue, grill*

Boerewors.................*farmer's sausage*

Gogo..........................*grandmother*

Hadedah....................*ibis, a big, dark bird*

Utshwala...................*homemade Zulu beer*

Impi...........................*Zulu warrior*

Isangoma...................*traditional healer*

Kombi.......................*Volkswagen vehicle resembling a small bus, used for taxis in South Africa*

Lobola.......................*bride payment*

Mielie........................*maize*

Muthi........................*medicine*

My liefling................*my darling*

Nkulunkulu..............*God*

Nkosi sikelel'
iAfrika......................*God bless Africa*

Rondavel.................*a traditional circular African dwelling with a conical thatched roof*

Sisi.........................*sister, woman friend*

Sjambok ....*whip made from hide*

Thakati.....................*witchcraft*

Taxi rank...................*taxi meeting place*

Tokoloshe ....*evil spirit, wizard*

Tsotsi.......................*young criminal, thug*

Ubuntu.....................*the belief in a universal bond of sharing that connects all humanity*

Umfundisi.................*priest*

Vuvuzela...................*an African noise-making instrument*

Volk ....*the people of a nation*